ACCESS ALL AREAS

ACCESS
ALL AREAS

BOOK 1 OF THE ACCESS SERIES

ALICE SEVERIN

Own Room Publishing
NEW YORK

This book is dedicated to
the following individuals:

*J, who made himself a lot of toast, understands proper tea
and biscuits, is smarter than he knows, and was and is a
trouper through all the ups and downs;*

*S, who never stopped pushing, who had the vision, without
whom this never would have happened;*

*S, who kept me going with her kindness, love, and
intelligence, and shared her dog and garden;*

A, who believes in tough love, but at least he believes;

*RP, who did some serious magic
that made anything seem possible.*

Prologue

I don't like anticipation. I don't trust it.

. . .

Maybe that's why I was shouting at my phone. Or why I was pacing back and forth in my small bedroom in my shared flat in London. And why I was trying—without a lot of success—to get the line right in my eyelashes. It had looked so easy in the video on the *Guardian* website. Like some terrible advert for kitchen appliances. Look, so easy, even an idiot can do it. I wasn't as convinced by that other video I saw, the one that suggested putting masking tape on your eye as a guide, before tearing it off to face your public. That seemed a little desperate. I wasn't a wall. But obviously a world of women could work the latest in feminine wiles, just not me. And time was running out for my transformation from hopeful also-ran to woman in-the-game. Not on the game, even if it felt that way sometimes.

I was on the verge of drawing pictures on my face with the blasted brush, when Sarah opened the door and started sniggering. Sarah, my roommate and tower of strength. Also accomplished producer of videos like the one that convinced me I could make myself look beautiful, as well as videos on actual important things like climate change and the housing crisis. She was a little intimidating. Still, it's better to be surrounded by those you admire than those you don't.

Of course, she quickly bustled about trying to calm me down, in her slightly impatient fashion. "Lily, what is wrong now? Why were you shouting? And why aren't you ready? I thought the cab Mark was sending was going to be here any moment?" She sighed, loudly. "Always so emotional. And swearing like a sailor. Look, shut your eyes, I'll do it for you. It's not that hard. Why didn't you just ask?" Sarah gave me a little nudge and sat me down on the bed. She took the brush from me, dipped it in the pot, then she carefully drew the rest of the line I had been struggling with and finished the other eye. She gazed at her work, then at the rest of me, critically as ever. "There. You look perfect. I know you, you'll win him over. Don't get hysterical."

"Bloody liquid eyeliner. Why do they think every woman can draw? I can't play piano either. Don't even talk to me about sewing. Doubt I would have even received an invite to the Assembly Rooms. A failure in the marketplace in any era. Spinster on the edge of no more time," I said irritably.

Sarah snorted with laughter. "Yes, you're the complete antithesis of feminine charm. A wallflower nun. Now please stop whinging and go admire my handiwork." I dutifully marched over to the big antique mirror that faced the bed and I looked at myself. I did look different. Dark hair pulled up. Moody green eyes flecked with blue and brown. A sardonic twist to my mouth that no amount of lipstick would soften. Dressed up. Distant. Harder. Pretty enough, but misaligned in places. The eyeliner made that better, I thought. Much better. A modern sketch finally pulled into focus.

Sarah's voice snapped me out of my vain reverie. "You're just pissy because you're nervous. Because you, my love, want it—that badly." Sarah cutting through the bullshit, as usual, always reporting back, razor sharp, on what she saw. It made me love her—and sometimes hate her. But I couldn't deny it had improved me, to have someone like that in my life—noticing things I'd hoped would just go unnoticed—and still sticking around. In my experience, people saw flaws, and flew away. I certainly did.

I tried to explain calmly, but failed. "It's just unbelievable. It happened so fast. Mark—knowing Jake Tully—the rock columnist—the radio personality. Sending him the link. The positive feedback. A possible freelance gig. Promising to introduce me! An awards show!" I sat down heavily on the bed. "Oh, Sarah, this isn't me. I shouldn't go."

Sarah laughed her choppy, barking laugh, then grabbed my elbow, hard. "You're going. Don't be a fool." She turned me around to face her. "Besides, who knows what is you? Who knows anything, definitively? Absolutes are for children. This is something you say yes to. You love music. Your blog. That article you wrote for *Confusion and Haze*. Didn't Mark say that Jake really liked it?"

"Shit, Sarah, I know, but why? Why is Mark doing this for me?" I started to wrench away to rub at my eye, but Sarah grabbed my hand and swatted it.

"You don't trust him? Hasn't anyone ever been nice to you?" I watched as her face registered what she had just said. "Right, sorry. Yes, he's a man, subject to whims and sudden distances. But that's not what I meant. Lily, good things can and do happen. It's the way the world works. Just because you haven't had a big taste of it, doesn't mean it's not out there. Waiting. For you!" She marched me to the door, and handed me my leather jacket. "And you're sure you don't mind Nick taking me out while you mix with the rich and famous?"

I sighed. Until about two months ago, Nick and I had been going out. He wanted me to be more regular. I wanted him to be less dull. It had been a stalemate, both of us feeling we should stay together, because we couldn't be bothered to do anything else. That is, until he met my fierce yet feminine roommate, Sarah, and suddenly I had a guilt-free way to let go. "No, Sarah. We are done. And he's a nice guy. Just not for me."

"Maybe you don't like nice."

I turned on the path and looked up at her. She was leaning on the doorframe, with her usual slightly distant and distracted look on her face. The wind blew my hair in front of my eyes and I wondered, not for the first time, why my hair never behaved and why Sarah was always right. My hand caught the offending strands and put them back into place. "Maybe I don't, darling. I don't know." We smiled at each other, and behind me, I could hear the diesel rumble of a black cab.

Her face took on an impish glee. "That's your ride...darling. Go lose your slipper—or something else," she said.

"I don't believe in fairy tales," I replied, waspishly.

"Yes you do. That's your problem. Well, it's all of us, really. Wanting to believe. Now go!"

• • •

That's how I found myself, twenty-five all too short and slightly panic-stricken moments later, at the venue for the big yearly rock awards down in Hammersmith, an area of London to the west, away from the center. I stepped out of the cab, slightly cowed by the small, yet intense crowd of fans outside, waiting patiently in the drizzle to see their obsessions in the flesh. I managed to slip by, unremarkable and unremarked upon, a little too early, to hand my credentials to the man on the door. He looked unimpressed, but that was his job. I hoped I didn't look the way I felt, a credulous newbie way too excited to be here, trying to play it cool, doomed to failure. At least my laminated card passed the test, and he handed it back to me, checking his list, talking to someone else through his headset, and I walked in over the red carpet, and proceeded to dig my nails into my hand until I felt the welcome pain. It was time to remember and to forget—all at once—why I was here.

I was more of an observer than a participant. Unlike the others, I would have to write about it, remain distant enough to give my view on the ceremony. My view, but told in a quirky way, according to the email I'd received from Jake. But quirky—that could mean anything. Everything I might see that others might miss. I liked the idea of me as outsider on the inside, a spy—because there was a beauty in invisibility. I could be made up to be just another normal face, useful, because people tended to watch out if they felt eyes upon them. Of course, the higher up they were on the food chain, unless for some reason they actually reflected upon the complications that came with wealth and power, the more likely they were to treat the "little people" like invisible dust motes—unable to hold any interest, much less understand the significance of what they were witnessing. Neither a problem, nor a threat– just a backdrop to a bigger, more important theatrical experience. The I and me show.

I had asked why they just didn't send me in as a server. Pouring wine. Taking away dirty glasses. Bending over shoulders, showing some cleavage, smiling benignly, remembering everything. The answer was unequivocal: it's been done before. Not only that, it's done all the bloody time. So celebs tend to go quiet when the waiter—ess is there, unless there's something they want repeated. But me, wandering around, masquerading as one of them, having a seat and a good pair of ears and eyes, could bring something fresh to it all. Fresh. Fresh. Fresh. They all kept repeating the word like a bunch of fucking greengrocers. I smirked. Every job, after all, has its jargon. And it could be so much worse, I said to myself. Fuck knows it's been so much worse. Now it was just up to me to not completely screw it up.

I ran my fingers through my hair, almost hearing Sarah's anguished plea—leave it alone!—and made my way further into the room. I'd find Mark, we'd sit down at the table, have a drink, chat to the illustrious Jake Tully. It was fine. I'd certainly done more frightening things before, right? No.

• • •

I made my way into the main hall—it really wasn't a very big place, all faded red and gold baroque glory in the way only aging London theatres can pull off, and walked around, checking out the meeting and greeting. It was, for the most part, the people behind the scenes. The people they don't show the close-ups of on TV, the expensive suits, the business deals, the people that treat the music like a product. Some of them loved it—the art, the craziness, the precision—the actual ears of the recording process. Some of them—well, it was the coolest place to be. And whoever was hot, was cool. That made good and bad interchangeable and meaningless terms. And it was a fairly ruthless world. I almost laughed out loud at the thought. No, scratch that. It was an incredibly cut-throat business, where the fever to be in was almost as sharp as the bloodlust to exclude.

For that reason, and a few others of my own, I stood for a moment at the edge of the dance floor, wondering if I should just call Mark, rather than wander around. No. I was stronger than that. I'd wander. And find a bar. A drink or two would make the effort of belonging, rather than fitting in, that much simpler. I spotted my bottle-covered goal on the other side of the room, and started making my way through the round tables, each covered with a crisp white tablecloth. The place cards were on the ones in the front; the tables towards the back had numbers, or one company name on it. They would sort out their own seating arrangement. The stage was covered in pseudo-Hollywood style TV staging—the curved staircase, the big bulb lights, now dim, the podium from which, later on, we'd get to watch the celebs receive their awards, trying to say something newsworthy and memorable in under a minute. As we were in London, these comments were going to be both more splintered with swearing, as well as more personally insulting. "F-ing and blinding" were what you could do here, as opposed to the other, supposedly sweeter side of the pond, and it pleased the crowd. Those naughty Europeans. Except we weren't in Europe, as the British liked to remind the unwise Yanks who waded in those muddied waters.

The tables were clean and clear now, but in a few hours they would hold the remains of empty bottles and glasses and food that would serve as proof that everyone had a good time. There would be a lot of bottles. A lot. Beer, wine, champagne—I wondered what would be on offer at the bar and what I'd want. Champagne, why not? If they had it for the hoi polloi. Sure. I really needed a drink. But there was a part of me that wanted to go down front and scope out the name tags on the tables down there, see where people would be sitting. Who did I want to see most? Pure visual, no autographs. I couldn't even think straight. I'd never been in a place with so many famous musicians all at once. I looked around again. Me. Them. Fuck. I was glad Sarah had forced me to come. Even if I wished her calming, sensible self was next to me, reminding me it was all ok, because it was hard to believe I was even here. But I was.

The barman was pleasant, pre-crowd pre-stress, and was happy to pour some cheap champagne. After the first few sips, the taste improved. Nothing special, but drinkable. I stood there for a minute, tempted to make conversation with him, or with one of the couples at the bar. Then I changed my mind. What was the first rule of being mysterious, or at least not looking like a complete fool? Distance. So much more alluring than actually opening your mouth. I drank some more and contemplated calling Mark. I had looked around but hadn't spotted him. I finished the first glass and went back up to get a second. I rationalized away my small feeling of guilt by reminding myself this was the music business. Drinking alone was the least of it. Why pretend?

I moved away from the bar, filled with the immense sense of purpose that you only get with your second drink, and determined to listen in, look around. I did have a goal, I wasn't just waiting around. More people were coming in now and the buzz was beginning. You could feel it—that mixture of energy and sex and money and competition—and wanting a good party. These awards did matter. An increase in sales and your name in the record books for the winner, and a big bonus for everyone on the team that helped get the band or the singer to the top. That meant no matter your part in it, you'd be linked with them—the winners, shiny, disdainful, and up there—forever. Your little life would suddenly have a whole lot of meaning. The atmosphere was humming.

But my second glass was nearly empty, and I wasn't doing what I was there to do. I knew it, and I knew I needed to fix it. I also knew I didn't want to go back to the bar alone. I shrugged. Needs must. It was time to call on Mark, and get some reinforcements going. I pulled out my mobile, and was just dialing the newly memorized number, when a pair of hands went over my eyes. I jumped, I couldn't help it.

"Guess who?" the lightly accented public school voice rang out.

I turned around. "Mark! I was just calling you."

"I knew it. That's why I'm here." We did some air kissing—four for Paris, he always used to say—and he pulled back from me. "You look marvelous. Well done." His eyes raked over my outfit—put together by Sarah—high heeled ankle boots, a lace and fake fur loose vest over a pleated silk floating tunic with a slashed neckline, and I smiled, in spite of my nervousness.

"Why, thank you, kind sir." I winked at him. "Doing my part."

His tone turned serious. "Yes, well this is the moment. Now or never. How do you feel?"

I looked back at him, wrong-footed for a second. There was no compassion in his face. All cold. Fear turned to fury, then annoyance. "How do you think I feel, Mark? Why don't you tell me?"

His thin smile returned. "There, that's better. Anger suits your looks so much more than terror." He slid his arm through mine. "Come on, hellcat. I've got a table, and the good champagne's chilling." He took my glass from me, and left it on a table. We walked back through the maze of tables, talking of nothing in particular, while he pointed out some business players to me. "There's Kirk Leary," he noted, pointing to an older man with a perfectly knotted honey-colored silk tie and a sharp dark suit, gesticulating to two other men, his expression a mixture of bored hit man and evil child. "He's Leary Music. Been in the business since forever. Owns rights to everything. Discovered heavy hitters from disco to metal. Interesting he's here. There must be someone he wants." We moved along. Mark carried on describing. I tried to take it all in. "Lil, what you need to understand is the intense mixture of personalities and egos in operation here. The failed artists who became business, the people that sold their grandmother and the dog just to get here."

I nodded, not sure what to say. We'd reached our table, and I sat down, meekly, where Mark indicated. All these names, all this history. I looked over towards the thick-necked bottle chilling in the bucket. Mark smiled a toothy cat grin at me. "See something you like? Let me open this." He reached over, the arm of his long tailored jacket pulling back to reveal the perfectly fitted cuff of his shirt, just covering a tattoo. One of many tattoos, I'd discovered a couple of weeks ago.

He poured us each a glass. We toasted. "To your future success, Lily. Let's see how far we can get you tonight." He winked at me. "We've got some time, let me tell you about our table. Jake will be sitting over there, but he's also doing some interviews backstage, so we won't see that much of him." He crossed his legs with some care, pulling up the trousers so as not to crease the smooth line of the fabric. "So you will need to be on when he turns up." I raised my glass, saying nothing. I wasn't on show for him. I closed my mind to the rising irritation, and listened to him describe the remaining five. "Noelle Painter, she's a photographer. Does some album covers, some fashion. She'll be here with her girlfriend, Vanessa de something or other. Stupidly rich. Throws great parties. We won't be invited, so don't try. Then Jake's cousin, who works over in America, has come over for this. He's a PR guy, but for some reason, Jake tells me, he's trying to break into engineering." Mark paused. "Wait, was that it? No, part engineer, part DJ. Something. He runs a club night in Brooklyn." He laughed dismissively. "Doesn't everyone?"

I smiled back. I had no idea, but I guessed from his tone, that yes, they did. "Sounds like fun. New York's great." I was feeling the power of speech return with the end of the glass.

Mark snorted. "New York's great. Brooklyn's great too—especially if you're a property developer. Still, it shows people are interested in music again. That can't be a bad thing."

I felt bolder. "So remind me. How do you know Jake again?"

"We met at Oxford. Although apparently, we had played together at some wedding when we were about 9 or 10. Isn't that funny? I can't remember, but he claims I threw a glass of something at him." He looked at the growing crowd. "Surely not."

"Surely not."

Mark watched the crowd for a while, silently, then turned to me. "Lily?"

"Yes?" I responded. I wasn't really paying attention. I was looking at the bands, who were beginning to arrive. We were just a little too far away to see them as well as I would have liked. The Arctic Monkeys had just come in, along with Kylie Minogue. Bob Geldof. Paul Weller. Was that Kanye? Jesus. A band I didn't recognize in t-shirts and jeans, looking like they'd just come from the pub. I suddenly felt overdressed, until I looked around and noticed that most of the men were pretty low key, but the women had obviously all just been shopping and hairdressing. The whole double standard of it pissed me off, until I wondered if Mark had been late because he was getting ready. This thought amused me, until I realized he was staring at me.

"Sorry, what? I was watching the bands come in."

As an answer, Mark put his hand around my arm, and lifted me up. "Come with me," was all he said.

Unless I wanted to make a scene, I really had no choice. So I let him drag me away from my star gazing. We went towards the back, and he started to open the door to the men's room.

"What are you doing?" I hissed. "I can't go in there. What's wrong?"

"Come on, it's less crowded than the ladies. I promise not to make you use a urinal. Now, quickly." And he pushed the door open and led me inside. There was one guy in there, who was arranging his hair, who gave us a quick double take, before shrugging and looking away. This was the music business, after all, I supposed. Laws were not only meant to be broken, but it was a law to break them.

Mark opened a stall, and closed the door behind us. He started looking for something in his inside pocket, then stopped. "Look, Lil. Do you want this?"

"You know I do. You decided I did enough to bring me here. What's going on?"

He frowned. "Lily, stop. Stop lying. Do you want this? Want it. As in, I want this so badly I will actually do something to get it? Because at the moment, you're acting not so much like Cinderella at the ball as her librarian."

I looked down at the tile floor. There was nothing to say. I felt the tears stinging at my eyes.

Mark shook me gently by the shoulders. "Lily, believe me. I'm your friend in this. It's going to work. You look fantastic. You're smart, witty. But you've got to stop apologizing for existing. You are here. Everyone else—they don't matter. Except they do matter." He took a bit of toilet tissue and blotted my eyes carefully. "I'm sorry, but it needed to be said. You've got to step it up. You'll have, what, two minutes with my old friend? Two minutes where you need to be actively engaging. Not building up to, not worrying about if you belong, or whether you're worth it. Do you understand?"

I gulped, and breathed in a big balloon of air. I shook my head vigorously. He needed to believe me.

Mark pulled out something from his inside pocket. "Luckily, they make supports for moody artists such as yourself." He quickly undid the vial and snorted up two little spoons. "And they say this stuff's out of fashion. Yes. Of course. We're all thin just through willpower." He looked me up and down. "This will help with that as well. Not that you're fat."

"Thanks. You're so kind."

"No, stop it. Look around. These people aren't just regular, they're...demanding. Let's put it like that. They all had an idea, and they all made it exist. So they came up with what they wanted. But made it better." He smirked at me. "You look fantastic naked, by the way."

I warmed to the compliment, in spite of myself. "Thank you. So much. And thanks for the offer, but I don't do drugs anymore. I think I mentioned that at some point."

"Yes, you alluded to some misspent youth—but I'm suggesting you deserve a misspent adulthood." He smiled, and his smile reminded me of the night we spent together. It had been pretty good, actually. I wasn't relaxed enough and he wasn't talented enough to make it all it could have been, for me anyway, but I'd enjoyed it. Not everything had to be great. Good worked too.

"And this is the way?" I wasn't going to tell him that coke had been possibly my favorite drug at one point. Yes, there had been a few nights where I'd waited for the dawn, alone, quietly shaking. But everyone else had been asleep. Maybe that was their fault.

"It will keep you chirpy. You will be able to drink more, that should be a plus for you. You will lose a dress size in two weeks. And it will feel good when you, or should I say when we—go to bed again." His hand slipped down under my dress and slowly slid up between my legs and pressed against me. I closed my eyes. But just as I moved against his hand, he pulled away.

"Oh no. There's a party out there, and your future. Besides, there's bound to be a fight. I heard there's going to be some trash talking on stage. One of these giant egos is bound to take offense." He held up the vial. "Come on." He unscrewed the top, and filled a little spoon. "Come on."

One spoon and then the other side. And that sparkle. God, could it still be the same? That slightly burning, bright sense. And a taste that brought back visions of hundreds of little folded up packets, and single-edged razorblades, and that starry cold that slipped to your tongue and made worry irrelevant.

We each did another spoon, and he took a little on his finger and rubbed around my lips, sensuously, before dipping back between my legs, and tracing a line there with his finger. The slight numbness mixed with my heat made me gasp, and he laughed.

"Oh, Lil. You've got a great future, if you'd just let yourself have it." He kissed me, surprisingly tenderly. "Come on, let's go. And for fuck's sake, keep talking. No more treats if you don't impress him." I looked shocked and he laughed. "Should have done this ages ago. Never mind."

We walked out of the men's room, casually, and headed back to the table. Everyone was there, except Jake, and all the introductions were made. Mark poured more champagne, and we all made idle chit chat, wondering aloud who would win what, while pretending we weren't actually scanning the room every so often to see who we could see. I was a bit fixated on Jake's cousin, partly because he was wearing a plaid shirt, which I found strangely appealing in an unappealing way—red and blue amongst what was pretty much a sea of muted grey and black, but also that he was completely silent. I couldn't decide whether I admired this or just found it irritating. I wondered briefly if that was what I was like, but then Mark caught my eye, and I quickly turned to the person on my left to make conversation. Mark was chatting to someone who had just wandered over to say hello. Words, everywhere, about nothing and everything. A couple of phrases struck me, and I thought I'd go put them on my phone for the article. I excused myself, and Mark slipped me the vial as I went past. I felt giddy like a schoolgirl as I headed into the bathroom. I almost had a moment once I'd closed the door behind me in the stall as to what to do first. Notes? Drugs? I pulled out the phone, figuring I'd forget, and saw I had a text. It was from Sarah.

> How's the show? Isn't it due to start? Having fun here. Much love.

Everything seemed right. I did two more of the tiny metal spoons, more indents, I thought, giggling, than actual cutlery, and one more for good measure. Jake would be coming soon. I'd be ready. And I stumbled out of the bathroom to find that we were being asked to take our seats. I walked quickly over to the table, and arrived in what seemed like no time at all. Mark was standing, talking to an attractive man with dark oversized glasses, and what looked like an alpaca sweater over a t-shirt, and dark blue jeans. His hair was short, nearly brush cut, but it suited him. I walked up, wanting my moment in the spotlight so badly I could taste it, like metal on my tongue. Mark turned to me, smiling. "Lily, I'd like you to meet my old friend Jake. Jake, this is Lily, of blogging fame."

I burst up to him, and held my hand out, clasping his tightly. His eyes were an interesting color of blue. There was something friendly in his manner that made me like him. He seemed genuinely happy to be there, happy to meet me. "Jake, a real pleasure to finally meet you in person. I wanted to thank you for the kind comments you had about the article."

"Lily, pleasure's mine. Really rated the article. I thought—still think—the blog's great. You're very funny. Interesting, usually good-looking women don't have much of a sense of humor." He spoke very quickly, his accent Northern via London, but he enunciated every word with a clipped clarity that made his words feel a little like gunfire. I guessed that came from being on the radio.

I fluttered at him. "I'll take that as a compliment—from both sides."

He looked amused. "So you're enjoying yourself—a music fan, obviously."

"None of us would be here if we weren't."

"True enough. Some more than others perhaps. So you think you're going to find something interesting to write about this for a 1000 word piece? Turned in? I'll be kind and give you hangover time—say in thirty-six hours from now? 8:15 a.m. in the morning after tomorrow."

"Absolutely. And 8:15 a.m. in the morning is a pleonasm."

He grinned. "Just make sure there's nothing redundant in your piece."

"I try not to repeat anything that isn't worth repeating." I winked at him.

"Does that include your many conquests?"

"Some places you need to return to. Others...," I paused, and looked him in the eye, "you'd like to visit."

He held my gaze, and went quiet for a moment. I noted how his glasses had barely any prescription. I wondered if he needed them at all. "It all depends," he said, "on how much you want to get there."

"I'm not turning back."

"Sure?"

"Certain."

His smile returned, and his line of vision took in Mark again, who must have been standing there watching the whole thing. I had forgotten he was there. "Then email me the article, on time, I'll call you and we'll tear it apart over lunch. Deal?"

"Done. I'll add my phone number to the email. I'm looking forward to you enjoying...the piece over lunch."

"Excellent. Mark, mate, a pleasure seeing you. I'll be back in a little while. I've got to go interview Razorlight and try and get them to express something negative about someone. Shouldn't be hard." He waved, and walked away. I stared after him. He looked shorter from behind.

Mark patted my arm, and I turned towards him. "Well?" I asked.

"I'm proud of you." He coughed slightly, and poured us each a fresh glass from one of the new bottles that the wait staff had brought around. "And just so you know, we're not exclusive, and you did the right thing even if we were. Some things can only be measured by how far you're willing to go. I was worried you'd choose that moment to suddenly get moral. Not that he'll carry through with it. Although, if he does, I'd love to hear about what he's like in bed. Of course, don't tell me if he's better." He made a little choking laugh. "Not that he would be."

"I'm sure it won't come to that. A bit of friendly banter, nothing more. And I don't kiss and tell."

Mark snorted over the top of his glass. "How am I supposed to get any publicity then? Why do you think we men like it when the girls all go to the bathroom together? Lil, I will never understand you. Tell everyone. Sex is like publicity. The only bad kind is none."

More Prologue

The presenters presented, pretended they hadn't rehearsed, and tried to seem too drunk/blind/natural to read their cue cards. Carefully scripted comments like—"Isn't this a laugh—an awards ceremony?" I was surprised they didn't add—"Aren't we ironically self-referential? And post-modern?" Their studied poses and their wry laughter all went into trying very hard to show they didn't care. Of course it only made it patently obvious they did. So the losers lost, the winners won, and then came up and thanked a variety of people. The more politically savvy among them remembered all the A and R people, their manager, anyone they'd met who might help them in their slippery scramble to the next rung—and oh yeah, the fans, love you guys, thrown in for good measure at the end. After only an hour, it was getting fairly predictable. I did feel compassion and irritation in equal measure for the people who I guessed we'd never see up there again. Some people just seemed off, their jokes fell flat. The group didn't accept them. Others—they were playing it so hard. Too hard?

I drank more champagne. How many glasses? I'd lost count by this time. Mark disappeared briefly, claiming it was business, waving the phone at me. Seeing as he had no business to do, I gave a brief nod and scanned the direction he went in, and wondered who he was hooking up with. Then I finished the rest of the champagne, and waited for the next bottle to arrive. I was more annoyed at what drifting off with such a lame excuse said about how he rated my intelligence. Was he kidding? How stupid did he think I was? I was riding this horse to the next town and getting the fuck off.

Meanwhile, the night was progressing towards its inevitable conclusion and climax. Now we were starting to get somewhere with the presenters and the awards. One of the hosts, who obviously decided that things were getting a bit stale, made such a snide, sarcastic comment about the famous presenter he was paired with, there was an actual little gasp from the crowd. That was breaking the rules. This was rock and roll royalty. You weren't supposed to actually say what everyone thought. Maybe just allude to it, a little. Everyone looked up to watch how the star was going to react. His face was still and grim, and he gave a brief little smile as he walked up the stairs to the stage. He stood and faced the audience for a moment, and waved, then turned towards the presenter. "Let's hear it for Graham Mills everyone. He really is a fucking asshole, isn't he?" And while he said this, he was looking right at the man. I had expected him to turn away, deflect, face the audience. But he didn't flinch. The host, Graham, let a momentary twitch cross his face, then settled back into his edgy half smile. But the rock royalty didn't move, not until the applause kicked in. That's how you do it, I thought. You look right at them. You go right up to them. No sideways movements. You stand your ground and wait to fight, up close. I sighed. That's how these motherfuckers had gotten here, I thought. Even the most seemingly mild mannered had balls of steel and will to match. They were either too stupid to notice how far there was to fall, or too determined to give a fuck what anyone thought.

The next bottle had arrived, and the waiter was having difficulty opening the bottle. I felt like grabbing it out of his hand, and doing it myself. But I stopped myself, hating my good behavior, and sat there, waiting, listening with half an ear to the speech that Rock Royalty was making. He was not only standing up for himself, but making the other guy, the main host, look like a complete wanker. Unless you were on the host's side, that is; then it sounded a little too defensive. Either way. They were both fighting it out up there. I felt like having my own fight. Now. The waiter finally opened the bottle and I held out my glass first, preempting the man in plaid who had been about to take the whole bottle for himself. I smiled at him sweetly, while glaring, and thanked the waiter, while continuing to stare at Mr. Plaid Shirt. No peace and love on your farm, I thought. He grimaced back, and I smiled. Hate me, love me. I'm not going anywhere.

Mark had returned, looking a little flushed. He waited for Mr. Plaid to pour for himself, then gestured for the bottle. He drank down a glass, and poured another, before replacing the bottle in the bucket.

"Thirsty work?" I said. "Or just washing out the taste of her personal perfume?"

He looked down his nose at me. "Life is short, and none of us are getting any younger. You got what you wanted, so behave." He smiled. "Besides, you have to be nice to me. I know your boy, and I've got the coke." He winked. "You are so much more fun when you're loaded."

"Yeah, whatever. I have a glass too you know." I waved my glass at him until he fetched the bottle and refilled it. "Ok, I'll behave. Now everyone's happy." I replied, looking away from him, and back at the stage. "In more interesting news, what's up next, Mr. Fingers in All Pies?"

"Let your fingers do the walking." He laughed.

"Must be why yours have calloused edges."

"So witty. Didn't you say you liked it rough?" He smirked at me, when I turned to glare at him, and I looked away. Nothing to say.

I drank for a moment, and glanced around, wondered if anyone had heard us. "So, what's the next band?"

He laughed. "It won't matter to you, you're a bit too young to remember or care."

"Yeah, yeah, of course, whatever. Who is it?"

"See, you don't even know. Who was it, more like." He was starting to slur his words a bit. I had the feeling his meeting had involved a bit more than the exchange of phone numbers. "He's dead, poor fucker. That's why I'm telling you to make haste. Carpe diem, bitch." He clenched his jaw, and his forehead tightened. "Joe Strummer. They're going to do a tribute to him."

"The Clash. The only band that matters," I threw back at him. "One of the greatest. More relevant now than ever. A seed band for things now. 'White Riot, I want a riot, White Riot, a riot of my own,'" I sang out. Mark looked at me in shock.

"This is why I keep you around, Lily. Full of surprises."

I ignored him. "So who's going to sing a song, and which one are they going to do?"

"Pay attention, and you'll find out."

"So there is something you don't know," I retorted. "Aren't they going to have a hard time finding a song that isn't too insultingly political for this lot?"

"No one listens to the words anymore anyway. Whine about it in your blog. And I do know, by the way. Just didn't want to spoil the surprise for you. It's Devised."

I squealed, drunkenly. "Really? I love them. What a great choice. They've got some of that attitude. Apparently Joe liked them, too."

Mark imitated my squeal. "Really? Great. Now stop talking. My head hurts with it all. Talk talk."

I shrugged. He was high, I was high, I was numb enough not to care. Typical. I turned towards the stage, feeling relieved that I'd already met Jake. Maybe I wouldn't have to put up with this shit for much longer. Maybe. Maybe we were just drunk and aggressive. Couldn't we just all get along? Couldn't we just settle this over a pint? I laughed. Plaid shirt dude looked over at me. I turned away. Seriously. This was supposed to be fun. It was all starting to go a bit wrong. I closed my eyes and took a deep breath. Ok, that was a mistake. Maybe a little too much champagne. After this, I'd borrow the little vial again. That would smooth it out.

But the presentation was starting. Mick Jones was up there, talking about the band, modestly immodest. He was a player—one of those people who was in the thick of it, whether you saw him in the magazines or not. Another one, I thought, who had stuck with it, love or hate. Some clips of the band were being shown. Joe. Looked so young. Was so young. A smart street fighter with a heart of gold, according to the rumors. I felt suddenly horribly sad. We were all sitting around, liggers, drinking to his memory, most of us didn't care. Shit.

Then he announced Devised, and someone ran out to strap a guitar on him. Mick hugged them all as they came out, and

there was this electric feeling again, partially brought on from
the meeting of past and present, making all the differences in-
significant. Something so right about it. And from the first
chords of "London Calling," the sting hit, and you felt wired,
illuminated. It all still mattered a lot. "War is declared...come
out of your cupboards, you boys and girls..." And it went on,
insistent, persistent. The frontman, Tristan Hunter, screamed
out "and I live by the river" and Mick grinned at him, and they
went at it with a fury, like they were trying to bring Strummer
back from the dead. By this time, I was standing, but I wasn't
the only one. Tristan called out the crowing battle cry of defiance and I felt the words. "Yes I was there too." And I was
there. There I was. All I had to do was ignore the assholes, who
were everywhere, and cut through it and stay standing. Then
the choppy guitars moved into "Tommy Gun" and I think I actually screamed. I didn't give a fuck how uncool it was. The
man had died trying to move us. Fuck 'em, I thought, and I got
up to head down to the front, ignoring the brief tug of Mark's
hand on my arm. I couldn't believe they were playing this song.
The rapid fire drum beat, Mick and Tristan screaming into
the mic together, Tristan's face, beautiful and intense, Mick's
face, intense and knowing, the guitar blistering through the air
like a flash bang. I was over by the side, but right at the front,
me and the photographers, and the cameras. I didn't care. The
wood of the stage was like an altar and I was ready to sacri-
fice myself to get up close to this, to feel it. Now they were all
singing, standing in a tight line, shouting out the words, "kings
and queens and generals...learn your name..." Then it ended,
sharply, and we were all on our feet cheering. They were all
smiles, arms around each other's waists, sweat dripping down

Tristan's forehead, as he leaned into the mic and said, "thank you to Mick! And to Joe—we wouldn't be here without him." He saluted the audience, and they all bowed, and filed off stage. Tristan threw one last wave to the crowd, as he disappeared into the wings.

And I knew. This was what the piece would be about. I would get backstage, and see them somehow, and I would have to go right now, or I'd lose my nerve. There, that was where Jake had disappeared through the curtain when he went off to do his interview. Now, right now, while the crowd was still milling around and talking about it. I pushed through, said "all access" to the bouncer, while pretending to reach under my dress for a pass, my voice stronger than I felt. I would fucking do this. I would not be the one on the sidelines. No.

I walked further into the backstage area, not having any idea where I was going, but figuring if I followed the noise I would get to the center of it all. And then I came around some sets stacked up, and I saw them all, being photographed, still smiling. "One more shot," one of the two photographers called out, and Mick and Tristan sat down again, while the rest drifted away. "We're done," called out the guitarist, "they're who you want anyway." I filed that quote away, while I watched the two of them pull a few faces for the camera. I'd interview the two—the leads. The links between times. Yes. I watched them get up, hardly looking at the photographers who just a minute beforehand had had their full attention, and move towards the side. It looked like they were all leaving—a breeze was coming in. I could see the metal stage doors open to the outside, the street beyond.

• • •

Now. I ran over to them, and they both looked over at me, startled, wondering who this was speeding towards them that they didn't know, and on guard, guessing what it was all about. But just as I was about to speak, my heel caught on one of the sound wires, and I went down, right in front of them. The grey painted concrete floor was even harder than it looked. I could hear Mick laughing and for a moment, I just lay there, wanting to die. That was my great professional entrance, oozing sex appeal and charm, lying like a spilled drink on the ground. Then I felt a hand come under my arm, and lift me up as though I were weightless. The first large hand was joined by another one, and I was placed gently back down, and brushed off. And then I found myself face to face with Tristan. All the air left my lungs in a big rush. I looked up at him, into his eyes, and they were a strange green and brown color, light and dark all at once. Funny, I'd always thought he had very dark eyes.

His voice broke the dream feeling. "Are you all right, sweetheart? That was quite a tumble you took." He smiled, and I had the odd sensation I'd done this before. I still hadn't said anything, stunned both from what had just happened and having Tristan in front of me, asking if I was ok.

What do you say, face to face with your musical heroes? I tried to rouse myself. Be polite, I thought. Before you ask for the soundbite. "Thank you. Thank you for helping me up. I'm sorry to intrude—but you," I looked over to include Mick, "both were incredible up there. Two of my favorite songs. It was amazing." I was starting to babble. "I'm supposed to... Jake wants me to write something about tonight. I wanted it to be different. And it was going all wrong. Then you reminded me why I was even here."

Mick cut in. "So why are you here, love? Be quick."

The pressure. A test. How many times had he been asked to justify himself? Trial by fire. Now it was my turn.

But I had no idea what to say. I'd have to say anything. Something. The first thing that came to mind.

I had gone blank. I looked at Mick. He seemed to have a clock face where his eyes had been, ticking away my precious seconds. I turned to Tristan. His eyes were warm, and then they lit up with an unworldly shine, and I thought I could see down a long tunnel, through space, past time. And I felt it. I knew I was where I was supposed to be, and doing what I was meant to do. And then the words came.

"It's the only thing that matters. The feeling you get when it's right. When it means something. Making it happen." I stopped for a moment, a Clash song had come into my head. "I'm not 'turning rebellion into money', I promise."

Mick smiled, a brief light breaking across his face. "Amazing how it keeps going. Follow that feeling, love." He turned to Tristan. "Come on mate, time to go. You can't have them all."

I glanced over at Tristan. He had an odd look on his face. I wondered if he had seen that strange sort of vision in my eyes too. I wished I could ask him. But all that came out was, "Thank you again."

He nodded. "Knowing it means something. Now there's a quest." He put a hand on my shoulder and looked down at me, his face serious, the circles under his eyes suddenly very apparent. He was about to speak, when someone called out from the direction of the stage door, and he seemed to come back to himself. "Nice meeting you." And he turned with Mick, and headed out towards the street. I watched his long figure move away, following Mick, until his dark head was lost amongst a group of people, watched as the small crowd thronged out the door.

I looked down at my hands, so recently covered with his. They had work to do. The Isley Brothers song flashed through my mind. "I've got work to do...I'm out here trying to make it." I suddenly wanted to know more than anything if he had ever heard that song, a million miles away from what they'd just been playing. But it was all music. More important than anything, genre, class, falling on your face in front of your heroes. "Knowing it means something," I whispered to myself. I walked down the now empty corridor to the stage door, and pushed the metal handle and leaned on the door until it opened. The fresh night air, cool and wet after the rain, washed over me. The dry spot where the limo had been was evidence that any of this had happened. It did all mean something. And I was going to go home, and prove it.

Five years later

Chapter 1

I was reading over my notes when I turned the corner in the long hall, and ran straight into someone. I looked up to apologize, and froze. I tried to speak, but my chest suddenly felt heavy, like a large warm hand had just pressed me back into myself. My mind had left my body, and thought just wasn't happening. My neck was in a vice. I struggled to force some willpower back into my limbs and managed to slowly raise my head. The vision before me was calling up some strange language in me, some pre-verbal reaction blocked by lifetimes of conditioning. My response seemed to be in my blood. His lips were full, not quite red, made to entice. His nose was fine, yet all about fighting and determination. I finally made it up to his eyes, which were dark and staring back at me. That part of his face set something up within me, something more, a firestorm of heat. He continued to look down at me, while I fought an internal total surrender. I pulled myself away from those eyes—but adding in the rest gave him the look of an angel, and softened the burning stare that went through me like an arrow. Courtly love, I thought, from the eyes straight to my soul. So it was true.

My entire life seemed to flash before me. Foolish. I had the feeling that nothing I had planned was going to be of any use anymore.

Then his eyes widened slightly, and suddenly we were both human again. And I instantly felt guilty. This beautiful, talented man was normal, just a person. How exhausting it had to be, the focus of a million fantasies and obsessions. I tried to smile, in some sort of acknowledgement of my failure to realize this right from the start. His mouth turned up at one corner slightly, and his face transformed again, and he seemed at once lighter and more serious, as though he had taken something into account.

"Hi," I managed to squeak out. God, my voice. I had effectively managed to cut off the rest of my body. It was probably just as well. I had the feeling that some kind of groaning plea was still lurking just below the surface. I tried again. "How are you doing?" and attempted a rough smile. In my mind, I was busy slamming the gates on my otherworldly experience. I tried to think of something professional, something that would allow me to speak. I cleared my throat.

"Hi."

"Yes, we did that part. I'm Tristan. And you are?"

Unfailingly polite. I yanked myself off the floor of shame, and met his eyes.

"I'm Lily...Lily Taylor." I wondered for a moment if I should tell him we'd met before. I wondered if he remembered me. I thought about how many women he must have met, and decided against it. "*The Core* sent me to interview you. I'm sorry, I'm a bit early. I didn't mean to startle you."

His smile grew wider, and for a moment I thought he was going to laugh. "No, you didn't startle me—I haven't run off, have I?"

Now my determination not to make a complete fool of myself was wrestling with the fog in my brain.

"I haven't either, so we're both lucky." My tone was more cutting than I had intended, and it had the horrible consequence of chasing away his teasing smile.

He looked at me seriously. "Let's make a start then. I'll show you around."

He guided me through the long corridors, stopping to pop into little offices and introduce me. Everyone seemed very pleasant, but severely uninterested. Another journalist, come to flounder in an interview. I shook hands with his manager, James Max, who I thought looked vaguely optimistic until he said, "You won't make this one of those hatchet jobs, will you?"

I assured him that I didn't really believe in writing controversy in order to gain readers. I guessed it was the right moment for The Quote. "What was it Frank Zappa said? 'Rock journalism is written by people that can't write, about people who can't talk, for an audience that can't read?' Or something like that."

They both laughed. Tristan looked at me, quietly reflective. I could only glance at him out of the corner of my eye. The effect he had on me at this proximity was still too new, too overwhelming. His manager spoke first. "Well, doll, I don't think you'll last long as a rock journalist. But you're a joker."

Then I bristled, and snapped back at him. "Thanks so much. But this isn't American Idol." I gave him my best fuck you smile. "Your opinion won't send me home crying." It was impossible to let your guard down in these situations. "So, where's this interview going to happen then?" I spoke more to the room than to either of them.

Tristan's voice was neutral. "Leave it, Jim." He stretched out his arm in the direction of the door. "Let's go get a coffee and you can see my room."

He turned quickly and began striding down the corridor. I followed him, two steps to every long one of his. He had reached the kitchen and was opening the cupboard, taking down coffee beans. "Fresh coffee all right?"

"Yes, that would be great. Thank you." I looked around the room. It was a fairly spacious kitchen, with white linoleum tiles and white doors with chrome fittings. A large silver refrigerator was on the other side of the room, and I watched him cross the room in one motion and retrieve the milk. Each rack of the painfully bright white interior was filled with beer, and champagne and soda cans. No food. He turned to me and saw me looking. "It doesn't bother me, all the alcohol, if that's what you were thinking." He stared at me, his eyes dark with challenge.

I looked back at him. "You're right. But you're wrong. I was thinking that actually, I still find it hard to be around a lot of drink."

"Have you stopped?" Tristan asked.

"Working on it."

He nodded, satisfied. "Milk? Sugar?"

"Just milk please." So far the interview was looking like it was going nowhere. If he had already taken a dislike to me, and I was alternately angry and disturbed by his physical presence, it was unlikely we'd get anywhere. I felt there was nothing for it; I had to try and be honest with him.

I waited until he sat down. "I feel like we've started off badly, and I'm sorry for that." I felt my face color. "I've been really looking forward to doing this interview—I'm a big fan." I took a sip of coffee and felt his eyes upon me.

"Well thank you. Isn't that something you have to say?" He sat back in his chair, hands around the cup, looking vaguely smug.

"I'm not sure I have to say anything. A bit like you perhaps."
I sat up straighter. If there was going to be trouble, then I was
ready. "I'm not here to trip you up, but maybe you'd prefer that."

He laughed. "I'm used to a fight. Maybe you want to get in the
ring with me?" He winked.

"Oh just add me to the queue. But I don't like waiting, so
move me up faster, ok?"

"How fast?"

I looked at him. His eyes were sparkling with some kind of
infectious glee. Jerk, I thought. Pretty jerk. "As fast as you like,
darling."

"Oh we're on to darling now. That must mean we are making
progress."

"Aren't we just? You make a mean cup of coffee. I feel so much
more relaxed and welcome." I raised an eyebrow. "This is great.
Listen, why don't we cut it, and you can tell me what you want
to have out in the press, and I'll try to ask some questions that
you'll deflect. But I warn you—although I'm tempted, I'm not
going to label you an arrogant ass in the article, if for no other
reason than it's been done so often."

He really began laughing then, and the sound of it bubbled up
inside me and I couldn't resist joining in. "You are funny. Come
on, let's do this." And with that, he swallowed down the rest of
his coffee. I found myself strangely fixated on his neck muscles
and tried to cover my confusion by drinking down the coffee
grounds at the bottom of my mug, which only made me cough.

We stood, and he put his arm around me. "Come on, I want
to show you where I work." I nodded. All my attention was on
the warmth and size of his hand around my shoulder, the closeness of his body. I felt my face going a bit red again. Fuck, the

man was a tease. I took a deep breath, and tried to relax into his arm. "It's going to be ok," he whispered in my ear. The rumbling velvet sound of his voice that close to me was screwing with my mind. I knew he knew it. I tried to breathe.

"Yeah, it's fine. Sorry, I'm just not used to being touched." He sprang away. Shit. Wrong answer. I turned to him. "No, it's fine, it's good, I'm just..."

"Just what?" He stayed very close to me as we went through a door and up a flight of industrial stairs. The large window, pierced through with chicken wire, let a white glaring light in that showed the hollows under his eyes. He really didn't seem so bad. It wasn't his fault that the press had fucked with him. That he was beautiful. He was human, and in the bright daylight of the stairwell, he looked exhausted.

We went through another door, and turned right. Tristan made a sweeping, old fashioned gesture as he opened the door. "My inner sanctum." He smiled again, but his eyes were serious.

I looked around. It was a large rectangle of a room, with fairly high ceilings, the pipework and ducts visible. Filled with windows, it nonetheless had a dark feel to it, from the black leather chairs and the big stained oak desk. It was neat, an ornate rug in the center of the room, and a coffee table with a vase of flowers placed exactly in the middle. The papers on the desk were ordered and placed in open letter box type shelves. There were some posters on the walls from the first two releases, and a big picture of his old band over the sofa, on a white painted brick wall. But it was the smell that struck me, and I tried to pin down what it was. Some kind of mixture of expensive men's cologne and frankincense? Candles with flowers and pine? Something else entirely, slightly sweaty and musky? I stood there and suddenly realized he was looking at me, the corners of his mouth twitching slightly.

I smiled at him. "It smells wonderful in here."

He looked animated. "Do you like it? It's a combination I've assembled myself."

"You're bringing out a perfume?" It seemed so unlikely, such a sell-out thing to do. But maybe he was branching out, making the money while he could.

"You're kidding, right? This is for me. Just me. Don't write this down." He sat down in one of the leather chairs, suddenly looking huge and forbidding.

I had to smile, but I felt the message. A little too well actually. In all the wrong places. "No, I'm relieved actually. I was having trouble figuring out how the infomercial was going to come across." He laughed, an irresistible sound. Damn. Keep to the truth. "But if you ever have some left over, I'd love to have some."

"I can think of ways for that to happen." There was that look again, and now, alone in the room with him, the intimidation felt physical. I wondered if he ever took it further, and the look of him surrounded by leather, staring at me, made me think that he did. And made me wonder what I would do if he did. I ran a hand through my hair. Focus. And then he snapped me out of it. "Sit." It was an order, and I backed up and collapsed into the matching leather chair that was behind me. It was soft and smooth, and against my legs, it reminded me of his hand on my shoulder, warm, strong.

I swallowed. "I'll just get my notebook and recorder out, then."

"Fine." He rolled away from the desk and a bit closer to me. I set everything up, and asked him to say something to test the level. "Are you comfortable?" he drawled, his voice a kind of slow pouring velvet, and I felt like I'd crashed into a wall. I literally did not know what to do with myself, and felt dangerously close to losing whatever control I had. Avoiding looking at him, I shook my head, and turned up the volume on his deep voice.

He took the head shaking for discomfort, and jumped up. "Let's go sit on the sofa, you can put the recorder on the table, and we'll be closer—easier to talk." He grabbed all my possessions, and brought them over, setting it all up. He flashed me a big smile, and looked delighted with himself, like a small child figuring something out. I couldn't help but smile back. He really was adorable. Dangerous, but adorable. He sat down and patted the cushion next to him. "Come on, let's do it." He looked up at me from under his dark lashes.

Such a fucking tease, I thought. I'm being played like a piece of music. He smiled again as I sat down, and I tried to find some of the anger that pushed me to action before, but I couldn't manage it.

Tristan jumped up again, startling me. "I'll get us some water." He was at a mini bar in the corner of the room, grabbing two small bottles of Perrier, and back in a flash. "Do you need a glass?"

"No, this is fine, thank you." I needed the water, though. My mouth was completely dry. I had a moment of wondering if he felt any of the insanity I was experiencing, and searched his face for any kind of confirmation. I thought my heart stopped when I saw his throat again, pale and muscular, swallowing and I looked up. But now I was unable to tear my eyes away from his mouth, wet from the water. He put the bottle down, and his tongue darted out, quickly, smoothing over his lips.

I think I groaned. As I was opening the bottle at the same time, I prayed that whatever sound I'd made had been covered up. A slight twitch at the corner of his mouth worried me though. I sighed. I was done for. The writer who became prey. Easy prey.

His voice broke through. "Shall we?" He pressed the start button, and before I had a chance to speak, he was all business— talking about the new release that was due out in a month, the direction he was hoping to take the music in. I made some notes, and was glad I was recording it all. He didn't seem reticent, not the monosyllabic artist some interviews had said he was. He jumped up and went to his computer. "Do you want to hear some songs?"

Now I was excited, but for a different reason. "I'd love it."

He smiled, and pressed play. "You will."

The first song was driven by EDM keyboards but then turned into a spiraling rock epic, with hints of Queen and symphonic orchestras. The next song was a straight out punk rock shout, his voice the drawling snarl from the very first CD. It was amazing.

"This is incredible."

"You like it? That's great. Really?" He seemed like a small child again, delighted at the praise. The next song was another rock song, but more like the Stones, harder, a growling rhythm, whining guitars, arguing and winning, but an insistent counter melody kept rising up to change the tone. I was trying to make a mental list of questions I could ask him, and started scribbling things down, not wanting to miss anything. It was thrilling, and was going to shut up every critic that ever said anything. I told him so, in between songs, and he laughed. "I hope so, doll, I hope so. I just want to get better—come up with something that will help people through their shit." He stopped the music for a minute. "Here, I'm skipping ahead a little. I want you to hear this one."

Another swirling song began, all delicacy and orchestration. Another strange melody served as counterpoint to a repeated line that stopped just when you expected it to reach a conclusion. The lyrics were about losing what you always thought you'd have, getting old alone, having to share what was most precious. Then the chorus began, hard and angular, furious, but the scale was sad and melancholy. By the end, his deep voice was reaching higher, the pain in it sharp and transcendent. It ended on a screech of guitars, and then there was absolute silence.

I sat there, slowly coming back to myself, and realized I was staring out the window, my hands clenched, eyes wet. I uncurled my fingers stiffly and reached up to stop the tear about to go down my cheek, and pinched my nose. I had a lump in my throat. I couldn't cry, not now. Not in front of him. I wanted to laugh and break the moment, but I didn't want to move. I didn't want to be fake and false, turn it all into a joke. Not now.

I turned to look at him. He had a sort of look of wonder on his face, but was equally silent. We sat there, his eyes locked with mine. I felt another tear start, but he was quicker than I was, and I closed my eyes when I felt his slightly calloused fingertip wiping it away. His hand cupped my face, gently, then I felt him pull me towards him, his strong arms wrapped around me. His hand was stroking my hair. "It's going to be ok, shh, I told you it was." I couldn't stop the tears then, and my arms went around him, the feeling of warmth ripping me apart. "Shh, shh, I've got you, it's ok." His voice was gentle and slow, and the closeness of his body felt huge and comforting, a sanctuary. A warning chimed through my brain, but I pushed away the fear and breathed in the smell of him, the softness of his touch in contrast to the leather jacket I now realized my face was pressed against. He held me against his chest, and I could hear his heartbeat in the silence.

I felt him move, and my return to consciousness was a shock. I knew that meant that the moment was ending and in that same second, I knew I was lost. He squeezed me tighter and then his soft lips were against my cheek. "I'm sorry," I whispered.

"Don't be," he murmured. "You're beautiful."

Chapter 2

I looked up at him, so close now, and suddenly saw a moment of confusion in his face, a worried frown pulling at his brow. Tristan started to speak, then stopped, his mouth in a tight line. He began again. "I'm really...um...never meant..." He was interrupted by a knock at the door. "Shit," he mumbled to himself, "excuse me." He loped over to the door, and opened it slightly, blocking the room with his body. "Yes, it's fine. Going well. Yeah, tell them I'll call back. I don't know where my cell is. Just ending, yeah, fine. See you in a minute."

Ending. Right. That was my cue to pull myself together. I started putting away my notes and the recorder in my bag, rubbing the back of my hand over my eyes. By the time he turned from the door, I was already standing, bag on my shoulder.

"I'm sorry...something's come up." His face was still.

"No, that's fine. I've got a few more questions, but we can always finish up over the phone." I wasn't breathing. I could not think of the implications of what I was saying. Images of blood flowing, like a fresh wound, came to mind. I guessed it was my heart. Maybe I'd get a tattoo. Pain for pain. But I spoke, said the same words I'd said many times before. "Your manager has my number. My deadline is in a couple of days, if I don't hear from you, I'll just write it up with what I have." He started to shake his head. "No, thank you. It's been a pleasure." I swallowed. "The music is brilliant. I hope...I want to get that across to people."

James, the manager, suddenly stuck his head through the door. "I'll walk her out, Tristan." His eyes were cold as he opened the door wide enough for me to pass.

I ignored him as I held out my hand to Tristan. "Nice to meet you." One more touch.

His hand covered mine, his voice a deep rumble, his face unreadable. "Um, yeah. Take care." We all walked back down the stairs. He was behind me, so I couldn't see him anymore, but I felt his presence. Too close. I wanted to hit him, push him away and touch him, but I didn't do anything but watch my feet go down the grey painted stairs one at time, carefully. One more step away from whatever it was that happened. And on to the rest of my life.

At the corridor, I turned to him. One more look. It was going to have to last, a long time. I looked into his eyes. I was dead anyway, there was nothing I was frightened of now. I searched beyond his beauty for something, some memory, but all I saw were the too bright white walls in the corridor, and his body, a strip of contrast, dark hair, leather jacket, serious expression. I smiled. The tumbrel was behind me, and I was reminded of the lines from the poem:

> *The door as sudden shut, and I,*
> *I, lost, was passing by,—*
> *Lost doubly, but by contrast most,*
> *Enlightening misery.*

"Goodbye."

"Bye doll." And he turned away.

The manager made as though he was going to grab my elbow. I shuddered, and glared at him. How dare he try to touch me, be where... I snapped. "Closing time, I get it. I'll see myself out. You've got my number if you want to check on the article before it's sent to print."

"I'll call," he sneered. "You're not the only interview," he paused, "he's had."

Bastard. I laughed, nervously, with all the tension of the moment in my voice. "You don't say. Well, you have been so helpful. I'll be sure to let them know over at the magazine. I know just how surprised they'll be." I pulled open the door. "Thanks again." The door closed hard behind me.

I walked to the lift and stabbed at the button. I was starting to see black spots in front of my eyes. I had to get some air, before I fainted. The beginnings of a headache were pinging sharply right in the middle of my head. The service elevator finally came, and I stumbled through the opening door, grateful that it was empty. I leaned against the back and closed my eyes. A vision of his hands, long fingered and graceful, handing me my coffee... I felt the tears burn at my eyes. I had to get the hell out of here before my body completely betrayed me.

Out on the street, I turned and looked back at the building. I couldn't help it; I counted floors, and added one. Those windows at the end. That was...it. I could imagine walking past here in years to come, remembering, silently. Maybe I could tie a flower to the railing, a shrine to what I'd felt. As I was imagining that, a dark shape at the window moved. I started. Was it him? Did it matter? Without any more thought, I raised my hand and waved. I thought I made out a movement, an arm raised. A cab pulled up next to me. Oh right. I waved. Deep breath. I did need a taxi, and I couldn't spend the rest of my life here, staring. So close to a kind of madness. I pulled open the door handle and gazed up at the window, one last time before I got in. The dark shape was still there. I smiled up at it. Ducked into the cab, and closed the door. I told the driver my address, and burst into tears.

Ten minutes later, my breathing started to ease up, and I felt the ache begin. I took out a tissue, and looked up to see the cabbie looking anxiously at me in the rear view mirror. "It's ok," I said, trying a smile. "I've just met the love of my life and lost him all in the space of an hour."

He looked confused. "Still same address?"

I nodded, waving my hand towards the road. Yes. "Yes. It's fine." He kept driving, and I pulled myself into the corner and watched the traffic go by. It was the end of another cold New York City winter, bitter and sharp. Hats and puffy coats. A mother with a stroller, baby wrapped up inside. A black suited bicyclist, Lycra covered against the cold. We finally pulled up in front of my building, a slightly run down walk up in a good neighborhood. I fished out some cash, and didn't wait for change. I flipped open the handle, and climbed out, slowly, checking behind me that nothing was lost. As much as I was dreading having to hear his voice again, I didn't want to lose the tape. It was all I had of him. All I'd ever have, said a voice inside my head that sounded remarkably like the manager.

I took a deep breath, feeling the cold hit my aching head, shut the door and tapped on the roof of the cab. Watching it drive down the one way street was like another link being snapped, something else broken between me and him. I would not cry again. No. I fished out my keys, and opened the heavy door, and slowly climbed up the stairs. I still felt light headed, and I gripped the railing as I went up. Six long twists later, I was at the top. I leaned on the door, breathing, and caught a whiff of that smell. No, it couldn't be. I held up my bag to my nose, and inhaled. There it was, just a hint. The stairwell, the ugly tiles, the sparkles in the flooring, my headache—all receded—and I was left with that strange heaviness in my chest again, the feeling that had come over me when I first met him. I sank down, my back to the door, and buried my head in my bag. I didn't care what kind of fool I looked, I just wanted to breathe in that…smell…and let it take me under. It will fade, I thought to myself, and the pain hit me again.

Eventually, I stood up, shakily. This was not normal. I needed some normal. I unlocked the door and went in, but instead of throwing my bag on the floor, I walked into the kitchen and placed it gently on the table. A symbol, of something. I wasn't even sure what anymore. I felt stoned. I went and washed my face. A glass of wine. That would settle me. And then I thought of him, facing that kitchen, facing his demons, and my stomach twisted. Coffee. I could drink nothing but coffee. "Oh come on!" I shouted. This was crazy. But I made the coffee and sat down again, running our conversation over in my mind. I was not looking forward to writing the piece, listening to the music, and his voice. That voice. Again. My headache was returning. I put the mug in the sink and walked across the hall to my bedroom. I needed to lie down.

In the shadows of the windowless hall, I noticed the red light flashing on the phone, but ignored it. I was sure it was Alice, wanting a blow by blow of the afternoon. Well, that would have to wait too. I wasn't even sure I could describe what had happened, even if I wanted to. Because I knew I didn't want to. It was ours. A moment we had created together. I wasn't going to tell anyone. Maybe just myself, and even then I probably wouldn't believe it. Like that movie. Yeah, the movies. They made them for a reason.

I returned to the kitchen, and picked up the bag. A few hours, alone with my thoughts, and I'd be able to return to life. Sure. I lay back down on the bed, and holding the leather bag to the pain in my chest, I closed my eyes.

Chapter 3

I was awakened by the sound of the door slamming. It was dark out, and I felt disorientated. Was it early morning? What had happened? Then I took a deep breath, realized I was still holding on to my bag. The faint scent was still there, floating ghostly on the surface of my consciousness. His voice, the music—I tried to grasp at pieces of it, but like a dream, it fragmented under my mental touch. I lay back down on the pillows, trying to make shapes out of the darkness on the ceiling. There was a knock. My American roommate. Alice.

The door opened a crack, letting in a bright strip of light. The white lit corridor of the music offices came back to me. I shut my eyes, the door opened wider. "Hon? Are you ok?" Alice crept over to the bed. "What happened honey? Do you want to talk about it?"

The lump in my throat rose up again. I would not cry. But it was hard to talk; my voice came out in a croak. "Hey." I took another gulp of air. "I'm ok, just a bad headache."

"Oh no, I know that voice. Come on, I bought a bottle of scotch."

"I'm not drinking."

"I know that. We'll say it's medicine. This isn't for fun. Look at you." Alice's voice was stern. The bad nurse.

I'd thrown off the duvet, revealing that I was still in my skirt and top, which were twisted around my body. I pulled everything up and down under her searching look. "Yeah, I felt like crap. I'm ok now."

"Bullshit. I'm making you tea and a shot. This is what friends are for. I tried to call you, to tell you I'd be late, but everything went to voice mail. Get up." She held out her hand, pretending to be rough, but there was a bit of sadness in her eyes. "Come on, hon, face the world. You can sleep later tonight."

I creaked out of bed, carefully placing my bag to one side.

"Since when do you nap with your bag? I know you're dedicated, but..." She faltered under the look I gave her.

"Come on, it's a long story." I took her hand and squeezed it. Of course, she was right. Of course. I needed a lifeline back to the world, and here it was. We walked hand in hand to the kitchen and she turned the kettle on. Spinning around, she pulled the box of single malt from the carrier bag.

"Oh, the good stuff, huh? You must really want me to talk." I laughed.

"Hey, life's too short, right? It was on sale." She turned up the light and I winced. She leapt to switch it off.

"Sorry, my head's a bit sensitive."

"Candles?" She ran around pulling out some tea lights and holders. She was always like this, a whirlwind. But everything got done, and it always looked beautiful. I couldn't move at that speed, I'd break things. Within moments, the table and counters had lit candles scattered at artistic intervals. With the sleeting rain hitting the window and the distant sound of the horns of evening traffic, it made for a cozy, almost romantic setting. Romantic. I winced. She didn't miss it. "Isn't that better? Maybe you should take something." She ran out again, and was back in seconds with some tablets. "It's prescription, stop looking like that. You know I wouldn't give you just anything. Even for a story."

She pulled out two shot glasses and filled them expertly to the top. The tea pot was already on the table, along with a small pitcher of milk. "Alice, you're amazing. I feel better just watching you."

"Yes, I'm wonderful. Sláinte." And she clinked the glass with me, and we downed the whisky. I felt the burning sensation pour down my throat, making my eyes water, but melting some of the cold plate feeling I'd had there. Maybe I could make it through this.

"Again?"

"Yeah, I think this might work."

I sipped at some tea, and we downed the second shot in the same way. Ok, I did feel better. My head had loosened up, and I felt the muscles in my shoulder for the first time all day. I started pinching the spot to try and get some more blood going in. Oh. That shoulder. I dropped my hand like I'd been burned.

Alice didn't miss it. "What?" Did someone hurt you? What's going on? This morning you were excited like a crazy person to go out and finally do a big interview—with the super-hot Mr. Hunter no less. You thought you'd hit the big time. What happened? Did it get cancelled?"

I grabbed the bottle and filled our glasses again. I took a little sip before I could answer her. "No."

"No? No, it was cancelled, or no, you got to meet him?" She was bouncing in her chair a little bit. I couldn't blame her. Tristan Hunter had been a bit of a legend for the last several years, an enigmatic figure, either loved or hated. But a lot of the haters were guys who couldn't handle the effect he had on their friends, particularly but not always, of the female variety.

I had known most of the story before I'd gotten the call that I would be interviewing him about the solo record. It was the standard tale of hard work that got called overnight success. Then the sparkle took a few years to start tarnishing. But the weird factor had been turned up about a year and half ago, when it was announced that Tristan was splitting up from his wife and the band, and concentrating on the solo career. No one could get near him for any kind of comment. The band seemed a little confused as well. The two guitarists were openly split on the causes, which finally devolved into a drunken and bloody fist fight in a restaurant in LA. It all had started when one of them, Paul, had said in an interview that Tristan deserved to be dumped, both by his wife and the band, he was a selfish ass. The other guitarist, AC, defended him, but the blood didn't flow until Paul had started getting a little too personal.

I asked Alice if she'd heard the whole story. She only knew what had been reported—which was filled with half-truths and cover-ups. She poured again, and I told her what most people on the inside knew. "It was supposed to be a reconciliation meeting. To talk. But after a few drinks, apparently Paul had thrown out that of course AC would be happy about it—he could go back to being Tristan's fuckbuddy again, like back in the good old days when he was Tristan's personal bitch. Then he said maybe if AC had been a "power bottom," they'd all still be together. And AC went ballistic. Naturally those quotes didn't make the newspapers, but the broken glass and blood over the tablecloth did. And then the next day, the center of the controversy himself released a brief statement. All it said was 'I'm sorry for the unhappiness

I've caused those I've cared about.' There was a picture of him, wearing the ubiquitous sunglasses. It was the least sorry picture they could find, he just looked like he couldn't care less, but that's why they did it. Trouble in paradise. The fall of the gods. Media goldmine." I took a swig. Talking around it. Going back to what my reality was...yesterday. Yes, this was working.

Alice was still talking though. "Ok, some of that I knew. He's been slammed for being a hypocrite, arrogant, above it all. But not to everybody, right? He just had that interview last month where he said the new material was ready to come out, and whoever did the interview..."

I interrupted her. "Clarice Close, *NME*. They've always loved him. They captured the whole tortured artist side. Misunderstood. Misquoted. Emotional pain of the breakup. Could happen to anybody. Music is all that matters, blah blah blah." I took another drink. "But she'll write whatever she's told. Somebody probably played her all the mp3s on her way to DJing a party for the kids of some wealthy businessman."

"Yeah, ok. But they didn't give out interviews to just anybody. Then you got the call."

"Well apparently they liked my credentials. The fact I wasn't the typical rock journo. They'd read something I had written and liked it. So the management thought it would be better, be more sensitive to the 'art'. But..."

Alice leapt in. "I know right? They need damage control. After his ex came out with that In Style article. What a bitch, saying how much happier she was in LA, showing off a new boyfriend. What a relief it was to be 'out in the sun, metaphorically speaking, away from the pressure and the moodiness'."

"Yeah. That was a shock. Someone helped her spring that

one. No one knew until it was too late. They were going to put back the release date, but the suits decided all publicity was good publicity." I sat back. Better to think of it as a story. A fractured fairy tale.

"Jesus. So he's touchy, right?" Alice's face was animated. She loved all the gossip, and I usually didn't spill.

I laughed. I poured out another drink for us both, drank some, and started laughing again. Then I couldn't stop, and pretty soon she was giggling as well. I hugged myself. "Ok ok," I gasped, "that's enough. Touchy. Ha."

"Was he a prick to you? He probably hates all women now. He was always a bit gay anyway, right?"

I took another gulp and the burning felt like it was reaching through my whole body. This was the moment where I decided what and how much to tell. One more drink. I threw back some more, a little more slowly this time, and looked over at her.

She looked back. "Oh."

"Yeah oh."

"You fucked him?" Alice bounced out of the chair, waving her hands around. "You finally got some, and with him? Girlfriend!! It's like a dream come true! Well done you, you sex goddess you. Come on, details. How big, how many, which way?"

"Jesus Christ, Alice! Slow down!" The increasingly drunk part of me was finding it ridiculous. Maybe I should just make stuff up to tell her, I thought to myself. Or I could just sit here quietly, getting smashed, and she could tell me. I started laughing again. No, I couldn't lie. It wouldn't be the first time I wished I was better at deception. I pretended to be angry. "What's with the 'finally got some' crack? Thanks."

"Oh bitch please. It's common knowledge you're shut up

tighter than a vault. Use it or lose it, honey." Alice swung her long blonde hair around and sat back down. "Come on details details, let's have them."

I pretended to be offended, but I shrugged. It was true. All the offers I'd had since the last breakup, which seemed to be further away every time I checked, just didn't do it for me. Alice kept telling me it was like getting back on the horse after falling off, while winking slyly at me and inviting me out. And I went out. But I was bored. Bored with the pick up lines, the way the most obvious women were the most obvious targets. I didn't like what was too transparent, too readily taken. A little mystery. Alice said I was hopelessly old fashioned and primitive. I'd always answer back with the same thing. Primitive like a temple harlot. And she'd laugh. But lately I'd been wondering what I did want.

Then this chance to meet Tristan had come up. Really out of left field, the way luck is, unexpected, and you are just grateful you'd done the prep work so you could actually take advantage of the small miracle. I'd always liked his songs, particularly—well I loved the band, but the idea of solo stuff made my head swim. I'd always thought he was seriously underrated, one of the most intelligent artists to come along in years. And with swagger. Yeah, I'd always thought he was beautiful. In pictures. Then I went to see them and was blown away. His physical presence set the place alight for me. I walked all the way home that night, miles in the rain, seeing nothing else. And feeling the pain of waking up, like pins and needles. At the time, I'd been sort of starting to see Freddie, a friend of a friend and of all things, considering the home life I'd rebelled against, a banker. I'd been busy convincing myself that money was more important than love, that expensive fabric covered up an emotional vacuum fairly well. And it wasn't like I was a great beauty. I thought I was finally being smart to be grateful. But after I saw Tristan and his band live, I had slowly stopped seeing the banker. And I'd stopped pretending. Just like that. I changed my life, and started trying harder to do what I loved. Someone had once said to me "don't should on yourself," but I'd never really seen the truth of what all my lies had done to me. Before he'd come on stage with his leather jacket and his intensity and reminded me what road felt instantly like the right one.

But that was a while ago. In between there had been Mark. And Jake. Coming face to face with Tristan at that awards ceremony. And that path had led me here. Alice was talking. I hadn't heard a word of it. I poured another half shot, feeling guilty. But the drunk was working, I felt better. I bet I could almost listen to the tape...I shook my head, violently.

"What? What is it? You haven't said a word about Sean taking us out Friday. You're not the only one with the rock star connections." Alice looked annoyed.

"Oh hon, I'm sorry. What? I was miles away." I tried to look guilty. At least the questions had stopped.

"Oh no. No no no. You're not getting away with it that easily. I know that look. But Friday—the secret show? It's going to be a blast. Secret guests, free champagne. A chance to get out. And Sean's all right. He'll look after us, not like your last guy. Say you'll come." Alice was smiling at me in that "I look nice, but no is not an option" sort of way that she had.

"I'll think about it. I think I'm drunk." I got up to get some water and had to hold on to the back of the chair.

"I thought that was the idea." She filled the shot glass again. "Now talk. You didn't fuck him, but you wanted to."

I nodded. I could nod. I could take another drink.

"He was incredibly gorgeous and he started a major thaw downstairs." I smiled. Alice was so funny, so funny.

"He looked at you with those big eyes and you lost your mind."

I found my voice. "Something like that." I closed my eyes and remembered seeing him for the first time. Then his hand on my shoulder. His voice in my ear, telling me it would all be ok.

"He touched you."

I couldn't help letting out a sigh. My emotions had been twenty ways to hell fucked with today. I put my head in my hands. "He did." Why was I torturing myself? "Ok. He put his arm around me and said he wanted to show me where he worked." Alice looked excited again. "He whispered in my ear and said it would be ok. His voice…" I looked away.

"Holy hell. What a player." Alice shook her head. "But come on, when you look like that, you almost have to. It would be a waste, especially when there are people starving…" She pointed at me accusingly. "You. Did. Not. Turn. Him. Down. No. Don't tell me if you did."

"No, no, it wasn't like that. His manager thought he'd had me though. But it wasn't like that. It was…" My words were lost in the shards of memory I was looking at. I held on to the table and grabbed the glass, very carefully. I got it to my mouth, and sipped. Ah. Better. I was drunk. Ok, I couldn't have her think I'd turned him down. That would be certifiable. And I wasn't crazy, right? Just a little weird. That's why I had collapsed by my own front door, smelling my handbag. Right.

"Tell me. Now." Alice wasn't generally a mean drunk, but she looked pissed off.

"Ok, ok. We went into his office, room, whatever. It was very neat. It smelled fantastic."

"Like what?" Happy Alice was back.

"God, I don't know. Leather. Flowers. Wood. Him." I stopped. "Don't say it. Don't fuck with my memory."

"Don't worry, go on." She was gentler now.

"Then he played me some of the new stuff. It's amazing, incredible. Did I tell you we had moved to the sofa? He was so close, but...listening to him talk about the music. I never meet anyone brave enough to care about anything that much!" I realized I was shouting. I took another sip, and tried to regain control over my voice. "Then he said he had something special to play for me."

"Oh here we go." Alice nodded. "Something special."

"No, it wasn't like that." How many times had I said that now? I had a feeling it was going to be my new mantra. Everyone would just think that of course he took and of course I gave. Of course. No. "Listen, no, the song was just like everything I've had in my head for a while. I mean, he's just been through being betrayed too, so it's not surprising, but..." I fell silent.

"So he played the song. Then what?" Alice was bouncing again.

"I started crying."

She made a face. "Oh man, that's a passion killer. You should have just said no." She shook her head.

"But that's just it. He...held me. He was so...," I struggled to find some way to describe it. "So gentle. Then he kissed my cheek."

"Your cheek? Mr. Sex God. Whoa. That's unexpected. Ok, so you're a tearful mess and he's being kind. Then what?"

I heard the shouting in my brain and drank down the rest of the whisky in a shot. I would never tell her what he said. She already thought it weird enough that he'd been kind. Fine. Our memory. Our secret, then. "His manager came in. He had another appointment."

"And that's it?" Alice looked disappointed. I didn't blame her, not really. It wasn't the sweaty tryst his pictures made you think of.

"Yeah, I said I had a few more questions, and he could call if he wanted to finish it up. Or not. The manager was an asshole, implied he fucked all the interviewers who walked in the door."

"Maybe he does."

"Maybe." I grimaced. It wasn't the happiest thought, but it'd hardly be surprising. Except that one of them was bound to write about it. Maybe the one who acted like they didn't care. Maybe that's why he'd been so careful, maybe he did want to...my head felt light. "I don't know, he's got to be careful."

"Yeah, especially after Ms. the Ex did such a kiss and tell."

"That did suck. Something surprisingly mean about it."

"Well, maybe he is a dick. Love 'em and leave 'em—a lot. And all those rumors about the band—swinging both ways." Alice took another drink. Was half the bottle gone? Yes, it was. "It's hot though, come on, admit it."

I nodded. "Well yeah. But I don't know."

"Whatever. I can't think what it takes you to let go. I'd pay good money to see him shagging that bandmate of his, what's his name? The one he lived with. The guy with the wild black hair."

I mumbled agreement. It would be. It wasn't the point, though. I wasn't dead, not yet, but my mind was fuzzing up with the drink. Alice was talking again.

"So, he hasn't called then? That's why you're so upset."

"It just happened! Honestly, I don't know. Anyway, he won't. Come on, get real. I haven't looked at the phone since I got home this afternoon."

Alice jumped up. "Shit, girl. It's 10:00 p.m. Check your crack-berry!" She ran off to my room and came back, holding the bag. "Oh, what's that nice smell? Did you buy some cologne?" I grabbed the bag from her. "Ok, calm down, don't panic. Here you go." She watched me pull out the phone.

I checked my texts first. The magazine, asking for an update. The yoga course I was on, reminding me of the next lesson. A number I didn't recognize. I opened it and all the air left my body in a rush, making a noise somewhere between a gasp and a groan. Alice jumped up and read the words over my shoulder.

> Loyal once, lost once, stand over me, no
> security—maybe I got it wrong. Call.

Alice looked at me. "What? Is that him?"

I managed to move my head. I wanted to smile, I was smil-ing, I just wouldn't show the hurricane spinning inside me. Not even to Alice. I stood up. I had to move around. She followed me.

"How do you know it's him? There's no name." She looked at me quizzically.

"Song lyrics." I didn't mention that it was from a love song.

No need, no need. I pulled a bottle of water out of the refrigerator for something to do. This was all mine. For once.

"Oh that's clever. And no name, just in case it goes to the wrong place. Smart."

"Yeah." Oh, you have no idea.

"You're happy, right?" Alice wouldn't leave it alone.

"I am, hon, really," I said flatly. She looked at me, shocked. "Really. It's great. I'm just drunk and it's been a long day. I think I'm going to go to bed."

"Are you going to call him?" I looked away. That was the question, wasn't it? To me, the answer was already clear.

"Yeah, sure. Probably not right now, though. Alice, I really need to lie down, the room's spinning."

She gave me a hug. "Don't worry, babe, it's going to be fine."

"I hope you're right." I took the bag and my phone and watched my feet make patterns of the wooden floorboards. I placed the bag down on the bed and changed into a t-shirt. It was soft and cool. It felt good against my flushed skin. My pulse was beating an endless rhythm. And I could only hear those words, in that voice.

"Loyal once, lost once, stand over me, no security. Maybe I got it wrong. Call."

Over and over again, until sleep finally won.

Chapter 4

I had a busy couple of days trying to do work, and pulling out the phone every so often to look at the text. I hadn't called him yet. I wasn't sure if I was going to call. I wasn't sure any more about anything—if any of it had happened, if the text was legit, if I really was going to give in to something that unreal that easily. Alice kept giving me dirty looks every time she started to ask me about it and I would shut her down, and walk away. I didn't want to talk about it. Letting go like that...I thought of crying in the cab, sitting by the door, holding the bag. It was stupid really. Silly. I wasn't a teenage groupie, never had been. I had a job, didn't own any four inch heels, like Alice did, or see-through tops. The last guy I'd gone out with had taken me out for a couple of nice meals, after getting over the shock that I wouldn't sleep with him after the first one, then told me I was too complicated, and he liked 20 year olds because they were more flexible...with their time. I didn't feel like being made a fool of, again.

So I went out that night for a drink in a club that was breaking new bands, chatted to the manager, made plans to come back and see "Worms," or "Bugs," whatever the name was, for my piece following the start up of different bands. It was something I'd been working on for a while—thought it might make a good book. And maybe I'll get to see some of these people before the system works them over, I thought. Then I walked all the way home, only looked at the phone once, and looked forward to getting into bed, and not thinking about anything for at least a few hours.

But I woke up in the middle of the night. Something had made a noise. I groaned and fell back on the pillows. My head was starting to hurt. I grabbed the bottle of water by the side of my bed. It was cool and it felt good to drink. So thirsty. I grabbed some aspirin, and swallowed that down too. What time was it? I rolled over onto the other side of the bed and grabbed my phone. It was flashing. There was a text. I felt my heart rate increase as I opened it. Yes, that's what had woken me up, sent four minutes ago at 2:21 a.m. From "unreal," the name I'd saved the last text under. I sat up as I read it.

Aren't you going to call? I'm serious.

Serious. That was a strange word to use. But maybe he knew I didn't believe it was him, or that he would want to see me. The frightened part of my mind said to wait until tomorrow, wait until I could think it all through clearly, and have a rational answer in the daytime. And then there was a reckless side that didn't care about rational, or correct. Sense was getting yelled down by the need to start this. Whatever this was. I needed to know. I needed to find out what I wanted. I put down the bottle, and I texted back.

Some people sleep. But yes I was.

I pressed send before I could rethink it.

A minute passed. I put the phone down and was about to get under the covers when it beeped. I grabbed it.

> Obviously neither of us is sleeping. I want to see you.

Well, that was quick and to the point. I tried to rearrange my mind in a way that I could play it cool. It wasn't working.

> Yes. When?

The reply came faster now.

> Now. Or in half an hour.

Now? But I had to shower, fix up...no. It was better this way. No time to think about anything. Still, I couldn't resist teasing him. Just say yes, you idiot, my heart cried out. But I was already texting.

> Do you always get what you want?

The answer came back almost instantly.

> Mostly. Tell me your address and I'll meet you in the car.

My body felt like it was going to explode. Was I actually going to do this? See him? I was grateful now for the buzz which still lingered in my head and was calming me down, just enough.

I texted him my address. That alone was breaking some rules. His text came back almost immediately.

> Meet me at the corner of 93th and Central Park West. At 3.

I could only answer yes.

I rushed to the bathroom and quickly washed and brushed my teeth. I threw on some scented body cream and rushed to pick out clothes. 2:45. I didn't have much time. I couldn't over think it, which was probably a good thing. Jeans, a low necked t-shirt, boots. Some lipstick. More perfume. 2:51. Time to go. I emptied my bag of everything but keys and some money and my phone and tried to be as quiet as I could, but I heard Alice's voice.

"Lily, what's going on?"

"I'm going out. I'm going to see him. I need to leave right now."

She called out from her room. "Don't think too much. Remember—'je ne regrette rien.'"

And I was off, down the stairs as fast as I could. I half ran, half skipped to the park, my heart beating. Was this really happening? It had stopped raining, and everything was shining wetly under the streetlamps. A few cars went past. I reached the corner and looked around. Nothing. I tried to take some deep breaths of the cold night air. I felt more awake than I ever had in my life. I didn't want to panic. I didn't even want to think about it—who he was, any of it. I just wanted to act. I didn't even know what he wanted, it occurred to me. Maybe I should have brought the notebook. Maybe he just couldn't sleep and decided to finish the interview. And here I was, excited like a little kid. I shut my eyes. I could do this.

When I opened them again, there was a black limo slowing down. Holy fuck. It slid into place in front of me and the back door opened, ghostly. I stood there for a moment, stunned.

"Get in." That voice, used to giving out commands and being answered, went through me, electric. My body had already answered, but I took one last deep breath to try and fight it.

I climbed in and shut the door. There was a bottle of champagne, opened, and two glasses. I turned my head to the back of the limo. And there he was, slouched against the back, his long legs tightly encased in black jeans, ending finally at black boots with a slash by the ankle. A white t-shirt and a black leather jacket. His hair was an artfully tangled mess. And his eyes, under his dark brows, were staring at me with a strange intensity.

"You came."

"You asked me to."

"I'm glad you don't sleep either." He pressed a button, and the dark window between the front and the back came down an inch. "Harry, just drive around. Maybe the Park. Wherever."

"Yes sir, no problem." The window went back up with a slight mechanical noise and the limo pulled into traffic. The only lights were the small strip lights along the side, and the street lights from outside, made dim by the tinted glass. There was a sunroof as well, which was letting in a rhythmic flash of lights from overhead. But that glass was tinted as well, so the effect was oddly soothing.

He rose up slightly out of his seat. "Champagne?"

"I thought you didn't drink."

"Sometimes, a little, for special occasions. This is special. You agreed to come out." His 3:00 a.m. voice was like honey on fire. I wanted him to just keep talking. He came closer and poured us each a glass of champagne. It was a delicate rose color, with tiny bubbles. I held it to my nose, and inhaled. With the perfume of the wine I could detect his scent on him again, and I felt as though all my senses were being called from some other dimension.

"It's Billecart Salmon '97. A very good year." And with that he touched his glass to mine, and slid back along to the corner of the sofa-like limo seat. He looked at me. "I don't bite. Come sit next to me."

Feeling slightly foolish, I slid along the leather seat to sit next to him. I kept a small distance between us, and with a deep breath, I stretched out my legs and took a sip of the champagne. "This is one of my favorites; it's been a long time." I blushed, thinking of what I had just said, and glanced over at him. He was smiling.

"Ah, ok, a connoisseur. I like that. What other pleasures demand your refined tastes?" His voice was a low murmur again. I could feel his breath against my ear. I didn't dare move. "You're too tense, but I think I like that." He moved away slightly and drank some of his champagne. I felt cold where he had been that close to me, and I wished he would come back. I started to speak.

"I'm...I wanted to thank you for that afternoon." I turned to look at him. His eyes were beautiful; that mix of colors, grey and brown and blue. I realized I was staring, and turned to the front and drank another sip. My mouth was dry again.

Then his mouth was at my ear. "My pleasure. But don't thank me yet." I inhaled, trying to have some control over my body. I pulled my leg in, and rested my hand upon my knee as an anchor. I felt like I was falling into him, and his body was turned towards mine, I could feel it. His mouth was closer, and then his nose was against my ear. I gasped, and I felt him smile against my hair. "I like you." I took another gulp of champagne. Oh god. What was happening? His hand reached over and took my glass and put it down. "There's time," he whispered. Then his mouth was just touching my ear lobe, running down to my neck, his face on my shoulder. His full lips were soft, just like I remembered. My conscious mind was floating away. There was only the heavy liquid blackness that I wanted to sink into. He broke my reverie with a nip, fine sharp teeth biting at exactly the most sensitive junction between shoulder and neck. I moaned, and stopped myself.

"No," he said. "Go on. I like it, that's why I like you, you're all nerves." He turned me towards him more fully. With my shoulders facing him, I needed to move my leg to steady myself. He extended his long arm and placed a hand on the top of my boot. I could feel the heat of his hand through the leather. "Look at me." I raised my eyes to his. "I meant what I said. You are beautiful. You have a quick mind. And I think you would like to play games with me..." He drawled out the last vowel until it was a rumble in his chest. Oh god. Those words, in his voice. Like raw silk, the wind before a storm, fresh running water... "And you like me, don't you?" He lifted my chin with his fingers. I could just feel the slight callous on his fingertips.

"I do." His eyes softened slightly but kept their level gaze. He managed to move my hand up to touch his face.

"Touch me then." I tentatively reached out my fingers against his skin. A tiny bit of stubble, the raised moles by his ear. I let my fingers drift across his face as slowly as I could, letting each sensation take time to reach my fogged brain. He closed his eyes and smiled. I wanted to touch his mouth. To feel it, the heart shaped upper lip, soft, but unyielding. Capable of extremes. Only focusing on the lower half of his face, there was that violence there that I had seen before, something dangerous and wild. I ventured my finger to the center of his lower lip. His eyes opened, and they were dark, almost black. I ran my finger over his lips again, and then moved to my own mouth, just to see the difference. His eyes followed my hand, glittering. "I knew you'd be like this," he whispered. He caught up my hand in his and moved his fingers over my mouth, moving closer until he was touching my lips and I was touching his, softly. My tongue licked my lips, they were dry, but his fingers were there. I couldn't stop myself and my eyes closed as I darted my tongue in between his fingers. I had just lightly touched him with my tongue, but we both breathed in sharply. His voice juddered like a ship hitting sand. "Ah, that's good. Very good. I wonder if you won't teach me something."

My heart was pounding and I opened my eyes to look at his face. He had a roughened look to him, a dark determination. But he suddenly moved away, and reached for our glasses and handed me mine. "Drink," he commanded, and we both took large swallows of the delicate champagne. The taste on my tongue, the sweetness of the wine, the slight bitter saltiness of his fingers, was making me dizzy. But I made my decision. I needed to kiss him, I didn't want to wait, and I couldn't wait. I turned to put down my glass and placed my hands quickly on his shoulders. He was faster though, and his hands grabbed mine. His fingers circled my wrists and held them, firmly. "No," was all he said, and he looked away from me for a moment. My heart failed. Rejection? Already? My blood was pounding, everywhere. I looked at him, about to speak.

He brought each of my hands to his mouth, and kissed them. "You've been mistreated. Someone's made you feel you had to do all the work. They misunderstood you." He laughed. I stared at him. He held my wrists tighter. "What if I saw something in you that would respond to me?" He pulled me closer, the current running through me intensifying. He suddenly pulled me up by my wrists onto his lap and put my arms around his neck. He held me to his chest, and moved his lips to my neck, beginning a series of warm kisses and bites. I could feel the rough wetness of his tongue, as he slid up to my ear. I shuddered involuntarily. "That's it. That's what I want from you. Nothing else. Just hold on." And he pulled me more tightly to him, until I couldn't avoid feeling his arousal, evident even through his jeans. I made as if to move, but he pushed my hips down against him. "You won't break me, darling. I like it, I like the way you feel on me. Very much. You can feel that, right?"

He bit me again, and the warmth between my legs felt like a flood. He moved me again slightly, and I was just where I could feel him, warm and rock hard against where I was wettest. I lifted my head. I wanted to see his eyes. He seemed to know this, and moved his kisses around to my cheek, then held me away from him for a moment, staring at me. "Please,"...I didn't know what I was saying. The hypnotic quality in his eyes was back again. "What?" His voice insistent. "What? Tell me what you want. Never lie to me." His jaw was set.

I faltered. "It's not much...please kiss me...I want to feel your mouth..." He stopped my words by pulling me down on his cock again, which had shifted, pointing towards his stomach, the shape and size of it clearly visible. So all those rumors were true, I thought for a moment. Another burst of wetness flooded out of me and I wondered if I was soaking him through our jeans. He moved me slightly, and I shut my eyes again, shaking. Then without warning, his mouth was on mine, gentle, biting my lips, then pressed against me , his full lips overpowering mine, changing pressure, first nipping at me expertly, now full against me. He moved his tongue, softly slowly against me, looking to enter. He pushed in the tiniest of amounts then ran his tongue over my mouth. I gasped again, and he took advantage to invade my mouth, exploring, It was like being fucked—and the second I thought that he rolled his hips against me. This time we both groaned. He stopped for a moment and leaned his forehead against mine. "Fuck me, when you do that it makes me want to come." He plunged into my mouth again and I fought back, licking his mouth, that mouth which seemed to respond to everything instinctively, wanting to touch. Our breathing was like the need, insistent, repeating, endless. He suddenly stopped and lifted me up again. "Get on me." And he moved my legs so that I was kneeling on the seat, spread over him. He pulled me down, hard, and I moaned. I felt like I was burning, something was taking over my entire body, I had no thoughts. He did it again. "My god," he murmured into my hair. "Imagine what it's going to be like when we actually fuck, darling." I closed my eyes. I didn't know what was going to happen and didn't care. And then he began to rotate his hips in a kind of dancing samba like motion, and his hands went around my waist moving down to hold my hips, designing ticklish patterns over my ass, then pulling me to him, tighter. I moaned from the increased pressure. It was like torture, close, so close, but not close enough, then he pulled me to him so hard it almost hurt. A sort of sharp pain and I gasped again. Nothing had ever felt like this in my life. I didn't want to think, I wanted him to fuck me until I lost consciousness. I moved to touch his chest and ran a finger tip over his chest; and finding his nipples hard under the t-shirt I squeezed one. And he moaned. "Yesss," he hissed and he buried his head in my shoulder, and bit down on my skin. It went through me like a flash of lightning. I was delirious, I was soaked. This pleasure so close to pain was unlike anything I'd ever experienced. I couldn't think...

He was moving under me again and his mouth was against my ear, his dark voice gloating. "I can make you come...just like this I think." And he pulled me hard against him, dancing with my body. His hands moved my shirt away from my shoulder, and he continued a trail of light kisses and bites, but this time he was heading towards my breasts when he stopped. "I don't usually do this," he said. "Take this off." He pulled at my shirt.

I moved my hands away and pulled my shirt off over my head. He stared at my breasts, barely encased in a cream colored lace bra I'd thought to put on. I wanted him to...but no sooner had I thought it, than he was there, kissing me over the fabric, biting down hard on my nipple. I groaned. "I knew it," he said and he moved away and licked my mouth. "I will lick and bite you—everywhere. And damn you, I am trying to slow down, but I need this. I want this." And he returned to my breast, and pulled the bra strap off my shoulder. I thought I heard something tear and he had me in his mouth. That soft incredible mouth. It was so intense I wasn't sure if I could take any more. He lifted his head, running his long dark hair against my breasts, then capturing my mouth with his. He was starting his hip rolling again, but this time more seriously, with certain intent. His fingertips began to flick my nipple with his fingernails, each touch painful but...but not. Our breathing was coming faster. "I don't do this. But I can make you come. Just like this. And I'm going to do it. Look at me. Don't stop."

And I tried to focus on his beautiful eyes, even though every time he increased the pressure my eyelids fluttered closed. He grabbed my arms, and he pushed against me, sliding me down to meet him. "Fuck you're wet for me," he groaned. His breathing became more rapid, and he pulled at my nipple teasing me with his mouth and his hair. I cried out and all I could hear was his deep voice, emphasizing every word in between his breathing. "That's what I want, that's it darling...I am going to teach you to come for me. Only when I tell you to." And he ran his tongue over my mouth and increased his rhythm. My eyes shut, I had lost control over my face, my limbs, my sex. And he closed his long fingers over my breast, and held me, hard. "Look at me, look at me, so close." I felt a kind of trembling start in him that went through me to the core, he moved faster and faster and his eyes were now dark galaxies. "Oh fuck," he gasped and he began to run tighter and tighter circles and suddenly all the sensations moved together, and his fingers on me were like fingers on my clit and he pulled me into him, holding a rhythm as he licked my mouth and I cried out moving against him as fast I as I could, unable to control my movements, taken over by the intensity of it all. He held my sex to his cock and I could feel him, huge, throbbing under me, letting off another round of convulsions through my entire body. "Oh god, yess," he cried out, ragged, his eyes closed and his head falling back against the seat, his cock still pulsing between my legs, adding to the wetness I had drenched us in. He was still coming, his voice barely audible, "oh god, oh god." And then he cried out, almost a sound of pain, and he pulled me to him, pulsing out another series of moans from both of us. I was trembling, shaking against him. I had no power over my limbs. His long arms circled around me and he pulled my head down to his shoulder.

"Oh yeah," he muttered, and kissed my hair.

Chapter 5

We sat together like that for a while, dreaming, our breathing slowing, outside of time. Every so often, he would hold me a bit tighter, or kiss me, softly. It was warm, and all my limbs were heavy, sleepy. Yet I felt lighter, as though a vast source of energy was pulsing through me, and with no effort at all I'd be able to float off. I started to fall asleep on his shoulder, breathing in his smell, the slightly bitter smell of sex and sweat that hit all my nerves.

Finally, he shifted. "Come, darling, sit next to me." And he practically lifted me up, and placed me next to him, but he kept one arm around me. I needed that contact. As long as he was holding me, everything was ok. Nothing was going to stop. He handed me my glass and we both drank. It was quiet, and still dark. He spoke again. "You're very quiet—now," and he smiled at me. "Are you happy?"

I turned to look at him. It was such an unexpected question. Of all the things people had said to me after sex, this idea of happiness had never come up. I looked back at him. "No one's ever asked me that."

"Well, they're idiots. What else matters? So, darling, are you?"

"It's more than happy, it's…" I couldn't think of how to describe how I felt. "Yes. I'm very happy." I smiled. "You are…a very sensitive…oh hell. You're amazing. That was…"

He interrupted me. "I would have expected a writer to be better with words. No matter. We'll work on that."

I felt a smile coming up from the center of me. "We will?"

"Let's not do games, unless we both agree." He fixed that stare on me again. "I wanted you, you wanted me, I think what just happened between us was...quite unusual."

"Unusual?" I bit my lip. What did this mean?

"You are very receptive, responsive. I'm sure someone's told you that before." He took hold of my hand, as though he could feel my nervousness returning.

I squeezed back. And smiled. "Yeah, someone told me that once. A massage therapist. That's it though."

He raised his eyebrows, looking like he had made a discovery, and he nodded. "I think both our lives are about to...become a lot more happy." He poured us both another glass of champagne. "There are some rules we'll need to go over, but not right now. What I need to know," and here he paused and drank half his glass down, "is whether you want to see me again, and if you can be discreet."

I'd get to do this again. And more. I couldn't resist, my eyes took in his body. The boots, his legs, the long arms, his talented mouth, his very mobile hips, the... He was waiting, watching me look at him. That smirk was back. I didn't care.

"Yes. And yes." I met his eyes. I would have to learn not to be afraid of this, and just thank the universe for it, no matter what it was, how short, how long. His presence was like a drug, and I was pretty sure I would do anything to feel him, more of him. I shuddered. I wanted him again.

"I can't do girlfriend/boyfriend things. You know? Can you live with that? I don't want you changing your mind, then feeling hurt. I don't want to hurt you." And he pulled me to him again. "I do like you."

I whispered into his hair, soft and dark around my face. "I can." I took a deep breath. "You make me feel incredible." He kissed my forehead. I held him close. "Like something I've only glimpsed at."

He hummed in my ear. "Then let's toast to everything that's going to become a lot clearer." He moved away, clinked his glass with mine. When we had finished, he took the glasses again and put them down. "There." He pulled me to him. "I'll drop you at the same place. Better to keep the limo away from your house, unless you like being photographed."

I shook my head. "No, it's fine."

"I've got your number." He held my face up close to his and kissed me. I felt we were sealing some kind of contract, a kiss instead of a signature. "I will call you. And next time...well, maybe we'll talk a little." He chuckled. "Or maybe not. But there are some rules we need to agree to, ok?"

I nodded.

"Ok then." He pressed the button. "Harry, can we drop off my friend at the same place?"

"Of course sir." The window went back up, and after stopping at a light, we turned left. I couldn't help but wonder how many times this had happened. I closed my eyes. I wouldn't think about it. This was the real world. And I was happy. Harry was obviously a pro at this. There had to be a reason. It didn't matter.

Tristan looked at me. "You're brave. I see what you're wrestling with. But you being you is what is so appealing." He looked out the window for a moment, then back at me. "You'll figure it out."

The limo stopped. I looked up at him. This was it. I was happy, I felt incredible, but the idea of separating my body from his was painful. He was so...warm. Beautiful. He kissed the top of my head. "Go get some sleep darling."

I nodded. "I'll try." He smiled at me as I pulled my coat back on, and moved away. Cold. So cold. I wanted to be back by his side. Without thinking, I slipped along the seat and hugged him. I didn't care. He hugged me. "Naughty girl. Now go." His voice was severe, but he was smiling.

I opened the door, and got out, my legs still slightly wobbly, and shut the door without turning around again. I'd manage to keep some dignity. The cold air hit the wetness on my jeans and pierced through to my skin. The difference between the extreme heat of only a short time ago and the wintry cold outside was shocking. And I realized my jeans were soaked, from both of us. I smiled. Some proof. I turned to watch the limo join the traffic heading downtown. I stood there for several minutes, feeling the wind whistling down Central Park West, chilling my overheated body. I could feel and see and hear everything. A small bird. A hair on my arm. My ears, reddening in the wind. The yellow taxi-cabs accelerating at the light. My mouth, chapped and swollen. The muscles in my legs, slightly sore. The sky, growing lighter, imperceptibly. I felt like I could hear the sky growing lighter. It made a sound. I smiled. Like every nerve had been polished to reflect the world. I wanted to stand there forever and feel.

But my jeans were becoming uncomfortably cold and stiff, freezing in the wind. And the wind was stronger now, with the sunrise. The first shoots of pink were streaking the sky over-head, the wispy clouds a mixture of colors—gold, and pink and blue and black. It was so beautiful. Like his eyes, changing, as he looked at me. I watched for another minute, then reluctantly turned down the street to walk home. I pulled my jeans down a little so they wouldn't rub against me, tender from all the friction. A giant grin spread across my face. I could take a little pain. Oh. Did that just happen? I thought of Tristan, in his limo, and I hoped he was feeling good. Idiot! I never asked him if he was happy. I'd fix that, next time. I wanted him to be happy, so happy. I wanted to shout. I looked around and let out a whoop, and starting running down the street, hugging myself.

Chapter 6

I let myself in, quietly. I really didn't want to talk, and I tiptoed down the hall to my room and shut the door behind me. I wasn't tired, not really. I felt hyper-excited, delirious, slightly drunk from everything that had happened. I sat down on the bed, then jumped up again. My jeans were really wet, and as much as I didn't want to, I'd have to take them off. I removed my coat and flung it in a corner, then started unpeeling my jeans. Ow. I knew without looking I was swollen, but I didn't care. It was a reminder, his touch had marked me, and I was changed. I stripped off my jeans finally and shook them out. His smell filled the room, sending a wave of heat between my legs. I turned and looked in the mirror, and felt slightly embarrassed. My hair was wild around my head, and there was a certain animal intensity to my eyes that hadn't been there before. Whoever said sex was the best makeup was so right, I thought. And at the same time, I had a moment of doubt. He wanted this? Me? All my flaws and shortcomings? I was sort of pretty, but...

I knew I didn't completely understand his reasons for doing this, whatever this was. And there were the rules. What were they going to be? And how long would I have to wait to find out? There was no point even thinking about it. It was completely out of my control. And I took a deep breath, and sat down on the bed. It was freeing, in a way, to not have to worry about when to call, or if I should, or anything else. Because it was all going to be agreed upon in advance. Games. Would I be able to handle them?

I pulled my bag over to me, and hooked up the headphones. I needed to finish this article, and that was something I could control. But I couldn't control how I became instantly wet, again, the moment his voice started up. I tried to focus. I would not touch myself. I wanted it to just be him. I wanted to be desperate, even more desperate for his touch than I already was. I drifted off again into my daydream. Were we going to fuck? Really? The idea of that...what I'd seen...holy hell. I had a vision of his hips, curving under me, rhythm, complicated, swaying, more than one beat. I pinched myself, hard. Stop.

I wrote a few paragraphs, really just transcribing what he'd said to me, interspersed with some descriptions of his room, but not too many, I thought to myself, and I left out the way it smelled, the way he smiled. Oh that voice. He said he'd teach me. What did that mean? I was frightened by all the things I didn't know. He was obviously much more sexually experienced than I was. But I wasn't a complete novice. I'd tried a few things. Just no one ever took responsibility. I was shy. They thought it was too much. Just wanted to get off. Were all men like this? I rubbed my eyes. Why was I having this argument with myself? Why couldn't I just admit what I wanted? And accept that he was in charge?

I wrote another few lines. I was growing sleepy now, and my neck hurt a bit. My neck! I jumped up to look in the mirror. Yes, there was a small, very neat and very precise bruise from his sharp teeth. I smiled. Oh yes, I liked it. I liked it a lot. I could never understand when women complained about the kisses with teeth. I liked the way it felt when it was happening, and the way it felt afterwards when it was sore. It suddenly occurred to me that I'd never really finished that thought before, I'd just known it. I tapped it lightly with my fingertip. It stung, just a little. I smiled. Well, discreet it was not, but it could be covered up. I felt sorry that I had to. I'd like people to see that he'd chosen me, taken hold of me and...

I squeezed my legs together. This was pointless torture. I needed to rest. I had no idea when he would call. For I all knew, there were going to be a lot of 3:00 a.m. trysts. And I wasn't going to back out of any of them, no matter how tired I was. I'd never, ever get this chance again.

I looked at my phone. Nearly 9:00 a.m. I called and left a message at the magazine, and gave them a glowing update, told them they'd have the interview over the weekend. Checked my messages. Nothing important. I called back my agent and said I was working on something, and asked about a royalty check that should have turned up by now. It was only a message, but I was surprised by my voice. Almost as though I'd taken some of that power into me. I leaned over and buried my face in my jeans. The scent of us, together, was dizzying.

I laid out the jeans close to me, and crawled under the covers. Go get some sleep darling. I was obeying.

•   •   •

I woke up with a start. The sun was streaming in the window. For a moment, I couldn't remember anything, then it all rushed at me at once. Images, sounds, smells, feelings. Tastes. Like a drug that takes all your senses and concentrates them into one explosive drop. I felt the tension rising in me again and my heart sped up. God, had he called? What time was it? What was I doing? I threw off the covers and turned on my phone. 1:30. Not too bad. Had anyone called? Texted? I looked at the texts. Nothing. One message from the magazine, call them, no rush, glad it went well. One message from the agent. Check in post. We'd see.

I pulled on a pair of sweat pants, gently. A little less sore, but I could still feel it. It hurt, but I liked it. Since when had I been so into pain? Always, I thought. Suddenly, I wasn't sure I recognized myself. Really? As I made coffee, I reflected on some of my past experiences. There was a certainly a case to be made for looking for situations that might cause me pain. Not dealing with the subconscious, I thought. Maybe this would be different. I touched my neck again, and shuddered. I am insatiable. I need to calm down.

I sat there, drinking coffee. I couldn't remember Alice's schedule. Was she here now, or out tonight? What day was it? Thursday. So what. It was the name of a day. It did not take into account how the earth had shifted. I felt the arbitrariness of imposing a name on time, time that would bend and twist unexpectedly, shoot into the future and back into the past. Thursday. Thor's day. Hammer of the Gods. I laughed. Well, that part was true. I got up to run a bath, taking my coffee with me, and nearly ran into Alice, coming out of her room. I just managed not to spill anything on her. She was taking off her coat.

"Didn't you hear me come in?" Alice looked amused.

"No, hon, I was just drinking some coffee, going to have a bath." I wasn't sure how discreet was discreet. I hoped she had a cold. I had the feeling I reeked of sex. I started smiling, unable to stop the silly grin from spreading across my face.

"You look like you got the cream, pussy...cat. Well? Did you?" She looked hopeful.

Discreet. "We talked. He's really lovely."

She looked skeptical. "And you're this happy?"

Lies, lies. Say the truth, just not all the truth. "Well, yeah. I got to ride around and talk to the most talented man on the planet." Ok, maybe that was a bit much. Not good to lay it on so thick. "He's great. I had fun."

"No sex?" Alice tapped her nose with her finger.

"Nope."

"You lying wench. That's ok. I won't tell." She giggled and kissed me on the cheek, as I started to protest.

"No, really, we didn't fuck." There, that was true.

"Uh huh. Whatever. Like I said, no one will hear it from me." We smiled at each other. Whatever she guessed, she wasn't going to make me break my promise. Was she trustworthy? I wasn't going to risk it. As much as I wanted to tell her everything that happened, I couldn't be sure. She moved in those circles too. Her pillow talk might ruin everything. I suddenly felt sick, and unconsciously rubbed the bruise on my neck.

"Alice, you can't say anything. Not even about seeing him. Nothing. Please." Her eyes were fixed on the bruise on my neck. "Alice, promise me."

"Don't worry hon. But you owe me. Tomorrow, you're coming out with me and Sean to this private party."

I wondered if it was going to mean giving up a chance to see him. God. But I'd have to keep her sweet. I did trust her. But.

"Ok, ok. I'll come. But clothes...I need a dress, something party worthy?"

"Nope, taken care of. You can borrow one of mine. We'll

make sure you look good, you never know who might be there." She winked at me. "I think you'll need to purchase a good concealer though. I don't wear clothes that cover my neck."

I blushed. There really wasn't anything I could say.

She laughed. "You suck at lying girlfriend. Go have your whore's bath."

I couldn't help laughing. "Having a full bath. Not just top and tail. And I'm not a whore."

"Yeah, whatever. I'm working tonight, I'll see you later—around 3:00, right?—if you're heading out again."

"Alice! Come on." I tried not to sound pleading. I would kill her first then myself if she screwed this up.

"I promise. It's cool. Really. I do want details sometime, though. Is it true he's hung like a fucking moose?"

"Alice!"

She went out the door, still laughing.

I had my bath, which stung when I sunk into it. I'd have to get some cream if this kind of friction was going to be a constant. Now there was a thought. Back to reality. I got out after a while, and went back to my room, towel trailing behind me, then I dressed and put on a bit of makeup. I felt like I wanted to make more of an effort. I wanted to look like I felt, which was horny as hell, and possibly, desirable? Me? Obviously. Look at what happened. And it wasn't going to be just once, right? I'd have to get used to that idea. And not desired by just anyone, but him. And he was so…amazing. God. Really, my vocabulary had just disintegrated along with my brain. Maybe a walk around and another coffee. Oh yeah, and concealer.

I checked my phone as I put it in my bag. Nothing from him. That was ok. Wasn't it? I had to trust in this, give up the control.

A primitive desire within me was warring with a modern need to know what the hell was going on.

It suddenly occurred to me, that this was part of it. Giving in. I hated it. I didn't like feeling helpless. But then I thought about him, and his smile and his hair, and the way his head fell back when he felt good and what my body wanted. And I made a decision. I was not going to do things in the usual way. I'd learn, I'd listen, I'd accept. I would speak up, and say what it was I wanted.

But what I wanted most of all was him. And in order to get that, I'd have to play his game. And trust that what he wanted was our mutual pleasure, and not just some crazed power trip. I'd been with enough guys that saw every chance as a chance to be on top, literally and figuratively, but didn't care how or why. Or what happened afterwards.

He said he didn't want to hurt me. That was a start. I looked at my phone again. Nothing. Ok. I could do this.

Chapter 7

So, I had walked around. I thought the fresh air and exercise would calm my overheated brain. Had a latte. Watched people start to head home. And in the early nightfall, I felt scared. And lonely. Everyone seemed to be with someone else. Intense pleasure couldn't be worth the isolation, could it? There was no answer to that incomplete question, and I was sick of arguing with myself. I was starting to see that I'd just gone around in circles. I clutched the bag of new cosmetics I'd made myself buy more tightly. Act as if, said the sign. As if what? I didn't know anymore, so I headed home. I'd run out of energy.

Then the waiting game really began. I hadn't appreciated what a good distraction the streets were, despite appearing to be a teeming mass of happy couples. Tick. Tock. You're such a girl, I told myself. I would not look at the clock.

6:00 p.m. Another cup of coffee. Still no call, no text. I was trying to have faith.

7:00 p.m. Ate a yogurt. Made some tea. Tried to watch some MTV. Failed. Cleaned the kitchen. Thought about the deadline. The tapes. No. Not right now.

8:00 p.m. More tea. Another bath? Work? I was feeling scared. I couldn't help it. But I wasn't going to jump first. He said he would call; I'd have to trust it. But what I wanted, the minute

I closed my eyes and let all my thoughts drift back to seeing his mouth, in close up, so close up, his skin, his pores, his smell, his tongue playing complicated games with mine. No. No. No. I felt like punching something. How did people deal with desire? Not just simple want, but the twisting grabbing feeling, so close to anger? God. I jumped up and slapped the cup off the table, feeling it rather than watching it fly across the room and smash into the wall with a pleasing sonic boom. I looked at the mess on the floor and felt nothing, no remorse, no sense of attachment. In fact, what I really wanted to do was go walk barefoot on the pieces, just to feel something else, but I didn't. I just held my head in my hands. No. I needed to hold it together. I went to the cabinet and took down a shot glass and filled it up with the single malt. Medicinal, I reflected, as the fluid burned its way through me. Good job on the giving up drinking front.

I cleaned up the mug. Didn't like that one anyway. I'd have to break something I liked. Maybe that would work.

10:00 p.m. In bath. Surrounded by warmth and nice smells, my body felt somewhat appeased. I would not touch myself though. I couldn't even think about it. I was on lockdown. The music tearing through the iPod was clearing a hole in my mind. That helped keep my mind off his eyes, those hands, lifting me up like I was nothing. Leverage, sheer will, size and power. I sank under the bubbles. Shit, the headphones. I plucked them out of my ears and went back under. All I could hear was my blood pulsing, steady, and overheated, my heart beating like a machine. I could practically feel it throbbing in my chest. Hot, physical, large. No. I burst up, gasping for air. I watched my chest rise and fall. Watching. That's all I could do. Participate in this pain. When my breathing returned to normal, I got out, and dried

myself off violently, hoping to get blood moving. I tried smoothing the new scented cream I had bought over my skin. That was
helping too. I rubbed some over the most sensitive areas between my legs, it felt nice, I could just carry on, and make some
of the tension go away. But I stopped. It wasn't that hard. I didn't
want the dream, I wanted his hand, actual, nail bitten, long fingered, in me. I didn't want substitutes. My whole life had been
about the substitute, the stand in, the fantasy covering up the
sub-standard reality. Faith, fuck it, I was going to have faith until
I couldn't anymore. I pushed all the hands crowding my mind
out of the way and stomped off to my room.

12:00 a.m. In bed. Trying to sleep. Making sure phone was on.
Oh foolish, foolish girl. You should have stripped off his clothes
when you had the chance, got to see that expanse of creamy flesh
from stomach to hip and all that hidden strength, touched him,
held him. You blew it. Rubbing together like in high school. Oh
god it was so good. Help. I punched the pillow and turned over.

1:15. Was that a beep? Yeah, I was hallucinating now. Next
I'd be seeing him, body and flesh, standing next to the bed. No,
there it was—the flashing red light. Ok. Breathe. I could do this.
I reached over and grabbed the phone. Yes a text. Yes from him.
Yes! My body surged. I could climb walls, float above my bed. I
was superhuman now. Anything possible. Calm. Read.

> Did you sleep? Caught in rehearsals.
> Disappointed? I am. Work first, then games. Until
> Saturday. Beautiful when you come for me.

Holy fucking... Did he just fire these things off?
So cool, yet so hot. So fucking hot. Life finally felt magical.

And my body relaxed instantly against the sheets. You'd get what you wanted. Needed. I was addicted. Cocky fucker, assuming I'd be free. But he was right.

•   •   •

I woke up the next morning early, with my dreams escaping and leaving only strange incomplete memories. I was calmer. That was something. Tonight was the party, and Alice had arranged everything and the dress. It'd be fun to go and meet some of Alice's friends. So you can scope out who she's most likely to tell, I thought.

More coffee. And working on the article. That would clear my mind. Then the gym. A normal day. Doing work. I ran a check on my body. Calm. Relaxed. I thought of him. Nothing. Or almost nothing. It was nearly a relief. I'd been so wound up, the thought of him was scaring me a little. I could think now. I would not look at the text again. Not right now.

It was a cold, clear morning. I could see the triangle of frosty blue sky from the kitchen window in between the buildings. A perfect day to regain some control and get something done. I ground some fresh coffee beans and inhaled the deep, slightly oily smell. Fantastic. I sat down, feeling something close to happy. Not so jittery. I cupped my hands around the mug. I was back in charge. Thank god. I made a piece of toast and nibbled at it. Appetite still hadn't returned though. Food made my stomach twist. And my mouth seemed oddly discontent with chewing. Weird. I made myself finish the meager breakfast, and I grabbed my refilled mug and headed to my desk.

I could so do this. No effect. Mind over body. Control.

I set everything up, headphones on, pen out. I pressed play, ready to work. And then his voice started. I had to listen to check something he had said on the tape. But I was completely surprised by the effect his voice had on me. That urban drawl, just torn between elegantly wasted and cool. Grammatical, even in between the "I don't know" and "it's not for me to say." Unwilling to pin himself down, but eager, almost desperate to talk about the music. What he was trying for. How it didn't always happen, but you had to keep trying, because that's what art and maybe life was all about. How learning to listen to your own voice was the biggest lesson of all.

I wished I didn't agree with everything he said.

· · ·

 By the early afternoon, I had shaped the piece into something I was reasonably happy with. It was a struggle to tone down the fan girl quality just enough, not too much. I had to share my excitement about the music with people; it was my job, and beyond that, I felt a certain justice needed to be done. He had gotten so much bad press. Why do the mediocre fear what they can't understand? I had to put in some philosophy in there. And quoted a bit of Jung. I wondered what the magazine would make of that, but hey, they hired me. I was the social commentator, the pop philosopher. They had to take me as I was.

Did they? I sat back, almost stunned at my thoughts. I had always been more about what I liked to think was the truth. The soul of the artist. Only backing down when I thought it would serve the overall game, negotiating. But very rarely did I ever come right out and say something, and more often than not, my fights were for others, their injustices, not mine.

I could run from the whole thing all I liked, but there it was, his power and his sensuality forcing open energy centers in the back of my head, creating havoc. Fucker. Away from the pleasure, it felt almost annoying, like coming home to find all the furniture rearranged. Idiotic. I read it again and saved it. Almost done. I needed some food. And Alice. And her stupid party. I changed into my gym clothes and grabbed a bottle of water and my phone. I'd run this one out. No texts. Fucker. Can't handle this.

I came back from the gym feeling sweaty and aching. My legs hurt from running. My ears hurt from turning up the music so loud. And I had tried to ease the tension in my shoulders by lifting heavy weights, so now they hurt too. I needed a bath, and maybe a quick nap before this shindig which was bound to be strange. Strange was following me these days, it seemed.

I opened the door and heard Alice call out instantly. "Hey Lily! Get your ass in here! We've got to start getting ready."

I stumbled into the kitchen and said hello, grimly.

"Oh you've got it so bad honey doll. You just need to see him again." Alice punched my arm.

"Ow. Listen Alice, cool it. You're going to say the wrong thing and then I'll get upset." It just wasn't funny anymore. It was my fucking deal. She could just shut up.

"Ok, ok, hon. Sorry." She looked at me quizzically. "It's going to be fun tonight, don't worry. Come see your dress, I've laid it out on the bed." She started walking to my room, and I followed behind her.

When we got to my room, I couldn't help but gasp. "Alice! The All Saints dress I love! You mustn't!" We never discussed the little trust fund that kept her walks on the wild side less dangerous than they might have been and her closet filled with fashionable frocks.

"Of course I must. Hon, you deserve to have it, and it suits you. Come on, look pretty. For me. You're getting tense again. I think I liked you well fucked better." She laughed.

"Alice!" I actually yelled.

"Ok, ok, calm down. And I want to do your makeup too. Are you covering up the bite? I actually think it looks sort of hot, but I suppose it's such a red flag—don't touch, been claimed. Better cover it." Alice had returned to her organized self.

"Oh Alice, this dress is really beautiful. I'm going to have a bath, then we can get ready. I'm sorry I've been such a bitch. I really don't know what's wrong with me. I can't get my bearings anymore," I apologized.

She just looked at me and smiled. "Not saying anything." And winked and left me with the dress.

It was stunning. A tie dyed blue silk, with a slight tulip skirt and a very low cut front. It tied tightly at the waist. Designed to flow over curves, yet look very cool. It was sleeveless to show off a lot of skin. But the leather jacket could cover that if I felt cold or underdressed. And there was a lot of bead work at the front. Pretty. Interesting. Not just all tits out to there. And there were bound to be a lot of girls who were working the naked under the dress style. It was rock and roll, after all.

Yet when I looked at myself, all I could imagine is what he would think of it. He wouldn't even see it. But if I wore it, for him, would he slide his talented mouth from my neck down-wards, or start at the base of the v and work up? Stockings and suspenders? Or was that going to be too obvious? Garters visible through the silk. In some ways, it was made to be worn with absolutely nothing under it. But I wasn't 17, and nice lingerie couldn't hurt. Besides, I didn't really want to be naked. I didn't know the people, had no idea what it was going to be like, and although I could tell Alice was up to something, I knew I wouldn't have eyes for anyone there. I'd dance, I'd drink, I'd laugh. But I wouldn't be where my mind was. With that thought, I stripped off and grabbed a towel. But I caught sight of my body in the mirror. "Oh imperfect flesh," I quoted out loud. The physicality of things shocked me sometimes, the flaws, the shame. And then other times the body was all that mattered in the world. When the physical just came together so perfectly, a deep voice, a long neck, beautiful eyes. Oh god. Not again. I smacked myself and headed off to the bath.

An hour later, I was putting on the stockings, trying desperately not to snag them. Why did all these things seem so complicated to me? Other women just took them in their stride. I always felt like I was trying to follow some convoluted recipe. Fuck. I sat down on the bed. What was I doing? Playing in the big leagues, when I was hardly out of the farm team. Crazy. I wasn't going to cry. I attached the stockings, smoothing them out. I put on the concealer and the powder. I powdered my cleavage as well. The brush was smooth and soft, and the sensation, prickly and smooth all at once, was distracting. Alice knocked and came in. She whistled when she saw the stockings.

"Nice one girl. Sexy. He'll love it."

"I'll remember that for when I see him." I smirked back at her.

"Yes you will. Look, don't put on the dress yet, I want to do your makeup." And she sat me down and applied powders and mascara, until the reflection looking back at me seemed an idealized version of a pre-Raphaelite opium addict; slightly dissolute, with dark eyes and heavy lids, and a deeply colored mouth.

It suited me, I thought. In fact, it looked at bit like I had looked the other morning. When you were happy, a little voice mumbled. Ah shut up.

"What? Don't you like it?" Alice seemed startled.

"No it's great! Really, I love it. I've been having a lot of internal conversations lately, sorry. I think that one got out."

"You think about him all the time."

I was silent.

"It's ok, you know. You're allowed to like him too, not just want to fuck him senseless."

Discreet. "Uh, thanks? Look, of course he's amazing. Sure I'd like to hang out. Who wouldn't?" My laugh sounded pretty fucking false. Never mind. Distract, disturb. "So who's going to be there? What is this anyway?"

Alice sighed. "I told you. You really didn't hear a word I said, did you? Alright, it's a record launch, a mini gig, and some meet and greet. Lots of record people. Free champagne. Hot guys in leather jackets. What not to like?"

"You mean arrogant tools with small dicks riding on the coattails of some band's success so they can get laid too." I'd been to enough of these things to know the business. A lot of the music industry involved situations that were nothing more than pissing contests between guys who were still corporate, but wanted more action, and got it by showing off the hottest girl, the hottest band, the biggest stash, the longest line of coke. Music was a product, a means to an end.

"Yes, that's right. Ruin everything with your judgmental pronouncements. Look, put on the dress, wear those shoes, and your leather jacket. Sean is sending the car around for us at 8:00. Any minute, yeah? And Lily?"

I looked at her, from down by my ankles trying to adjust the strap on the high heels. "Alice?"

"Don't spoil it."

"Will try."

I put everything in my pockets. Checking messages, as I did every time the phone was within touching distance. No messages. Ok, that was fine. He did say he was busy. Oh shit. No.

"Alice?" I called out for her.

"Yeah, what? Sean will be here in five. Are you ready?"

"Yeah, ready as I'll ever be. Alice, did you ever say who the launch was for?"

"I don't know hon. Sean said it's top secret, just the insiders going. That's why you had to come along. Stop panicking."

Oh. Ok. That seemed safe enough. Still. I wondered, and as I thought about him, and his leather jacket and his rehearsals, I felt my heart actually leap in my chest. Oh god. No. It couldn't be. The release was a month off. I was just wishful thinking. Or not. Because suppose he was there, and he was with someone else. I'd die.

I stood there. Maybe I shouldn't go. "Alice?"

She came rushing in and looked at my face. "You're going. Don't pussy out."

I nodded. I was dressed. Two minutes later, the buzzer rang.

"Come on girlfriend, we're on! Sean's even got a line of coke for you."

Oh lucky me, I thought. Like I'm not wired enough. I focused on the heels and a future glass of champagne and enjoyed the feel of the leather against the dress as I walked down the stairs. And underneath, the swish of the blue silk, my bare arms nestled into the heavy weight of the leather, which smelled of wood and smoke, over the gentle flowery perfume I'd covered myself in. Everything in my mind seemed to be contrast, opposites, male and female, yin and yang, dominance and romance.

Where did that come from? I wasn't thinking like that. Was I?

And hands in pockets, I walked out to another limo. It was getting to be a habit.

Chapter 8

Sean, a lanky easy going guy who turned out to be from Nebraska, of all places, was waiting for us in the limo. It was a bit of a shock to me to see him sitting there, blond, short hair, friendly smile. My brain was expecting someone else, irrationally. He was in a good mood, possibly helped by the six lines of Peruvian marching powder lined up on a small mirror on the table.

I was about to say something but he interrupted me. "Lily, pleasure. Partake, then we can get to know each other. Alice has told me a lot about you."

I smiled. And instantly put up my guard. He had that industry fake charm, and the patter, and the drugs—and Alice, feeding him info. I tried to smooth my face into an expressionless mask. It was going to be one of those evenings, but I had figured that out anyway. But it'd been a while since I'd done any coke, and it wasn't something I was in the mood to pass up. Alice went first, looking happy, and throwing her arms around Sean with a torrent of giggles. I ignored them and focused on getting my breathing right. First one side, then the other. Ah, it was high quality, that was something. And the burst of white energy that went into my head and down my body made me feel buzzy and numb enough to ignore a lot of things. There was no reason to talk. They were still kissing, and I poured myself a glass of champagne, which eased the quick dryness in my mouth. That strange taste, slightly chemical, partly the taste of cold. Yeah, I could get used to this. The lift, the sharp feeling, the warm limo, my stockings, the numbing of inhibitions and ego worries. That's what made it addictive—the brain rush. I looked out at the lights, the traffic going by, trying to ignore what Alice was promising she'd do later.

Thank god. He was putting out another set of lines. "Come on ladies, we're nearly there. Lily, you're lovely. I'm enjoying the view of your garters. Alice said you were a dark horse, and she's never wrong. Here, gorgeous." And he indicated the freshly chopped up lines. They were thick as well. A good host. Well what the hell.

"Thanks darling. I see all the ways Alice told me you were... generous...were right." I smiled at him, and looked down, very obviously, glancing at his crotch, giggling inanely, and at the lines, and smiling to myself, bent over to grab some more numbness. Snowy goodness, keeping me from feeling my lost heart. Good. Play the game; it's a game, just play. No. Not those. Those games, that I didn't know how to play yet. For now, it was just a waiting game.

They were laughing. Alice looked sparkly, from the lust and the drug. "Oh Lily, you're so much fun when you loosen up." She ran a finger over Sean's mouth. "Maybe we can all party later, after this."

"You bet sugar," Sean replied. "Whatever you want." They looked over at me.

I smiled, obliquely. "Maybe." I didn't have to say yes or no now, that much I knew. Hell, it was nice to be wanted, even just like that. Weird, yes. Bad, well, that was a matter of opinion. What was that Interpol song, "There's No I in Threesome"? Right. Funny how desire engenders desire. But they weren't thinking that hard, and I needed to stop.

The limo slowed down. The club was over by the river, in a dark area of industrial buildings and soundstages. Sean got out first, and helped each of us exit the limo, as we were teetering a bit in the heels over the uneven sidewalk. Fuck, it was cold down here. I pulled my jacket in a bit closer, covering up my dress which had blown around when we stepped out.

Sean leaned down to whisper in my ear. "I can see you like the cold." His eyes were riveted to my breasts.

I laughed. "All kinds of cold, sugar." Alice really knew how to pick them. Still, work it. Champagne and coke the reward. She would be the one that had to pay that bill.

We went in and it was instantly, gratifyingly warmer. There was a long wooden bar with a traditional mirror running the length of it. Tables filled up the floor, and they were mostly full, with some people milling around, talking and some up at the bar, ordering drinks from the bartenders wearing jeans and leather vests, and nothing else. Nice. There was a buzz in the air, somewhat sexual, somewhat predatory. The suits were making deals, and you could feel it. Only a few ponytails, but a lot of sunglasses at night. A large handful of women who were definitely being paid to be there, but who looked great doing it. If you can wear heels that high, why not get a special payment for it? The usual band of models. A few trannies. Was that RuPaul? I was interrupted in my celebrity spotting by Sean taking my arm and guiding both of us to a table near the front. Nice one. That's why Alice had chosen him. Reasonably good looking, good manners, connected. Good coke. I wondered what he did exactly in this incestuous little world, but I didn't feel like getting into it. I really just wanted to feel the vibe and enjoy the scenery, while altering my perceptions of life. Alice was right; I needed to relax. This was pretty amusing, and with the added pharmaceutical enhancements, I felt pretty confident I could handle it. Sean came back with a bottle of Cristal. Nice. Maybe I could get some hints from Alice on the kinky stuff she did to get this. Games. Yeah, well we'd see.

Ah. There was my first thought of him. Oh no, it wasn't, I thought. You've been thinking of him since you got in the limo. Since you got dressed. Since you were alive. I shook my head a little. Sean noticed.

"You all right sweetheart? Don't worry so much." He poured out the champagne, and handed us each a glass. "To art!" And he laughed and drained half the glass.

Jesus, I thought. But I smiled. And drank. He handed something to Alice, and winked at her, and she immediately grabbed my hand and tore away from the table, my high heels in tow.

"Alice, babe, slow down."

"No, come on hon, show's gonna start, Sean's given us a little pick me up while we freshen up. Let's do it!" Alice was heading with intent to the back of the room, and we ducked into the Ladies. I reapplied some lipstick. The druggie look suited me. Yes. She was handing me the vial. "Come on girl!" I took it, one little baby spoon each side. Yeah. That felt much better, and the shock was going up and down my whole body. "You look great darling. Sean's going to hook you up, he likes you. Then you'll have a choice!"

"Alice, you talk way too much."

"Yeah, whatever. Come on, one more for the road." And I snorted up a couple more of the mini spoons.

Alice snatched it back and grabbed my hand. "Come on baby, let's go! Showtime!"

There was something in her voice, that when I thought back, I should have recognized. But I was high, and numb, and enjoying the feeling of my stockings under the silk dress rubbing against my half naked legs, and I just didn't want to care about anything, anymore. And I needed more champagne.

So I followed her out, and tripped along in my heels back to the table. The lights were going down further, and people were actually taking seats, and the talking was growing less.

One of the suits came out on stage just as we reached our seats. I reached for my champagne. My, that was fine. The tightly woven fabric of his bespoke suit moved slightly as he spoke. "Thanks for coming down and being part of this. We've all been looking forward to this release, and I think you'll agree the wait has been worth it. Can you put your hands together for..."

But here the buzzing in my head grew to a crescendo, as a tall, dark haired man loped onto the stage. His leather bracelets. Thighs covered in skin tight leather pants, boots. Leather vest. Black shirt. Big smile, quickly hidden. His arms went around the suit in a quick hug, and he bobbed a little bow to him, and then to the audience.

I was frozen. My fingers were growing cold clutching the glass. As I watched him walk to the mike stand and straddle it, reducing it to a toy in his large hands, I realized how I must look. I hid in my glass, and finished it down. And tried to pull it together, but my legs were shaking.

I looked over at Alice. She winked at me, and handed my glass to Sean, who refilled it. He looked amused.

I was fucked.

I gave a little forced smile, and raised my glass. We were there to listen, and that's what I was going to do. Would I have gone if I'd known it was him? Hard to say. Anyway, there we were. Alice had obviously mentioned something. But what? One more notch on the belt? Fuck it.

I drank some more, and watched his dark head count off to the band. I'd enjoy it. Now. And kill her later.

He began to sing, that drawling deep voice that you could feel. Everywhere. Absolutely fucking everywhere, I thought, strangely riveted to his long legs, tapping the beat. I felt like I could see the muscles in his legs moving under the leather. I closed my eyes, the rhythm in the song was just hypnotic, and his voice was wrapping around the notes in a complex dance. This was one of the songs he had played for me, that day. Was it only a few days ago? Were we really going to play games tomorrow, this vision of sex up there, leather and tall, and me, stoned and wet, sitting only a few yards from those thighs? Bloody hell, it wasn't possible. I had been straddling those hips, fuck. My heart was beating with the poly rhythms of the drums. Craziness.

The song finished and we all put down our drinks and applauded just enough. The usual cool as ice industry crowd. But there were murmurs. This was one buzz that was going to build. I felt proud of him. Show these fuckers, I thought, and I smiled.

He was just saying the name of the next song, when he turned his head in our direction and saw me. There was a flash of surprise, a micro moment of hesitation, and then his face was professional, impassive. What was that about? No, work before games, he had said it. This was his career, his life. What did I think he was going to do, wave? Never mind, I loved this song—it was the building rock anthem, lyrical, classical. It was stunning to see him sing it, alternately passionate and organized. He looked like he was completely lost in the music, but by his gestures every so often to the rest of the band, it was obvious that he was keeping track of everything, conducting them, practically without turning around. I couldn't take my eyes off him, his eyes closed, his long fingered hands wrapped around the mike like he was strangling it, silently deadly. Fuck. I felt dizzy for a moment, and looked over at Alice. She was watching as well. Yeah bitch. Me. That. Now where did that come from?

At least once, a little sad voice muttered.

No, I wasn't going to let anything stop this. Not her, not Sean, nothing.

The song ended. He smiled at the crowd, who mostly seemed to be smiling back, now. Charismatic fucker. It's hard to ignore that kind of power. Some of the men looked a little annoyed as their dates were drooling. Ru Paul looked like he had seen a ghost. It was funny, really. A little leather, legs up to there, a killer stare. Amazing what that could do.

I looked back at the stage, and found he was looking right at me. Did he know it was me? Did he know what he was doing? The warm, sticky timbre of his voice broke through my reverie.

"I'd like to dedicate this one to people that don't sleep." And he smiled for a moment, then looked away for the count to the band.

Oh fuck me, he knew it was me. And then the song started. The one that had made me cry, and I felt the lump in my throat start up again. He remembered. He said something. He cared, at least enough to send me a little message from up there, god like, the crowd lusting after him, the suits counting their money already, he was thinking of me. People that don't sleep.

I looked around. I wanted everyone to love this beautiful song. I felt like shaking them.

He was singing the chorus now, and I felt my eyes start to prick with tears. I wouldn't cry. My nose was numb, my face hurt from holding in all the emotions, and then he looked over, directly at me —

> *Whatever happened, it's not the end,*
> *I knew you and I were already more than*
> *friends...*

That hint of a smile appeared again for a moment, and evaporated just as quickly.

And in that moment, it became way more than a game. I was whipped. And there was nothing else I wanted in the whole world. Nothing. Just to see that hidden half smile every day.

He played a few more songs, all spot on. The buzz in the room was a roar at this point. This music was not only going to be a hit on the alternative charts, but it had a good shot at the regular pop charts too. That mystical combination that made record company execs weep with joy. Crossover. I felt like flying, proud of him, stoned, crazy with lust, delirious with the thought of touching those legs. I'd never really gotten off on legs before, but everything about him screamed "touch me." He glanced over a few more times, but was focused on his singing. Which was fine with me. I wasn't sure if I could have sat still through another message.

Finally it was the last song; he told us he was going to do a cover version of an old classic. Everyone looked intrigued. Sean poured us the last of the champagne and toasted us. "Ladies, I think this one's out of the park." And winked. I just drank and smiled, and turned back to watch him sing. It was the Al Green hit, one of his most famous love songs, "Let's Stay Together." The skinny indie kid who had become an artist, now singing old school like a pro. Jesus Christ, that voice, dripping over the notes, like syrup. I had always loved this song anyway, and he was so on it. Suddenly, he jumped off the stage, making contact with all the outstretched hands, working the tables. All these hyper cool people, but everyone wanted to touch him. He made a little circuit, and then started to head towards our table. I stopped breathing. He came closer, getting taller and more solid by the second, his impossible voice still singing the verse. He shook Sean's hand, and strode over to me, eyes staring with that strange faraway look, but his hand touched the back of my neck, quickly, and ran down my arm, his fingernail lightly grazing the skin, before he stopped, and carried on shaking hands at the next table. His touch was electric; my entire body was trembling from the unexpected contact. I looked down at the small white line his fingernail had made on my skin and traced it with my fingertip.

He hopped up on the stage and finished the song, bowing to the band and the audience. I was still in a bubble of sensation. Everything seemed very far away. I watched him bow again and walk offstage to huge applause. Presumably, he would be coming out to meet and greet, as this wasn't your normal crowd, but then again, maybe he wouldn't. I was aching to touch him. None of my limbs seemed to be working properly. Sean was speaking, but I wasn't listening.

He was waving a bottle of champagne at me. I tried to focus.

"Hey Lily, we got a present from the management company. Do you want some? There's a card. It doesn't make any fucking sense though. These artists. So fucking cryptic. Whatever."

I sat up and said things, went through the motions of holding out my glass, and held out my hand for the card, as though it was the most normal thing in the world to have this happen. We clinked glasses, and I sipped. Pink. Oh my. And I read the card.

No BS. But it's pink. Almost Saturday.

I laughed out loud. Sean stared at me. Alice leaned over. "What's up doll?"

"Nothing hon, just funny. This is nice champagne though."

I drank some more, smiling. People were milling around, talking, enjoying the party. I didn't feel like moving.

And then I felt my phone vibrate. I took another sip of champagne, trying to look calm. And pulled out my phone from the inside pocket of my leather jacket, where I'd stashed it.

Saturday starts at midnight. Go backstage.

Oh fuck me. Yes. Right. It was 11:35. Did he mean now, or then? I guessed then. He probably had to finish up what he was doing. Why was I being so calm about this? I was not calm at all. But if I didn't keep it together, I was going to start screaming. Oh wow. Oh. My. God.

I looked up from my phone to see Alice looking at me. "Good message?"

I shot her a look.

"It's cool, it's cool. Keep your panties on…for now. Come, let's go do a line." She held out her hand. Probably was a good idea.

For staying awake. And keeping my feet moving. I followed her again to the bathroom. When we were in the cubicle, she pulled out the little vial and held the first spoon up to my nose. Ah, better. Or different. It was like extra. I didn't need it, but I did the second as well.

"Are you coming home tonight?" Alice seemed offhand.

"Not sure. Are you going to stay at Sean's?" I tried to be off-hand back.

"Yeah, think so. Might go to a club after this though. Do you need a lift?"

"Nah, I'm good."

"Yes you are. Remember baby, you deserve this." She was grinning at me. I gave her a big hug.

"You're awesome babe. I was mad before but..."

"...not so much now, huh?" Alice laughed. "Come on girl, let's pee, and get out of here."

We walked out, arm in arm. Any two rock groupie chicks, right? Happy and high. Tomorrow never happens. We got back to the table, and Sean was deep in conversation with a guy with crazy hair. We sat down and I had a sip of champagne and checked the time. 5 to. Early and often.

I leaned over to Alice. "Be right back. Or not."

"Have fun." She gave a little wave.

And I headed over to the stage, trying to look casual, like I was looking for someone, or something. Where was backstage? I tried a door, but it was locked. There were a couple of stage hands packing up, and I called over to one of them.

"Hey, sorry, excuse me—how do I get backstage?"

They pointed to a door on the other side, and I went back through the tables, feeling like everyone was staring at me. I just kept my eyes straight ahead. Focus. Smiling. Moving through the crowd. I finally got to the door, and tried the handle.

It flew open, as a group of people came out, talking excitedly. "Yeah, very cool, very cool. Going to that new club. Brilliant."

I slipped through them and in. The door closed behind me and it was suddenly very quiet. I kept going, careful not to catch my dress on the various metal power transformer boxes sticking out, stepping over the thick cables on the floor. I heard voices and suddenly felt cold, and even more nervous. It sounded like his manager. Fuck. I hesitated for a moment, then carried on. I'd do what I wanted.

I walked on a bit more, and there they were—Tristan, towering over his manager, still in the leather gear, exuding a just ran energy, toying with his bracelets. The manager was smiling at him. "Brilliant job Triz, you totally nailed it. Let's set up the rest of the dates tomorrow—I think on this buzz we can get a lot of places to confirm without the full contracts yet."

Tristan was nodding. "Just run them by me first. I want to make sure this is doable, not some up and down tour where none of the dates make sense, ok?"

At that moment, my heel made a loud clacking noise on the concrete, and they both looked up, their expressions exactly the opposite of each other. The manager looked annoyed and bored, and Tristan had that little smile again.

"Hi there, how are you doing?" The manager spoke first. "Probably not the best time to finish the interview, but I'll leave that up to Tristan."

"Nice to see you again. That's fine, just coming by to congratulate you." I smiled at the manager, but I turned to Tristan.

I was sure he could see the question in my eyes. I was ready to turn around and go, but his arm shot out and grabbed my hand.

"I'm sure I could do a few questions. Be great to get the concert in the article too. Lily was out there, so she got to hear the comments. James, I'll see you later, ok?"

His manager rolled his eyes. "You're the boss."

His reply was laconic. "Yup. Go have a drink."

We stood there and watched him negotiate the wires and head out towards the party. We were completely motionless, my hand still in his. It was as if we were frozen to the spot, waiting to hear the door open, then shut.

When it did, he pulled me closer to him and held my hand up to his lips and kissed it, softly. I looked up at him, petrified suddenly. What was I doing with this gorgeous creature? His eyes looked down at me, and softened.

"You're here. Are you sure?"

I was sure I'd agree to pretty much anything, if it involved being this close to him. "Yes," I mumbled breathily, "I wanted to see you again."

He pulled me against him until I was flush against his body. He was hot, still warm from the performance; I could feel the heat coming off his back as I wrapped my arms around him. He had that scent again, sweaty and hot and soap and leather and that strange perfume all at once. He bent his head down and started kissing me, his mouth full and soft, his tongue pushing slowly into me, his leather clad leg pushing between mine, until I could feel it against me, right where I wanted his hands, his mouth. He kissed me harder. His mouth had taken control of mine, his tongue exploring and teasing and I was pulsing with need. I was so wet, I thought there would be a mark on his leather trousers when he pulled away. God. My head was spinning and suddenly he took his mouth away and leaned over my neck. And bit me, hard, right over where the other mark was. I cried out, and he held me closer.

"Jesus fuck I want you. Let's get out of here. I want you in my bed. Now."

He let me go and I tottered for a second before he grabbed me. "Oh I like you. So much." And like I was nothing, he scooped me up and started carrying me to one of the big double doors in the back. I started laughing.

"I'm such a Neanderthal, I know. Come woman. To my cave." And he laughed. He knocked against the metal bar with his hip, and pushed it open, careful to not catch me on the other door. I couldn't understand how he had the energy to do this. I wasn't exactly tall, but he was obviously even stronger than he looked.

He put me down by the limo. And opened the door. And we slid in along the seats. Again. Like before. Except we were doing this together.

"Harry, home please. My home that is."

"Yes sir."

He turned to me. "I'm not even going to touch you. No, I lied. I'm going to hold your hand. I don't trust myself, and this isn't where I intend to have you."

He smiled then, wickedly. And began to take each one of my fingers into his mouth. I watched them disappear between his reddened lips, one by one, and I looked up to see his eyes, blacker now, staring at me, unblinking. He was on my fourth finger and I couldn't take anymore. "Oh fuck, I can feel you everywhere, how do you do that, fuck..." and at that point his mouth was on mine again, his tongue flicking out, precise, controlled. All I could think of was feeling his mouth on my sex, those same flicks, oh god, I was losing it. I pulled him closer and moaned into his mouth. "Oh fuck, I just want to feel you on me, in me."

He held me tighter, which was good, because I was shaking. "Oh girl, I want to make you scream. Make you beg for me inside you. Tell me you want this." He raised his voice slightly. "Tell me, now."

I tried to kiss him and he held me away. "Tell me you want me to fuck you, hard."

"Please."

"What?"

"Fuck me...god, please." I didn't know what I was saying anymore. "Fuck me, please, as hard as you want, until I don't know where I am, god I can't stand it. Tristan. Please? Touch me..."

His eyes were glittering.

Suddenly his long slender fingers were sliding over my thighs, pulling my dress up, over the stockings, where he hissed, mumbling "fuck so beautiful," and...and then without warning, he slid two fingers deep inside me and thrust in again, pulling his fingers around, curling up in me, the pressure and the wetness, and sliding in me, over and over again. I looked up into his eyes, dark and intent on me and he forced me onto him so that his fingers were now deeper into me and I fell against him, crying out, "oh god oh god, no," closing around his fingers again and again, unable to stop shaking, wet pouring out of me, buying my head in his hair, his hands all over me, I was biting at him, his groans of pleasure, feeling him hard against me. I started trembling again and tried to slow my breathing. Feeling the pulsing around his fingers slow, as he pulled them out, slow, and long and steady. "Open your eyes," he ordered, his voice rough with tension.

I looked at him in time to see his fingers go into his mouth, up to the hilt and his eyes flutter shut. Jesus. And I watched him pull them out again, equally slowly, his tongue working them.

"You taste divine. So wet for me."

He removed his fingers again from his mouth, and placed me slowly, gently on the seat. I watched in amazement as he fit his large hand over the sizeable bulge now very obvious through the stretched leather and pressed down, hard, a groan escaping from his mouth. "Fuck I want you so badly. It hurts." And he pressed again. "Oh god, I want to come in you right now. It's all I can do not to fucking have you right here. I said I'd wait..." He pressed again and groaned.

He turned to me as the car stopped. "I am going to fuck you like no one ever has. You beautiful girl. I'm going to ruin you for anyone else."

* * *

He pulled my dress down.

"Thank god, we're here." He took my hand, and pressed it over his cock. It was huge and hot and stunning. I squeezed it. Holy fuck.

"That's what you do to me. And you will feel it."

He flew to the car door, opening it, and practically pulled me out of the car.

He bent over to the window, "Thanks Harry." And turned and slapped me hard on the ass, in full view of the driver. Another act of possession.

"Let's do this." And he laughed.

And for a moment, I was a little scared. But the wetness sliding between the tops of my bare thighs was telling another story.

He pressed the code for the building. Those fingers. And he turned to me. "Ready?"

Chapter 9

I followed him into the building, shakily. I didn't want to hold on to him, even if I didn't feel like I was still in the world. Everything was gliding by. It was just a lobby of an apartment building, but it was as though I was going through some tunnel, Alice through the Looking Glass, about to fall straight through. He was walking ahead of me, holding open another door that he had pressed a button to access. I couldn't tell if he was intent on his destination, or if I had slowed down. Suddenly my head hurt and I couldn't think anymore. I was tempted to run back out to the street. But I wasn't going to let my stupid errant thoughts ruin any of this, and I kept my eyes up slightly, focused on his leather clad shoulders. I let my glance drop down his body, oh my there was a lot of him. What the hell was I going to do with all that? He was so tall, exuding masculinity, yet there was something about him, sensual, strange, other worldly. I was admiring his haunches, the way they sloped down to impossibly long legs, the view of him from behind just screamed sex. No wonder the boys loved him too. Not many people look truly fuckable from both directions.

We were waiting for the elevator. I was still just behind him. He still hadn't turned around. I wasn't going to paw at him though. I kind of liked the distance. It gave me a chance to feel I did have a choice. I wondered what he was going to do to break it down. It was pretty obvious to me by now that he liked being in control. And that was ok. Usually I always had to keep it all organized and going. There was something thrilling about his silent darkness, his ego needing this and actually admitting it.

Now what was I going to have to admit to? The door opened with a noise that startled me. He put his hand out behind him, and I took it, and went with him into the lift. He squeezed my hand, then dropped it to fish out a set of keys, one of which he used to turn the lock to the seventh floor. The elevator door closed.

Funny how some things impress me. "The whole floor, huh?"

"Yup."

His silence was unnerving. We stood there, the elevator making its little whooshing and clicking noises as it passed each floor. My ears were echoing with the quiet. I felt like I could hear my blood flowing.

The mechanical door slid open and he used another two keys to open the door to the apartment, which was a forbidding wall trapping us in the box of the elevator. It sprang open, and he held it open for me.

"After you."

I stepped out into a raised foyer, looking down on a long living room that ended with three large windows, facing the skyline. It was simple, slightly old fashioned, elegant. Wood floors covered with rugs. A mix of modern furniture and some antique looking pieces. Wood and plastic. Paintings. Interesting.

I looked over at him, to see him smiling. I instantly relaxed. He didn't look nearly as forbidding from the front, not like that.

"You like?"

"Yes." I could be quiet too.

"Ah, you're nervous. Amazing. I really didn't think girls like you existed anymore."

I couldn't resist. "Maybe it's the circles you move in."

"My circles brought you here. Don't knock them." He hopped nimbly down the three steps to the main living room. "Come on." He walked to the end of the room and went through another door to the left. There was a large kitchen with a wooden table, another vase of flowers in the middle, and some books scattered by the end, along with an old mug of coffee.

"I'm a slob," he grinned. "Sorry." He walked over to the fridge, a repeat of the one in the office. "Do you want a drink?"

"I think just some water, please. I had quite a bit to drink at the, at your show." I felt shy. What was going on with me?

"Yes you did. And tripping off to the ladies like that. At least you'll be awake, huh?"

I looked at him astonished. "You were watching?"

"Always curious to see people when they think no one's looking."

I nodded. Fair enough. "True."

He took out a bottle of Perrier and poured a glass for each of us.

"Come on darling, let's go sit somewhere more romantic than the kitchen. Although it could have its uses." He laughed to himself and I followed him again, as he went through another door, again to the left, and down a short hall leading to yet another door. I felt like I was trying to keep track of where I was, in case I had to run. It was crazy, I wanted to be here, but I was scared. I almost wished we were back in the limo.

He opened the door and of course, it was his bedroom.

Ridiculously large bed, or maybe it just seemed that way. Shades of coffee, mocha, copper, amber. Rugs on hardwood floors. Pillows covered in raw silk. Another three windows, with curtains between them. Bookshelves at the end, another raised area, with a sofa, a guitar casually resting against the cushions. Lamps, tables, an ornate quality. I couldn't decide if the bed was the stage and the sofa the audience. I wondered if it had ever been used that way.

Again, I looked over to find him watching me, a predatory look on his face, a tiny smile pulling up the corner of his mouth. I let out a breath I didn't realize I was holding, and his smile increased. It wasn't exactly friendly though.

God, I was so confused. I looked at him, willing him to understand some of what I was going through. I wanted him to make it better, whatever better was. I didn't want to feel this fear and awkwardness. I just wanted to feel good.

"You know, coke makes most people a bit paranoid."

I'm sure the shock showed on my face. "Yes, but..."

"You're scared."

I took a drink of my water. We were standing by the bed. It all seemed so...impossible. "I am, a little. I don't know why. I'm sorry."

"It's ok. Really. You just need a minute to get your bearings. You don't strike me as someone who walks away from a challenge."

"Are you a challenge?" I raised my eyes to his. I wanted to see what they showed of how he felt. Where were his emotions? Did he have any?

He looked at me, and sighed. "Of course I am. I'm never only me, I'm everything you've ever read, everything you've heard, all the rumors." He walked towards the windows and looked out. "I think I used to enjoy that part of it more than I do now." He drank some water. "I'm actually not happy that you're scared of me."

"I'm not. I don't know. I think I'm scared of myself." I looked at him. What was I doing? I could not fuck this up.

I walked over to him. I was going to be stupid and honest, but all the show of strength had worn me out. He held out his hand, and took mine and smiled. His smile melted a bit of the crazy fear that had come over me. This was right. To trust what I felt. Not what I'd been told.

"I really do like you," he whispered. "When I saw you out there..." he trailed off. "I was happy. But then you know, it was like I was worried." He stopped again and shook his head.

"Worried?"

"Yeah." He let out a huge sigh, and kind of blew through his teeth. "Yeah. You don't know what it's like, well maybe you do. The usual deal." He put his hands on my shoulders, and left them there, heavy, as he looked down at me. He seemed even taller, with the black twinkling backdrop behind him. I felt like I was in a photograph, pinned down for all eternity. "I can't explain it. I saw you out there, I still wanted you, but..."

My heart had stopped. "But?" I had blown it. I wasn't going to cry though.

"I wanted to frighten you. See what you'd do. Whether it mattered to you. Or if you'd just ignore my coldness."

"I tried to ignore it. I figured that's what I was supposed to do." I was starting to babble. It was all ruined anyway. "Alice, that's my roommate, she plays this whole scene. I haven't, I just don't..." I stopped. What the hell was I about to say?

He was looking at me, intently. I felt his presence like a furnace next to me. God this want. If I just let my brain loose, maybe it would know what to say.

"I get scared of what I want. It gets too intense. I don't do pretend very well, I usually go for what seems the safe option, but that hasn't worked very well for me, because it's never right, and I dream of what is, and I never see it, and then, well, that song you played for me, and everything it said, and the way you held me, and shit, you're beautiful anyway, and I'm totally out of my depth here. Fuck, I'm sorry. I'm sure you'd rather have somebody with...oh fuck I don't know." He was looking at me, with that same sort of gaze he had when he was watching me cry. I tried to return his steady look. "I'm sorry. I'm way too honest, and I'm not even telling the whole truth. I can play the game, better than this anyhow, it's just..." Then his finger was resting on my lips, and he looked amused again.

"No, it's all good. That's why I like you. I've got to apologize to you. We got here, and I thought to myself, she's a journalist, she's just playing you and you're about to take her to your house." He shrugged. "I could have just fucked you into tomorrow, and sent you off, and switched off." He walked away from the windows, and sat down heavily on the bed, his leather pants creaking with the motion. "Fear's a common thing, little girl."

Jesus. There went the rest of my heart. God, had I been that shut down? I closed my eyes. Ow. What to do, what to do.

I put down my glass on the window sill, and flew at the bed and jumped on him before I could stop myself. And there I was, having knocked over the glorious, messy haired god, and I was now straddling his lap and looking down at him, as he gazed up at me, stunned.

I was about to start apologizing, when he started giggling. Laughing, like I'd seen on the videos from so long ago, not just cut off, but actually laughing. It made me giddy, like a teenager with the giggles, and he pulled me to him, until we were both hysterical with nervous laughter.

We lay there, his arms around me, my face resting on his chest, and slowly stopped laughing. I didn't know what to say anymore. I just wanted to stay there forever, warm, feeling that strange happiness that was bursting out of the desire. He was stroking my hair, smoothly, gently, his large hands reassuring and warm. I felt sleepy and contented, yet the desire for him was still there like a beacon. It was so hard to just accept this warmth, these feelings of...tenderness. He was incredibly tender. Paradox, the man a walking contradiction. But he smelled so fantastic. And this leather was so soft, I could touch his arm, his skin was soft too...

· · ·

I woke up, and it was chilly, and I wasn't sure where I was. I looked around, and I heard water running in the bathroom. Great. I fell asleep on a rock star. Useless. I lay there and spread my arms out over the bed. Well, I was still here. That was something. And I breathed in the scent from the duvet cover and the comforter, and it was all him, yet soft and warm, like he was, after all.

The bathroom door handle turned, and he came out, wrapped in a silk kimono robe. I could hear water running. My god, he was stunning. Pure sex. He couldn't even help it. He was walking towards me; I noticed and shook myself out of my reverie.

"Good you're awake."

"I'm really sorry. Great date, huh?"

"Hey, you're tired. It's not a crime. I dozed off myself."

He looked at me, like he was deciding something. Here it comes. I sat up, ready to be escorted out.

"Would you stay? Would you like a bath? With me, that is?" And he smiled, that wicked schoolboy smile, and I felt all the blood rush to my face. Then descend.

I took a deep breath. "I'd love to."

He held out his hand. "Come then. Leave your shoes."

And in stockinged feet, I walked up the little stairs hand in hand with him towards the running bath.

Chapter 10

Of course the bathroom was tasteful as well. The floor had old fashioned NYC apartment tile, small squares of black and white, and the bath was black and huge. There were Jacuzzi jets, and he had already put in some foaming bath soap. It smelled divine, and there were two huge towels hanging on a warming towel rack. I guess he'd already thought this through a bit. It wasn't just a spur of the moment decision.

"You always observe your surroundings quite intently," he said.

"I suppose I do."

He tilted his head slightly, and scratched his cheek absent-mindedly. "And what conclusions have you reached?"

"About you? Hmm, secret sybarite. Paradoxically tender. Traditional. Elegantly wild."

"Elegantly wild, interesting. And do you think you trust me?" He bent over to turn off the water, and looked over his shoulder at me, a strange sort of expression on his face. Daring me, almost. I just looked at him. He stood up and came over to me, and tipped my face up towards his. "Tell me what you think."

"I think I want to."

"Wanting doesn't always make it so."

"How about if I really want to?"

He looked at me with that stare. I felt myself dissolving under his gaze. I didn't really understand the mood changes, the switching back and forth from kindness to questioning. I wanted to say something, tell him he could trust me. Maybe that was it, again, the need he had to feel that people were not thinking too much about what they did around him. Or that he could control it. The look he was giving me was going through me again, taunting me, waiting to see what I was made of. I closed my eyes. I couldn't figure out the rules to this one. I'd grab at any idea I had.

"You can trust me, though." I reached up and ran my hand through his hair. God, I'd been wanting to do that.

"You haven't even told me you like me. Now you want me to trust you." He smiled, but it didn't entirely make it to his eyes.

"I like you. I like you—a lot. More than I should. More than I'm comfortable with. But that's my problem, not yours. But I promise, I'm not in it for anything but my own selfish wants, which is to spend a lot more time with you. Being confused." I paused for a moment. "And a strange, wild, irrational desire to see you happy."

He smiled, and it lit up his face, the room, the entire world. There it was, that light pouring off him. I felt elated. I'd done something right. I'd made him smile.

"Really?"

"Really."

"Well, let's get to work on that. You know what would make me happy?" His face changed slightly, and looked more amused and bored than elated. But I'd take it.

"Tell me."

"Take off your dress."

"Help me then." I thought I'd try to play, but the game had already gotten beyond me, and his eyes were darkening.

"No. Take it off—for me. Slowly." And he leaned back against the enormous sink, arms crossed, looking every bit the bored rock star.

"Ok." I felt idiotic as I said it, and reached behind to undo the clasp and start pulling down the zip. I reached up a hand to pull the wide straps off my shoulders.

"Slowly, very slowly. I'll never see you naked for the first time again. I want it to last." His eyes were trained on my shoulders.

I spread out my fingers and swept the silk off my shoulder as slowly as I could, the fabric tickling my arm which instantly came up in goose bumps. He watched me with a strange intensity.

"Now the other side."

I repeated what I had done, and was now holding the dress to my body with my arms pressed to my sides.

"Let it drop." His voice went down an octave as he said it. The tone of his voice was hypnotic. The dress fell to the floor, and I stepped out of it and picked it up with one finger.

"Where do you want it?"

He took it from me, and ran a hand down it, as though he were caressing a person.

"Lovely. Did you know I would be the act at the party tonight?"

"No, Alice didn't tell me." I didn't tell him that I could think of nothing else but seeing him, that I didn't know what to think.

"Were you thinking of me when you got dressed?" He looked impatient, waiting for an answer.

I breathed in. Was he going to ask every question I didn't want to answer honestly? It appeared he was.

"Well?"

I had to. "I've thought of nothing but you since we met." I paused. "Isn't it obvious?"

"Not to me." He gazed at me, now clad in nothing but matching lingerie and stockings. "I ought to throw you in the bath like this."

"Why don't you?" There was something about his animal physicality that made me want to fight with him, literally. I wanted him to grab me, touch me, pick me up like he did before. I also wanted to resist.

"You'll learn that it's not always a good idea to bait me."

"Good for whom?"

His eyes lit up. "There is a bit of steel in you, after all."

"Glad you figured it out," I replied.

"Oh, I'm pretty sharp. You'll notice that if you stick around." He drawled the words out.

"Touch me, and I'll stick around a lot."

"You might get bored."

"Are you bored?" I snapped. There was something boiling up here, getting quickly out of control. But neither one of us could stop it.

"I'm bored that you're so far away." And he pulled me to him, and held me, just close enough, his eyes searing into mine.

"Are you a fan of the classics?" He began quoting. "You should be kissed and often, and by someone who knows how." He pretended he was going to kiss me, and then pulled away. "Can I assume that the same thing that cured Scarlett will cure you?"

"Do you think you know how?" I batted my eyelashes at him.

He smiled. "Oh, I know a few things."

"Do you now."

"Oh you minx." And with that, he picked me up, and lowered me with surprising gentleness in the tub. In my underwear. Which instantly went transparent. I looked up at him, and he was incandescent. He followed me into the bath, still wearing the black silk robe, which melded to all his curves, and his entire body became geometric, planes and ridges, and smooth muscles, all shining under a layer of wet silk. He ducked his head under and came up, dripping wet, his mouth glossy, his dark hair flat against his face and neck. "Now look what you've done."

I was looking. I was certain I never wanted to look at anything else again.

He held my wrist and dragged the back of my hand up the inside of his leg. His skin was smoother than the wet fabric, yet taut underneath. He let go when my hand made contact with his balls, and we both gasped. Actual skin. "Touch me. I want to feel your hands on me." I traced circles over his skin, silky, wet, unbelievably hard. His cock was thick and sculptured, just like the rest of him, and long, like his fingers. I ran my hands all over his hips, his balls, cupping his ass. He was made for sex, I'd never been this enticed by a man's body before. But his was mysterious, and huge and responsive. His eyes were shut, and he let out a long low moan when I ran my finger over the wet top of him and put my finger in my mouth. Oh my god, he even tasted good, that same dizzying scent, salty, like sand and ocean. I bent my head down under the water, and took him in my mouth, managing to get about half of him to taste before I had to come up for air.

"You taste fantastic. Let me...?"

And he nodded, and slipped off the robe and sat up, out of the bath, on the wide tiled shelf. I felt like I was swimming over to him in the huge bath, a mermaid who'd found someone she would walk on knives for. I suddenly wanted him to hurt me, touch me, something. Out of the water, his sex appeared even larger, and I wanted it like I had never wanted anything in my life. I kept swallowing him down until I had nearly all of him, then moving back and running my tongue over the ridges at the head, gently squeezing him, licking him. I felt crazy with lust, it was almost too much.

I suddenly felt a hard slap on my ass through the water and it stung. I raised my head as quickly as I could, being careful to lick the wetness from his head, and I looked up at him, as innocently as I could manage.

The muscles on his neck were standing out, and there was a hawk like fierceness in his expression. "You," he muttered, "are driving me insane."

I smiled. But I had to catch my breath as he attacked my mouth with his, and licked me, thoroughly, effectively, my face, my mouth, my neck, until we were both wet with his kisses.

I could barely breathe. All I could feel was an ache that made me want to do crazy things, and not care, never care. I tore myself away, and was about to start kissing a trail down his stomach, when he pulled me back to look at him.

His voice was a low rumble. "I can't wait." And he stood up, lifting me up, both of us dripping water, and got out of the bath, then helped me to climb out.

He peeled off his wet robe, hanging it over the bath, then turned to me, and unsnapped my bra in one motion and watched as it fell to the floor. He then flicked open the clasp on the garter belt and began peeling off the stockings, kneeling naked in front of me, my foot on his shoulder, first one then the other. He did it slowly, carefully, rolling down my stockings as his knuckles brushed the skin on the inside of my thighs. I held on to the towel rank as he placed my foot back on the ground, shaking. "Nice," he said, "now take these off too," snapping at the elastic of my panties.

"You do it," I whispered.

He ignored me, instead pulling a towel down off the rack, and took my hand and pushed me ahead of him. "Bed. Now." He herded me out of the bathroom and down the few steps. When we got to the bed, he pulled the quilts off in one massive flourish, the muscles in his back fluttering with strength. He flung down the towel. "Lie on it." And the look in his eyes was dark with something like rage. He pulled open the drawer next to the bed and pulled out a condom. He nodded to me. But I obviously wasn't moving fast enough, because the next thing I knew he had thrown me on the bed, and was now straddling my legs, staring at me possessively. His large hands were taking hold of my underwear and tearing them with a frightening ease. And there was that smile again, satisfied, as he neatly ripped open the packet with precision and rolled the condom over his cock, his enormous hands finally looking comfortable. He ran his hands over himself a few times, and suddenly groaned.

I was riveted to his every motion. He was stunning. I would do...

And without warning he was buried inside me. I cried out, half from the unexpected pain of him opening me up fully, partly from sheer relief.

"Fuck," he rumbled against my mouth. "Fuck. Stay still for a moment. You're so tight, god, so wet, for me...tell me it's for me."

"So wet, only for you, please..."

"Say it, or I won't move."

I tried to wriggle to get him to move, but he wouldn't. He held me pinned to the bed.

"Beg me, little girl."

I thought I was going to come just from the sound of his voice, the sheer size of him filling me up. Oh god I wanted to move, I just wanted to move, against him. I wriggled more, and fought against him. Oh there, some friction. A moan escaped from my throat.

"Beg for it. God please."

I wriggled some more. His eyes were black, and he couldn't help himself, and he moved a little against me. We both gasped.

"Say please," he whispered against my mouth, and licked me, wetly, and moved –just imperceptibly. I moaned again. I wanted to torture him, I didn't know why. But I needed to move on him, now. I wriggled against him again, his stomach touching mine, and he pulled on my arms roughly.

"Now, damn it," he rumbled around my nipple as he sucked down hard. I felt it all the way inside and I clutched around him.

"Ahh, fuck." And he bit down, and I started to come. I couldn't hold on any longer.

"Now, baby, fuck me please, you're making me come, harder," I gasped.

And he let out a low wail as he pushed as far as he could inside me, and set off another long rush of convulsions. My entire body was trembling. "God, baby, please, harder, please, I'll do anything you ask, please." And he started fucking me hard, holding my wrists. I was arching my body into his, sliding on him.

"More, give me more," And he pulled me up to a sitting position, and he held me in place as he moved deep inside me, over and over, not stopping, until I was trembling over him again. Then he pushed me down on the bed, and kissed me, listening to my moans. And he sped up. I was boneless, weightless, and still I could feel him, and I felt myself tightening again around his cock.

"That's it, let go, come for me, come for me. Now... "

And I fell apart on his words, finally, under him, my hands trying to hold on to his strong back. I couldn't breathe, my heart going too fast and then another vibration went through me and he was coming, inside, throbbing, warm. And he was crying out, "fuck fuck fuck, that's it, that's it, that's it!" And his voice disintegrated into animal moans that made me come again, clutching around him, thrusting my hips on him as hard as I could. And he held me tightly as he shuddered, again, like he had in the limo that first time, still coming, beautiful, his face torn up with his orgasm.

His body convulsed again, and held me closer, kissing me by my ear, whispering, "Incredible girl, incredible." And I held on to him as hard as I could.

We stayed like that for a little while, until he said, "wait just a minute darling." He pulled out and we both groaned. He peeled off the condom and dropped it over the edge of the bed. "Later."

He reached instead for all the covers and pulled them over us, then wrapped me in his arms, and kissed my head.

"So beautiful," he murmured against my cheek and held me even tighter. I held him back, just clinging on.

I kissed his cheek, and I felt his smile.

"Good night darling," he said, in that incredible voice, and kissed me, gently. But we were still clinging to each other, and there was nothing gentle about it.

Chapter 11

We slept like that, amazingly enough. When I woke up, I still had my arms wrapped around him, and comfortably, his around me. I tried to zero out my brain before it registered who this was and what we had done, and simply listen to the sounds of traffic reigniting down below, and his heartbeat.

His heartbeat. And his breathing, regular, soft, deep. All of him there, like some kind of gift. His incredibly soft skin over the hard muscles, his nearly hairless chest, which paradoxically exuded masculinity. A strength that just was, yet complicated. He made me not think clearly. Some kind of non-apology for what he was went on there. No excuses, nothing hidden. His beauty creating a kind of force field.

But I really needed to get up, like it or not. That was real, right? He would probably have to do the same, I was just up earlier.

I tried to slip my arms out from under him and I moved a pillow closer to try and take my place. He was still sleeping. Amazing, and beautiful. The circles under his eyes were more pronounced, and he looked exhausted with the effort he had been putting into the work. There was a certain tension there, even in sleep, which made me anxious for him, and his deep set eyes looked pained.

I walked as quietly as I could up to the bathroom, and shut the door. I had no idea what time it was, but it seemed right before the dawn. It was still quiet out, but you felt the energy of the day coming.

I was washing my face when I remembered my dream. I had been out on the ocean, in something like a homemade jet ski. And there was a beautiful floating hotel, and strange mini float- ing docks scattered around it, all glass and chrome, surrounded by miles of empty ocean and the strange resort, hovering above it all, smashed repeatedly by the rough seas of the mid ocean. It reminded me of all the pictures of that island they had been building off the coast of Dubai, the one that was sinking anyway, the one that was losing money and would be destined to return to the sand bed it had come from. And I wanted to park at one of the docks, but someone told me I needed a yacht to be able to do that, something big enough to anchor it down. Then I was living in a trailer, and trying to sort out used canvases to paint on, and plant a garden, and someone was telling me I couldn't, it was all my fault I was there, living in such squalor.

I dried my face, and hung my discarded bra up on the heated towel rack, along with the garter belt. The stockings were ruined, but it didn't matter. But I suddenly felt very out of place, and disposable and just wrong, like the underwear. I used some toothpaste, and rinsed out my mouth. I felt like leaving. This just wasn't me, I didn't do this, and like the dream, I needed a yacht to navigate these waters, when all I had was a rowboat, able to capsize at any moment. I knew some of the feeling was just the comedown, the depression that always followed the euphoria of imagining oneself capable, desirable, the high of possibility, the drug and ego fuelled dream where you can do anything.

I wasn't going to panic. If I had been home, I could have made a cup of tea, crawled back into bed, maybe read for an hour and just let the anxiety wash away. But I was here, with him, and I didn't feel comfortable wandering around his kitchen. You didn't do that, not with people you didn't know, and I suddenly realized that I really didn't know him, I didn't really know anyone, and neither did anyone else. Out in the world, like a star in space.

There was nothing for it. I was here. I'd have to deal with all the night terrors and pretend it was ok, as much as I felt like grabbing my clothes and running back home. I drank some tap water with my hand, and turned off the taps, drying off and carefully opening the door. I wished I had a t-shirt or something to put on. I felt very naked and exposed. But I tiptoed out, and went back to the bed. There he was, asleep, looking more capable unconscious than I felt awake. More dark thoughts. I brushed them aside, and focused on the idea that I could get back into bed with him, I was supposed to, and I'd be mad not to do it. He was startlingly real in sleep, sharp features cut out against the white pillowcase, dark hair and moles and cheekbones. I wanted him to be flawed in some way, so I could relax, and it occurred to me how bizarre an idea that was. And how hard I had fallen for him. And how I was desperately trying to back pedal my way out of this danger.

I took a deep breath, and crawled under the heavy duvet, keeping my back to him, trying not to wake him up, or touch him with my hands which were cold from the tap water. I was just arranging myself to try and sleep, when a heavy arm stretched out over me, and pulled me in closer to the huge soft warmth that was his body, bones and skin and muscle, and his scent, and he hugged me to him, like a child's stuffed toy, I thought. And he sighed. A soulful, beautiful sound, yet light, floating over to me like a seed pod on a summer breeze. And all the fears I had came to the surface, reflecting back at the delicious sensation of comfort and calm and reassurance I felt being held like this, at the last minutes of the night. I sighed as well, involuntary reflex reaction to feeling my body melting into his. It was so good, it'd been so long since I felt anything like love. Love. There it was, that word. I was drowning in it, and I wasn't sure if I would be able to anchor myself, just like in the dream. But for now, he was holding me, and the weight of his arm and the size of him were comforting like nothing else. Love.

I closed my eyes, and my last thoughts before sleep were how one complicated, beautiful, long, heavy arm was managing to chase away all the fear. And that I didn't have to get up early.

Chapter 12

Consciousness came slowly for a change. First, the light, brighter, shadows made by the curtains, but sunlight still filtering in strongly. Then, the faraway sounds of honking, engines, a million people talking on their mobile phones. Afterwards, a very long leg wrapped around mine, heavy, smooth. Then breathing, mine, his. I was still here, and so was he. I'd slept again, dreamlessly and quietly, his body seamlessly touching mine. I was so close to him, in the light. Daylight to make it real. But it all felt so normal, not like something that was about to end. And the next thought. It was that word, that love word, again. And in the light, that was dangerous territory. I was going to have to survive, whatever this turned out to be, and getting too attached...not a good idea. I pushed it away. But this felt so right. I looked over at him, dark hair tickling his pale shoulders. He was real. It was easier to touch than look sometimes. Looking at him made my heart stop. So I breathed out, and closed my eyes, and tried to remind myself that not everything was down to me. I was here, he was here, it was warm—a cave— my memory brought back what he had said—and all I needed to do was feel it, for just a little while longer. Later didn't matter, I told myself. Forget later.

A few minutes on though, I really did need to move, and

cursed my bloodstream for wanting circulation. I rolled over, extricating my pins and needles leg from under his, and put my head against his back. The gesture felt intimate and tender, and I wondered if it was too much. Never mind. He was waking up now, and we'd see what would happen.

He yawned, rolling over and stretched his arms overhead and then around me. Smiling. He was smiling. I smiled back. Those lips. His deep set eyes, examining me. Then he closed them, his movements languid and dreamy, his hands running over my body as though he were memorizing it. His hands were large and slow over my skin; alternately comforting and erotic, pinching here, circling there. No words. I was tracing patterns over his back, his arms, his chest—his skin was soft, velvet warmth. Oh, this was nice, so nice. I didn't want to say anything out loud to break the dream-like spell, and it was a dream, a really good one. His hands covered so much of me at once, like he'd taken hold of me and all I had to do was let go. I couldn't help letting out a sigh of pleasure at the combined sensation of his fingertips lightly drawing lines between my hipbones, and the way the small of his back felt under my hands. His skin under my fingers was soft, and the muscles underneath were hard.

His hands were going lower now. His fingers opened up my lips, both his hands exploring me, possessing my sex, and finding me wet and swollen. I tried not to moan, not wanting to break the spell, the silence that was building like a secret. But his hands continued their circling. I didn't recognize the sound that erupted from my throat as his long fingers drew a line, over my sex, over and over. My hands had fallen away from him and as I felt my body start to spiral, and tense, I clung to him, but then just before it was all going to break apart, he stopped. And quickly rolled over, away from me. Something like a strangled cry emitting sounds of pain started up, that was me. No. No please don't stop.

But he was back, kissing my ear, murmuring something I couldn't understand, again alternately soothing and erotic. But I was so wound up, I couldn't relax. I had to have him; he had to make me come, now. I reached out my hand to touch him, and found his hands wrapped around himself. Putting on a condom. Oh god, yes. To feel him, now against me, in me, coming on me, in me, I didn't care. I joined my hands to his larger ones, and surrounded his cock, one hand dropping to squeeze his balls, gently, putting pressure between his legs, that bit of flesh, smooth, inbetween. That made him gasp, and I pulled him to me, rubbing the tip of him up and down against me. Even with the condom, he was warm and wet and huge, sending shudders through my legs. So close. I looked up at him, his eyes were shut, his face all sensation. He pushed against me. But when he tried to enter, I was still sore from last night, and I was suddenly tight against him. I felt like a virgin, newly deflowered, unskilled, too sensitive. But there were his lips against my ear again, murmuring gently. "I want you, darling. Does it hurt? I'm sorry, I was too rough last night...we'll take it very slowly now..."

And he moved against me, tiny amounts, then backing away, more tiny amounts. So much sensation in such a small space but every motion took over my entire awareness, everything larger, the tip now burning into me, both of our breathing labored with the effort of doing this so slowly. He was moaning now. "God, you're so tight, I like it, I don't want to hurt you, but I have to be inside you." And he pushed in a little further, and I felt his cock open me up and send a wave of desire and heat through me, vibrating in me, all my nerve endings on fire but wet, so wet. And he slowly, agonizingly moved further in me. It felt as though his entire body was inside me, and I wanted him, more than the pain, and little by little, I was taking him in, throbbing, moving past whatever pain was left, until he slipped in, heavy and thick, all the way inside, touching the very back of me. His fingers began twisting at my clit, again alternately gentle and rough, and I felt myself tightening around him, as much as I could, his huge cock fighting back, moving now inside me, gently, a rocking motion, like water, steady, rhythmic. He was kissing me now, and I was lost in all the sensation, his tongue against mine, his fingers tickling me, teasing me, and his body, smooth, dreamy. I'd never felt anything like this, the rhythm was constant and obsessive, perfectly slow, the head of him reaching the furthest point he could inside me, over and over again, just at the same time, slowly. I knew he was close when he suddenly jerked, out of time, syncopated beat, and moaned against me, incoherent noises. He moved his fingers away, and he was in me even further, pulling against me with every motion, and his tongue moved down my neck, and began sucking, hard, on the mark he'd already left. It was so sensitive already, and when he bit down on it, teeth sharp enough to break the skin, the bolt of electric fire it sent between my legs pushed me over the edge. I was trying to speed up, but his hands were on my hips, holding me down, keeping me to the same rhythm, controlling me, and the agonized slowness dragged it out, each thrust bringing another tremor and he rode it out, pinning me beneath him, biting me, steady. Then his body suddenly was hot, his skin burning, and he pushed even deeper within me, convulsive, shaking, crying out, throbbing inside me, his voice ripping out of him, rocking into me, over and over and over, completely devoured by his orgasm. I felt a burst of wetness flood me, and I was coming again, around him, under him, part of him, just from the sound of his voice, delirium. We were breathing, like one, panting, together, gasping for air, blinded by sensation. His skin was wet and slickly animal against me, his mouth hot on my neck, his cock still hard inside me, the smell and sound of it hanging in the air around us.

And through the fog, the fullness, the burning pain in my neck, all I could think of was the word in French, apprivoiser. Hard r and teasing, drawn out oi sound, like an animal cry. Me. Tamed. Completely.

Chapter 13

We lay there for a while, not moving, not speaking. It was as though we had both been through something, a crash, a fight, a storm that we'd both witnessed and now were trying to process. As though we both knew what we had seen, but couldn't really understand it. Not right now.

He lay next to me, breathing, our sweat cooling on our skin. Finally, some of the spell lifted, and I turned to look at him. His eyes were open, staring at the ceiling, deep set and profound, a puzzle being figured out behind them. I liked that I could see that. It was a shame I had no idea what he was thinking. But his skin was so warm next to mine. And when his arm lifted me up slightly and brought me to rest on his chest, his underarm hair tickling at my shoulder, the scent of him sweet and strong, his nipples taut and brown if I opened my eyes to look down the length of his body, I decided I was past caring.

He kissed my head, gently. It wasn't just a gesture, and I thought I sensed a moment of fear in it. Maybe some of the anxiety I had felt was not just mine, but his. The worry at trying to start something, the blank sheet, and wondering how the fuck it would all turn out.

"I'll be right back," he mumbled into my hair, and pulled his arm out and climbed out of bed to head to the bathroom. Ah, now, him in the light. Reality. Pale skin, and hair, and his long back trailing down to the most perfect fucking ass in the universe. And then legs. When he shut the door to the bathroom, I threw myself back on the pillows and groaned. There was daylight, girl, you wanted to see him in the light, and there he was. Is. I heard the water running. Then it stopped, and out he came, wearing a pair of old fashioned running shorts, tight, banded in white, and an oversized grey sweatshirt. I smiled at him.

"Hey there."

He smiled back. "Hey yourself." He gestured around the room. "Have a shower if you like. I'll make us some coffee, ok?" He looked serious for a minute. "I wanted to talk to you...before I have to go. We never really got to talk." He sounded serious, but his mouth was curling up in a small smile, that made me smile back.

"No, we didn't really, did we?" I thought I'd take a chance. "We seem to understand each other though."

He gave me that searching look again, the one that made me wish I really could read his mind. And then he bent down and kissed me, a sweet, soft kiss, that dissolved all the resolve I had to not care. "I think we do. But a few words just to make sure." He walked to the door to the kitchen and the rest of the apartment. "I have to leave in an hour, ok?"

I nodded. He went out, and a moment later, I heard the coffee grinder going.

I stretched out against the sheets. Wow, I was sore. Everywhere. I looked down at my hips and saw neat, small bruises where his hands had been. Oh. It hadn't felt that hard when he was gripping me, but then again I'd been delirious. Did I even want a shower? Part of me felt like never bathing again, leaving his scent and sweat on me like a mark, the fresh bruises, the soreness.

I got up and figured I'd decide once I'd seen myself. I went to the bathroom, washed my face and looked at myself in the mirror. I looked a hot mess—lips swollen, eyes sunken and slightly bloodshot, hair tangled, cheeks pale from lack of sleep, yet flushed at the same time. No doubt what I'd been doing. I liked it. Clean was overrated. I rinsed out my mouth with the toothpaste, and put on my newly dried bra and garter belt. The matching underwear was torn...somewhere under the bed, I guessed. Torn stockings I stuffed in the trash. Dress went on slowly, over the bruises. The leather jacket would hide all that anyway. I tried to make something of my hair and vaguely succeeded. Well, it wouldn't be a walk of shame. I wasn't ashamed. He...it was incredible, and feeling covered all over, really all over, with the signs of his possession was thrilling, illicit, perfect in a way my brain could not explain. But my body could.

So in this way, ten minutes later, I was sitting at the kitchen table, drinking strong coffee with the man I had shared it all with. He smiled, a hard perverse little smirk, when I came in wearing my dress, barefoot, holding my shoes. "No shower, huh?"

I tried out a few smart answers in my head, and thought I liked the truth. I found my voice. "I like the way you smell on me. Don't feel like washing it away just yet."

He raised his eyebrows, his eyes growing rounder. And laughed. In a happy way. "I never thought I'd hear a girl say that. They're usually so keen on smelling like flowers, or berries or whatever else they think they should."

"No, I'm quite happy to smell like you for a while, at least."

"Good." And he sat down with his coffee. "So I gather, so far, you're happy with…" Here he waved his arm around, and gestured theatrically with his hand. "…all this." Then he gave me a strange little bow of his head over his coffee.

I took a sip of coffee. I needed it. "I am." I took another sip. "Shouldn't I be?"

His face changed slightly, but quickly returned to its implacable stillness. "You tell me."

"I'm happy. No, happy is a stupid word. Last night…this morning…you…yes."

The smile returned. "You're doing that mangling words thing again."

"Yeah," I laughed. "You seem to have that effect on me."

"Good," he repeated. "Now we need to sort out some details." And suddenly he was all business. He reminded me of that famous music publisher I had finally been able to interview, the one pointed out to me at that very first awards show. The same steely eyed, sharp nosed expression was there. Power. It was thrilling, and again I was awash with that same strange confusion, whether to fight him, or lie down and wait for the blessed inevitable.

"Listen," he carried on. "It should be obvious to you now. I like to be in control. It's the way I'm made. But not everyone likes that." He looked to my neck, where I'd washed off the small spot of dried blood this morning. Now it was just red. "But I have the impression that you do. Despite a certain…what should I call it… defiance is a good word…that seems to be part of your nature." He gave me another searching glance.

"True." I felt like if I weren't honest, I'd lose it all. It was terrifying, and I wondered if he realized how much he was in charge of me already. "Very true. I like to fight back, but I need to submit."

He smiled again, and it made me scared. "Oh—I want you to submit. A lot." He took a deep breath. Here it was, the kill. "So let's discuss terms."

I tried to sound brave. "Ok. Tell me what you want." He looked at me and narrowed his eyes.

"It's not that simple, but I'll try to explain it."

"Ok." I took another gulp of coffee. Where was the calm happy feeling now?

"I want sole access to you. No other boyfriends, girlfriends, sex toys, whatever. You come with me, and me alone."

This was promising. The little voice said, what about when he's away, and what about when he can come, and I drowned it in more coffee. Shut up. You come with me. That phrase alone was pulling me in. I tried to stare back at him. Those eyes. I blinked. "Ok. Nobody else and not me either?"

"Right."

"Ok, I can do that. What else?" I sounded like I negotiated sexual relationships all the time. Right. Bloody hell.

"When I want you, you come. I won't be unreasonable—obviously you need to work and you have responsibilities. So do I. But if I need...want you there, you need to do what you can to come to me, wherever I am, as soon as you can."

"Ok." I needed a new word. But my brain was still stuck on him calling me, wanting me. I could only come with him. No touching myself. After last night, and this morning, that had lost its appeal anyway. I looked up at him, waiting for more.

"I like control. Power. Dominance. Over you. There are going to be...demands...I will make of you. I'm assuming that you've got a safe word that you like to use that you'll share with me." He was drumming his fingers on the table.

"I...no. I've never done anything like this before."

His eyebrows went up again, and his eyes darkened slightly. He looked angry. Did he really have to leave? He could fuck me right here, on the table, and show me what he meant.

"You've never played in this scene before." He sounded disbelieving.

"Unless you count being tied up with a t-shirt. Oh, and once I got a nose bleed when someone tried to mildly asphyxiate me. So no, not really."

"Oh shit, amateurs. And you still want to do this?" He looked slightly annoyed.

It was my turn to smile. "I have a feeling you know what you're doing."

His eyes grew dark and faraway. "It's possible."

His long hair shadowed his face, with a sprinkling of stubble and his eyes stared off into space, his mouth pressed into a hard line.

He looked back to me suddenly, completely serious. "I don't want to do this. Take away your innocence. I don't know what you want from me. You're complicated."

I inhaled, sharply. No. This wasn't going to go down this way. "I think we're both complicated. That's why last night was fun. Ok, maybe I haven't had the best luck in finding people to match up with me. True. But I want this. I want you."

He looked at me, waiting.

"You see something in me, and I feel what you see." He was still silent. "For fuck's sake, help me with this. I want this, I've always wanted it, and I'm not even sure what it is. But I'll still want it..." And here an idea occurred to me. "And I'll still want it, whether or not you're the one to initiate me into it. I'd like to feel lucky enough to have you do it properly."

He stared at me, and then there was a hint of that strange smile. He held up his large hands facing me, in some parody of a gesture of defeat. "Well played, little girl. But when I'm standing over you with a whip in my hand, I want you to remember your little speech."

My mouth went dry. Jesus.

He smiled at me. "I do like you, you know." He got up, and put his cup in the sink and turned and came back over to me. Bending down, his soft lips brushed my ear. "And you make me come insanely hard."

He pulled me up by my hand, and kissed me, his tongue gently exploring my mouth. God.

"Come on sweetheart, I'll call you a cab. I've got to get ready." And he walked back over through the living room, picked up his jacket and pulled his cell phone out and made a quick call. Looking up at me, he nodded. "Five minutes darling. Have you got everything?"

I grabbed my jacket, checking for keys and phone and credit card in the pockets. I nodded. I still felt breathless.

He pulled me to him again. "The cab's all paid for, don't worry about it." He placed a line of kisses from my ear to my neck that made me dizzy. He stuck a bill in my pocket and patted it. "That's for the underwear. Don't argue." The tone in his voice settled it.

I looked up at him, and nodded.

His phone went. "They're here. Alright little girl. Expect to hear from me." He kissed me again. "Beautiful. Don't doubt it." And he opened up the door, and the elevator was there, the same one that had brought me up several lifetimes ago. I stepped in, feeling like I was in another world again. He smiled at me. And blew me a kiss.

I smiled back, bravely, and the door slid closed.

Suddenly alone, it was though the focus changed and everything looked sharper and harder. I was sure every feeling I had was written on me and when I walked past the handyman in the lobby, I tried to stand up a little taller. Nothing to be ashamed of. I just didn't know what I'd agreed to, or who I'd really agreed it with.

Sitting in the cab, with hardly any room for my legs because of the security glass, and inhaling the strange mix of very old cigarette smoke and oil from the taxi, I leaned my head into the crook by my breast, like a bird trying to sleep. And I could still smell him, that glistening wetness that made everything better. Deep breaths, heading somewhere that was supposed to be home.

Chapter 14

Did I imagine it, or did the cabbie wink at me as I got out? I went to give him a tip, and he waved his hands at me. "All paid, all paid," he said in heavily accented English, and shooed me away, smiling.

Yeah, all paid for. I couldn't decide whether I felt spoiled or bought and sold. Oh, shut up, I told myself, and let myself in the building. Quite a different scene here, and walk up stairs, no endless elevator ride. And it was afternoon now, not first thing in the morning, but it reminded me of that euphoric return after that first meeting in the limo. Nothing was the same. He'd been inside me, in me, god, it felt different, I felt different, why should it matter so much, but it did. It made all the difference. My body felt like someone had held it in their hands. Bruised, satisfied, and thoroughly fucked. I liked this feeling. Where had it been all my life? I let myself in to the apartment, and ran to my room and shut the door. And locked it. I didn't want anyone to ruin this feeling by looking over me, at me, whatever. I spun around, and dizzily fell on the bed, stupid giant smile on my face. I buried my head in the pillow and breathed in, and quickly flipped over on my back to get some air, my heart beating so fast. Too much to take in. Too much to feel, after so long of not feeling any-thing but a kind of distant prickly longing that only held echoes of what had been and what could be, but never had been. This was different; everywhere on me and in me, liquid emotion. His scent. His sweat, still part of my skin. Oh god.

A song I hadn't thought of for ages came through my head. What was it? Real love? No, true love? Sweet Love, that was it. "So sweet, so sweet, so sweet," sweeping up into the air, "oh baby, no sweeter love." Who was it again? I couldn't remember. It would come to me. "Sweet love…hear me calling out your name, I feel no shame." High notes. Anita Baker, that was it.

I didn't want to think words and I forced myself to think of nothing but the song, and its plaintive, soulful joy, so much like the feeling running through my body. A feeling that didn't ignore my body, or my head, or my heart. As I heard the voice in my head singing, I could hear his voice, crying out in pleasure, ripping through me. I fell asleep with the two mixing through me.

◆ ◆ ◆

I woke up when the front door to the apartment slammed. I felt disorientated, then as consciousness slowly swept up me, a divine liquid achiness took me over. It was though as with sleep, all the reactions of my body changed, just a little shift, and all the sensation came back again, now mediated through pain, or soreness, or a tightness in my stomach, the tiny thrill of knowing what happened couldn't be confused with a fantasy. I stretched out, toes to fingers deliciously all of a piece, instead of the fractured disconnection I usually felt. Even the background knowledge that there was something wrong with Alice, that I would have to hear about and deal with, possibly for days, if not weeks, could not take away my languid happiness. Everything felt sharp and up close from the ache between my legs to the throb of the wound at my neck, yet at a distance, like I'd been wrapped in some silk cocoon.

I stretched again. My usual impulse, to run to Alice's side, the fixer, was gone. Did I even care? Where was I, and who had replaced me? Or maybe this was the real me, divinely indifferent, scorched by the gods. Or god. I giggled. This would never do. She'd hear me, and this would only increase her wrath. Oh I didn't care. The whole world felt open, and warm. I'd move out of this apartment, and away from her moods, and life would be sweet and complete, and yes, I felt I being somewhat unfair, but it was all ok. It was finally, blissfully, completely good. At last.

I lay there, smiling, and listened to more things being banged. Maybe I could just go back to sleep, and dream sweet dreams of a certain dark eyed, dark haired divinity. Yes. That's what I would do. I didn't want to talk. Bathing could wait.

I rolled over and checked my cell phone. No messages. That was almost a relief. I needed a little time to myself, to readjust, and introduce myself to this new happy, selfish, achy person who seemed to be me. I shut my eyes against the setting sun, and vowed a few more blissful hours of sleep wouldn't hurt me. My weekend. My time.

I buried my head into the pillows. Yes, I wanted a text from him. Telling me how fabulous I was. How happy he was. Yes, I did. But I wanted even more than that just to cuddle into the bed and not let anything ruin this feeling. But I sat up and looked at the phone one more time, just in case. Nothing. It was ok. I sank back down into the pillows and closed my eyes. Just a little while longer.

When I woke again, it was full dark outside, and there was just a strip of light falling onto the floor. I did feel achy now, and thirsty, and I needed to get up. I'd have to face the music. Hopefully, she was asleep. Or maybe she had gone out again. I creaked out of the bed, and grabbed a bathrobe. I was sure it was still obvious what I'd been up to, but maybe she'd be kind.

I went to the bathroom first. I didn't look at myself—I didn't want to. There was time for reassessment later, after some tea and food. I walked into the kitchen, and there was Alice, bottle of Jack in front of her. It looked like she'd been crying. This wasn't good.

"Hey girl, what's up?" I tried to sound neutral.

"Eh, life sucks. What else is new? Never agree to threesomes, that's my new mantra." Alice took a swig from the bottle. Whoa. This must be serious.

"What happened?" I didn't want to ask, but there it all was in black and white. I couldn't pretend it wasn't.

"He decided she—no, they, needed to go shopping, and I needed to go home. That's what happened." Her face twisted into a bitter smirk. "Fucker." She took another swig, and passed me the bottle. "Here, have a drink."

"Nah, I'm making some tea. You want some? I need a little caffeine first." I actually didn't feel like getting drunk and losing the buzzy euphoria of hurting so sweetly in so many places, but I wasn't going to say that. I turned to the kettle and busied myself getting out tea bags and cups. Don't look at me don't look at me, I repeated in my head. I did not want the interrogation. Would I luck out? I doubted it, but I could postpone the inevitable. The kettle boiled and I brought the two reddish cups of Assam, strong the way we both liked it, but no milk, to the table. Tea. I suddenly felt starving and horribly empty, and I realized it had been over 24 hours since I'd eaten anything, or drunk anything but champagne and coffee. Coffee. His sweet skin, and creamy coffee. I must have smiled.

"Hey!" Alice broke me out of my reverie. Shit. "Dream girl! I just remembered! So how did the dream date go with the dream man? Was it all dreamy?" Ah, bitchy Alice, out to play.

"Yeah, it was fine. Very nice."

"Nice? That's it? Sean told me he was a total player since the break up, a string of all kinds of girls. You're lucky—apparently he likes all shapes and sizes." Alice took another swig, ignoring her tea.

Bitch Alice was about to get bitch slapped. No, deep breathing. Ignore it, said some smarter side. Time for a bath. I picked up my tea. "Yeah, I am lucky. My size seems to be just right. Maybe you need some sugar in that tea, take away some of the bitterness." I felt on the edge. "Or maybe you should just mind your own business, you've got enough of it." I walked out. I didn't care anymore.

I locked the door to the bathroom. I wanted quiet, to drown out the hatefulness of her words, and I ran the water. I was horrified at the idea of washing off him, his everything, but I needed to soak. I was one big ache. When I got in, the mixture of relief and stinging sensation was disturbing. My body. What had happened? I calmed down in the hot water. It was all good. All good.

Chapter 15

I lay in the bath, playing idly with the bubbles, smoothing over the bruises and soreness. I could still hear banging in the kitchen, distantly. I didn't want to fight with Alice, but her casual meanness had removed my sympathy for her, for what had happened. Usually, I would have helped her, not now. And I was glad I didn't have to do it. I added some more hot water, and watched my skin color up with the temperature. Soaking up the water like a sponge. Soaking up all his energy, no wonder I had felt confused. And all my insecurities. Too much thinking. I swirled the water around with my hands, practicing the deep breathing that I'd been told would make me feel more grounded. I wondered how often I'd have to use it in the future.

The future. Whatever it would be. Completely unknown, you could hardly believe it would happen. But it did. Images swept through my mind. His leather pants. His face, dripping water, his hair slick and black, his body wet and hard. I felt my pulse racing and the ache start up again. But this time I had contracted to leave it alone.

Before, I only wanted to feel his hands tracing torturous lines across and down and over my weak and willing flesh. But it wasn't just a preference any more. Now it was a command. Don't touch yourself. All my orgasms, all my sexuality I had willingly agreed were dormant until he brought them to life. No, that wasn't it exactly. It didn't take a lot to remind myself of the sexual madness he brought me. But anything else would be betrayal. I'd agreed. I wanted to follow his rules. They weren't hurting me, I didn't feel diminished. In fact, I felt desired. His desire. I could still see his face, the first time he came inside me. Yes, there was the emotional attachment. But maybe this desire was intense because of the intelligence behind it, that preferences were acknowledged, secrets revealed. It was a game, and I was learning to play. The space between "won't" and "can't" was being confused. Yet the "I can't" part was as much my will as his. Strange.

I drained the tub, and wrapped a towel around me and walked out to my room. I called out "good night." There was no point in making more of it. Cowardice, or self-protection? I didn't feel like examining the point.

I curled up in bed and pulled the covers over me. The phone lay on the small white and blue table next to me. It was quiet. I realized suddenly that I had also signed up to never turn off the phone. I had to be on call. Me, who guarded my privacy and my space like a hurt animal, had just given it all over to a certain dark-haired man. I lay back and closed my eyes. What had I done? We'd had one night, one brief morning. Some people had that all the time with strangers they knew nothing about, and went on the next day like they'd done nothing more important than drinking a few beers. As much as I used to wish I was more like that, I wasn't. So what was going on? I heard my stomach grumbling, and remembered eating. Tomorrow. I took a deep breath and tried to feel comfortable in my cocoon, but it felt cold all of sudden. Lonely.

Finally I fell asleep, but I woke up in the middle of the night with a dream voice in my head, intoning, nodding intently that I should copy down the words. I reached for my notebook, which was always next to the bed, and scrawled down what it said in the dark. I knew from experience even turning the light on could chase away what seemed so vivid; it could make any vision, any phrase, suddenly other-worldly and distant and invisible. I wrote, checked the phone—nothing—then fell back on the pillows.

I woke a few hours later, the sky lightening dimly through the window. Another city end of winter day. I stretched, and remembered the writing, but not what I had written. I pulled out the pad. There it was, scrawled and confusing:

The future is metaphorical thinking.

Like describing a sound with a taste, or an emotional state with a color or sensation. This is where we are heading.

Strange, I thought. As the sensations from the bruises and soreness resurfaced, I wondered about describing them that way. What would my bruise taste like? Beyond the saltiness of blood, or sweat, or any of the literal descriptions. Fire, I decided, fire, like the coal in a grate, metallic and hard, dusty, scraping a trace on my hands, my thighs.

And his kisses? His mouth, large and swollen, elegant, sweet? Ah, I was obsessed. I was. I couldn't stop thinking about him. Where had I gone? Or was I there, more there than I'd ever been? His lips. Elegant, fine, like the graceful sweep of silver candelabra, formed and polished, yet heavy. A Venus with an axe. Dionysus with a whip. Literally. My skin grew hot again. He reminded me of the Caravaggio painting from the late 1500s. That sullen, dark eyed invitation to pleasure, one nipple the centerpiece of his half-clad body, his face a question waiting for an answer. The Maenads, the women who would leave all behind, and follow him, drunk, sky clad, trailing animal skins and ivy vines. Unrecognizable. A cult of secrecy and power. Death to those to tried to view their revels. I lost myself in a dream of dusty hills and sweet wine, searing heat and soothing rituals on the cool rocks, a temple in nature to desire and the incomprehensible.

I must have dozed off, because I woke with a start to the phone buzzing wildly next to me. I grabbed it without thinking and mumbled hello, sitting up with a start, noticing it was light out now.

"Hey Lily, it's Dave here. How are you?"

Dave, my editor at the magazine. The Editor. I hadn't expected a direct call from him. This could be either really good, or really bad. I held my breath and tried to think positively. "Dave, good, great to hear from you." I grabbed some water, and focused on waking up. "Did you see the piece? What did you think?" Why not just dive in? Why not?

He sounded cheerful. "Yeah, that's why I'm calling." Pause.

My heart stopped. I waited.

"I wanted to call you personally. It's just brilliant—and his manager—James, you've met him? He's a bit, what could I say, prickly, right? Even he likes it. He's passed it on to Tristan. And we're looking into syndication, not the rock mags, but overseas newspapers, magazines. I've sent it over to Huff Post in the UK, I know the arts editor pretty well. They won't run it, because we have it, but they are going to do a link to it."

"My god, wow. Holy shit. I mean, that's great." I was speechless. This was the big time, knocking on the door. Me? Incredible. I needed to say something more professional. "Overseas rights?"

"Of course we'll discuss it. You'll bring a lot of credibility to the magazine—amazing how these things happen. And you know the buzz around this release?"

"Yeah, I was at the party on Friday. Could add something about that to the article?"

He paused for a moment. "You were there? It was great, wasn't it? No, I think the piece is perfect as it is. There's a certain wistful quality to the ending that makes it very personal, as though the reader was really connected to the artist, and then it's broken. Like leaving a great concert. No, it's good."

I shivered a bit when he said that. I wondered if the truth got out, if it would change his perception. From illusion, carefully wrought, to truth.

He was still speaking. I needed to focus, fuck, my career at stake. I willed my brain to work. "Sorry, I didn't catch that."

"We want you to go to London and write up the secret gig over there. There's always been..."

I interrupted him. "London? You're kidding. When?"

He laughed, a short bark. "Look, like I was saying. There's always been a huge buzz about him over in Europe—they aren't as distracted by the good looks, maybe. Who knows? Anyway, he's flying out in two weeks, gig possibly at the Barfly, although it's—probably will be moved to Dingwalls. Do you know them?"

Now it was my turn to laugh. A series of images, this time of me, standing in a crowd, waiting in line, pushing my way to the front... "I do. Used to go both places a lot, in fact. Happy memories."

"Great, you can put that in too. Personal approach. Well, call it as you see it. I couldn't get you on the flight going out with him. Manager I think threw a wrench into that."

My heart stopped. Did that mean he was flying over with

someone else? Oh god, did he know it was me coming over to record the show?

"Does he know I'm going over to write the piece?" My voice sounded tentative, even to me. God. Lie lie lie. Sound stronger, not like some love sick fan girl. Woman.

"It's a bit odd, actually. James, you know, this manager person, said yes to it all first without checking with him. I caught the tail end of the shouting, and it wasn't pretty, considering I was on the phone."

"Odd." I didn't really know what to say. Had he read the piece? Were we not supposed to interact anymore on a professional level? What game was his manager playing? But Dave was talking again.

"He's a hardass, your musical hero, you know. You should have heard him."

My blushing was thankfully, invisible on the phone. I was desperate to know what he had heard him say, but I didn't want to alert him by seeming overly interested.

"Musical hero? What makes you say that?"

"It's in your piece—are you awake yet? Stop kidding around. Come on, I need you conscious for this. He's reading it now; anyway, you're due to fly out next Thursday evening, pending his final approval. Ok? Putting you up at No. 5 Maddox Street—very organic and central. And private. In case you need to bring your hero back for some questioning." He chuckled to himself.

Musical hero? Did I say that? God, I'd better reread it. Private? Life and art were mixing, obviously. I would deny everything. I blustered. "Right. Sure. When are you getting the final approval?"

"Depends how fast he reads." Dave laughed.

"So you think he'll say yes?" I was asking a question he couldn't have the answer to, because he wouldn't know the reasons anyone would say no. But I couldn't help myself.

"Yeah, I think he was reminding James who's in charge. I'll let you know as soon as."

I let out a long breath I'd been holding in, and tried to keep the light mood going. "So, Business class?"

"I think we can do that."

"Excellent, I want to get used to the high life." I was smiling. Professionally. I hoped he could tell the difference over the phone.

"Ok, Lily, I'll let you know when we hear from him. But start packing."

"You got it boss. What do you want from London?"

"Oh, you'll get a list. No worries there. Consider it my fee."

I hung up, feeling more and more like I'd slipped through the looking glass. I mean, I'd had some good press before, a small book tour. I wasn't a complete newb. But this. This could be big. I stared at my phone. And now he was reading the article. I almost felt more exposed. It seemed he was going to pass judgment on everything about me.

I wondered if we would be flying back to the States together.

London. Again.

Chapter 16

I lay back on the pillows. I hadn't even gotten up, but everything had altered yet again. So I was going back. London. The Big Smoke. Expensive. Tribal. The banker's paradise. The Queen, and her vast estates. Postcode wars, where kids were drawn into battles over turf that ended up with casualties. The march of centuries of architecture slowing down beside the new towers of metal and glass. Bitchy women and the distant men who loved them. A million people coming to the closest thing Europe had as a frontier of opportunity. A hard place, with a lot of fighting and ugliness and deceit. Yet it could be mystical, with illusion and darkness and light shifting past you to reveal anything, everything you could imagine. I wondered if the streets would look any different, and what it would be like to be there, again, after everything that had happened in between.

I closed my eyes and thought back. It was only a few years, but it felt like a lifetime ago when I had lived there. Seven years of putting up with the high prices and the tiny flats and general discomfort, until I moved to New York, and found it was all pretty much the same, except without the poetry. I wasn't sorry, not now. I hadn't found what I was looking for over there, partly, I reflected, because I didn't know what I wanted.

London and I had gone through a really low patch, where it

felt like I wasn't going to find anything I wanted, anywhere, ever. It had been a pretty dark time. I looked out the window, and listened to the New York traffic for a few minutes, thinking back. The whole experience was a little like a wound that hadn't really healed. When I had moved here, I tiptoed around what was broken. I had stuck to a routine, and that had helped me get over the memories of panic, working on what I could fix. Trying not to anesthetize the rest, trying to avoid cowardice. And all the struggling had paid off. The amazing irony of it though. Going back to see Tristan perform somewhere I'd gone to work off a lot of my nervous energy. I had some good times there, even if they had been a little weird.

The Barfly was a dive in Camden, where most of the up and coming bands found themselves at one point. Coldplay, Elbow, Muse, The Strokes...all went on to fame and fortune, in different ways and for different reasons. But once they'd all been just trying, hoping. And Tristan's first band had played there— I wondered if he found it ironic, or if he'd chosen the place on purpose to remind people of the history, the long standing devotion. Like he had said, he needed the control. So unlikely he wasn't aware of the links. This trip of course was all orchestrated. Lying there, in bed, it seemed easy to fit it all into the story to be written. But what about me and my old life? Where was all that going to fit in? And did it have anything to do with where I found myself now? I pulled up the covers, and drifted into my past.

It seemed a long time ago, once upon a time. I used to go to the Barfly on my own, none of my friends really being into indie music. Being alone in a place where everyone was at least in a couple, if not a whole group, was bizarre, but I got used to it.

My desires never seemed to be in sync with anyone else's, so I was alone. A lot. But my weird anxious shyness used to work for me, and people would come up and talk, maybe just to see what the hell I was about. I didn't know what they saw, or what they wanted, but we talked, we drank, I walked home alone.

Just like now, I didn't really do the one night thing. I didn't get all soft and swoony at the shouted endearments, hot beer breath in my ears, it just made me laugh. I was always looking at them, challenge in my eyes, I think, silently laughing. They never said the line I was waiting for, never stood up to me. Yeah, I wanted to be touched. But I'd forgotten, somewhere along the struggle and the ups and downs, how to give in, how to be welcoming. Maybe I didn't really want to be. So I waited, for a moment that never came, and so did they. And then there were the walks home alone, in the dark, in the rain. The silence at 3:00 a.m., listening to the night, was more poetically satisfying than the sickly vague hopeful looks on the skinny legged indie boys, who seemed to find me curious, like a lab project. But I wasn't laughing now, was I? Would all this be easier, if I had been easier, way back then? Impossible to tell.

I remembered the first time I went in there, surprised at how ratty it was. The Barfly had a dark, high ceilinged room with banquettes tucked into corners, with a big bar in the center. Too much fake looking wood. Red walls. Filthy floors. And that was the downstairs. When it was time for the music to start, you had to get in line, right through the bar, up the narrow twisting stairs, along the hall, to go into another big room, a big grey and white dirty square, with the stage at one end and the bar at the other. A few chairs and tables by the far wall under a few windows that looked like they hadn't been washed since before the

war. And then there was a VIP line too, right next to the regular queue of punters, which expanded as people grabbed friends
to join them, or a good looking girl in heels and lots of eyeliner
who looked needy.

There was that one night, when I got to join the VIP line. This
strange girl had come up to me. With her boyfriend. She was
pretty, blonde, all eyeliner and push-up bra breasts, covered with
a tiny t-shirt, and she latched onto me with a speed and per-
sistence that was alarming. She didn't wait for any approval—
and turned me into the one who was watching, wondering what
the hell was going on. She had grabbed my arm like we were
old friends, and murmured hazily in my ear. Her breath smelled
weirdly like yogurt, but the shock of the sour, milky smell somehow added to her air of mystery. Are you a gay, she had asked,
syntax throwing me as much as the question. I nodded silently,
figuring I could play along and be whoever she wanted me to be
for the moment. I was curious. So nothing had changed there,
not really. I liked it, just a little different. Like that song. "Alone
Together." The Strokes. Perfect.

Lucky for me, she took my nod for acceptance, and she held
me closer, and threw a triumphant look to her boyfriend, who
had a patient, bored expression. Then he disappeared for a
while, while she bought us beers, so I figured this little ritual
had been played out before. Sucking down beer, she asked me if
I was watching the band. I managed to speak, but still thinking
less was more, mumbled yes. She squealed, and hugged me, running her hands over my body. It was nice. I smiled. She seemed
so pleased with me. Happy surprise. It was so easy. And she
dragged me to the VIP line, so we would be right up front for the
concert. She was a fierce little thing, pushing back people that

tried to muscle in to our place on line. I liked it. Girls that acted like boys but looked like girls. Sort of like the Blur song.

When we got upstairs, she found us a place in front of the stage, planted me there to hold it, and went to get us another round. I wasn't sure if she'd come back, but she did, complaining they tried to give her warm beer and she made them open two new Red Stripes for us. We clinked bottles and she held me close to her as the band hit the stage. They were disappointing, they were supposed to be on the verge of something, but only hit it for a couple of songs. I had always paid close attention to this stuff, having worked in the business, my first job, my first serious boyfriend in the trade, but that had been the first time I'd gone home and written all about what might have gone wrong in between the CD and live show. Funny to think that's what had gotten me here, writing for the magazine.

It was always fun to play spot the A and R men, and they had not looked pleased. The week after I followed the band to the ICA, watched the suits give them another chance. It was sickening to watch them turn away, faces cold and grim, leaving as soon as the last note finished, knowing that was it for the band. They missed the golden ring. Disaster. Disappeared. Tristan was more of a sure thing, but the company people would still be there, watching the crowd closely, gauging the reaction. He was taking a gamble, one that hopefully would pay off. The element of risk—that could go in the piece. Remind people it wasn't as easy as it looked.

But that night with the yogurt girl was fun. We kissed a lot, even though the taste of yogurt and beer was only somewhat tempered by the Camel Lights we were smoking. I don't think I ever asked her a single question, not even what her name was, as we made out in a style that owed more to cool club display than actual passion. She was all over me, getting her girl on girl badge, but there was something, yet again, that made me want to leave it at the door. Was it her spacey attitude, or the boyfriend that checked in every so often and exchanged glances with me, that while not overly suspicious, seemed to acknowledge that I wasn't all I was pretending to be either? Or was it just the power trip in saying you had to go, and watching their faces register the refusal? I guess I liked a little control too. And leaving was easier than staying. I never saw either of them again. I thought about her sometimes though.

One story in all the history that was following me.

Going back. To be there. Watching him. I felt my throat constrict. What the hell was I going to say now that wasn't going to reek of desire? I couldn't pretend he wasn't sexy, hell, he was famous for it. I'd have to be very careful. It was all going to be written all over my face. And the past. The ghosts that were going to be there, in the club, watching me.

I checked the phone. Great. I'd spent a whole fucking hour daydreaming about the weird little moments of life I'd been through. I leapt out of bed, realizing the enormity of what was going to happen. I was frightened of what could go wrong, maybe even more frightened of everything that was going right, so fucking right. I threw on some jeans, and my very own push-up bra and black t-shirt. The bruises were fading, I was still a little sore. All that meant was that I was ready for round two. This looked right. Rock and roll lifestyle all the way. I could use what I'd learned, back then in those lonely days.

I pulled out some boots. Musical hero, what was I thinking? I wasn't thinking, I'd been caught up in his spell, and now I ran the risk of exposure. Indiscreet could mean losing it all. I stretched out and touched the floor. The ground, to ground me. That's what the yoga therapy had recommended. I stood up, slowly, and went to brush teeth and hair and put on some makeup. Out in the world. A strong coffee, some notes on the book. Maybe that strange dream idea would give me some direction.

Fifteen minutes later, I threw on my leather jacket, and left the house. My phone told me it was just after 12:00. A bit late to start out the day for normal people, a bit early maybe for the serious music crowd. In between—that's what dwelling on the past got you. I walked over to Broadway, and up to my favorite bagel place, the one that wasn't famous. They made really nice plain old coffee, regular, like the old men still called it. Half and half, that brilliant American invention and strong fucking coffee. That would chase away the demons. I smiled up at the sun. I'd walk around. Maybe sit in the park for a while. I checked my bag—notebook, and gloves. Phone. Still nothing. Fine. I needed some caffeine before any more calls came in.

The guys behind the counter were friendly as always, and one of them stuck a piece of rugelach in the bag for me. I smiled, said my thank yous, and walked out. I decided to sit in the middle of Broadway, on the bench, but when I got there, there was a homeless woman with all her possessions in a shopping cart, bundled up against the cold like a babushka. There but for the grace of a god go I, I thought. And I thought I had problems. I have no problems. I turned away, and walked towards Central Park, sipping at my coffee. I nibbled at the tiny Danish. It was good, buttery. Smooth. I wondered if Tristan ever ate little pieces of pastry, if he would ever just sit with me in the park, and talk and drink coffee.

He'd warned me. And as usual, I ignored all warnings, plunged ahead with my own philosophical imaginings about how this time I'd get what I wanted. Needed. And here I was, on speed dial to the gods, and I was thinking of more. Stupid idiot fool.

I threw out the bag, and stomped off towards the park. I crossed Amsterdam, and squeezed through the group of private high school kids coming out for lunch. I listened to their sharp chatter, wishing for a moment that I could feel that entitled and oblivious again. That had been me back then, sneaking out, or faking some kind of permission, and going to smoke in the park, beautifully indifferent and horribly self-conscious all at once. They completely ignored me as I walked past. I was backdrop, stage dressing to their loves and losses. Yeah, yeah, it's always been that way. All your belongings aren't in a shopping trolley, and you're out in the cold because you want to clear your head.

The red light changed to green, and I crossed Central Park West, and went up a block to get past the low red stone wall that only permitted access at certain points, decided long ago. Just like life, I thought. Access all areas. The secret gig. Was he going to think I'd planned it all, some career progression? Or would he see all these events as what they were, a group of happy accidents? Well, happy for me. Discreet. We were supposed to be discreet. If no one knew for certain, didn't that count? But there was Alice. And the boyfriend, Sean. And the manager. And the limo driver. What was amazing to think about were all the people who were witnesses to any liaison. Oh god, what a headline. "Fetish nights whip up good reviews." Any publicity, right? But we were going to have to be careful. Especially over there, land of odd libel laws. Any rumor could snowball. And no one could be trusted. Look what happened to Kate Moss, photographed in a studio, doing coke, by a "friend."

I walked by the bridle path that circled the reservoir, strolled past the sweaty, driven joggers, the older couples and what seemed like an endless supply of strollers and anxious looking mothers, some accompanied by their nanny, in case it got all too much. It's good to have back up, I thought. And then I remembered I hadn't seen Alice. She had been there for me, a million times. I felt a bit guilty, and pulled out my phone.

And there was the flashing light. Fuck. I'd had my headphones plugged in; I hadn't heard anything over the traffic. My heart was beating wildly and my fingertips felt numb. Shit. I sank down on an empty bench, and closed my eyes. "It's all ok," I said out loud. No, not now. Not yet. Ignorance, bliss. I postponed finding out whether it was good or bad news by sending a text to Alice.

Hope yr feeling better. Lets talk.

It wasn't much, but it was a little flag of truce. She'd bounce back, she always did. I wondered idly who the next Sean would be, or if she'd go back to him. He was connected, and she had a heightened sense of self-preservation.

Now. My stomach was churning, the coffee burning through me now. Voice mail first. Yoga. Fuck, it was like AA for yoga. Constant reminders and check-ins. Well, that's what I had wanted. Before. Delete. Next message. Dave.

"Lil. Ok. Yes. All go. Of course he liked it. Why wouldn't he be happy to have you come over? Said you were very professional. Apologized for the outburst before. Come by the office later in the week to pick up itinerary, chat with the *Guardian* newspaper and *NME* lined up, and brief interview with some new band from Australia that are supposed to be hot, who are playing next Friday. Ciao."

Well. It didn't look like I'd have a lot of time for fun and games or reminiscing. Maybe that was best. Interesting the damage control Mr. Control had done. Very nice. A chess player, thinking several moves ahead. But that was the story for them. What about how he felt about us? Was the relationship going to be professional or personal, one or the other? The idea of having to choose at some point between them...which would it be? If you had to choose. Call yourself an independent woman. Shit. There was my answer. Maybe.

And all this while, I knew that I had a text. At least one. But it could just be Alice. It could be anyone else I knew. I wiped my hands on my jeans, and unzipped my jacket. I was heating up. I slid the little track ball over to the symbol. It took forever to get there, and I pressed down. Yes there was a message from Alice. And from him. Was it a request...for...company? Or a rating on the article, and the new need to keep it strictly professional? I pressed the link for Alice's message first.

> Soz doll, that wz bad. All fixed, out 2nite, tlk
> laterz.

Oh, so Alice was all better. Great. As I knew she would be.

Now the serious stuff. I'd kept him as "unreal." I thought there was no point in leaving a crumb trail directly to his name. And "Master" seemed a bit much. I kind of hoped he wouldn't have me call him that if it came to it, it seemed a bit tacky. Yeah, like you'd complain, I thought. He's probably about to tell you the game's over, anyway. With a sense of fatalism, I pressed the button.

> Like the article. You write very well, but you knew
> that. Hero? Look up to me tonight. BTW, discreet
> London plans for you. My apartment 7.

The wave of heat that rushed over me as the image he had planted in my mind of standing over me with a whip came to me. My legs were shaking. The phone vibrated in my hand and I nearly dropped it, I was so on edge. It was him again.

> Text me yes. Now.

I had a purpose. It was so much easier like this. I jumped to obey.

> Yes.

An answer came back almost immediately.

> My fingers, in you. Now. Are they wet?

Whoa. Ok. What to answer? The truth, that's right, sticking to the truth these days.

> Now they are.

Again, the answer back in a flash. Was it experience, or eagerness?

Not like they will be.

I leaned my head back and closed my eyes. Holy fucking hell. My body was vibrating with want, like a pulse going through me. My phone went off again.

Hard...thinking about it.

The image of him, silken and ready, jumped into my mind. I needed to let him know. Everything.

Hard to obey when you tease me like that.

Another lightning reply.

Those who break rules get punished. Understand me?

Oh. Fuck. It was going to happen then. I closed my eyes for a moment, overcome, heart racing.

I do now.

And in a flash, he wrote his answer.

Steep learning curve. Tonight.

I put the phone away and got up and began walking. Anything to move this huge rush of energy around. Six hours, and he'd teach me something I said I wanted to learn.

His beautiful hands on me, again. And he'd make me understand.

Oh yeah.

Chapter 17

I checked my phone again. 6:50 p.m. The hour was finally here, and I was standing outside his building, looking up, trying not to look too conspicuous. I walked up the block again, and back, not wanting to be too early, nervous as hell. Too scared to admit I wanted it, badly. I just felt numb with anticipation. It had been the longest afternoon ever.

I finished my latest march up and down the block, and checked the time on my phone again. 6:55 p.m. I couldn't wait any longer. I went in; the handyman who was loitering this time wasn't the same person who was there the morning I left. I couldn't really remember who was there the first time I came in, though. I walked up to the small buzzer panel. I thought maybe the heels and short leather skirt might give it away, that I wasn't there for a chat, but his face was impassive as I walked past him and through the door which now opened. "The elevator's straight ahead," he said. I thanked him, while wondering if all the rumors were true about the frequency with which Tristan changed bed partners, wouldn't somebody like him know it all? Somebody ought to ask them, I thought. Except I didn't really want to find out.

I stood in the elevator and pressed the button for his floor. I wasn't scared like I had been the first time, but I was still on edge. What would he make me do? What if I didn't like it, and it was too much?

What if I liked it too much?

The little lights showed 5, then 5 and 6, then 6, then 7. The elevator slowed down, and came to an old fashioned stop, jerky and slow. The door seemed to creak open slowly. I resisted the urge to kick it. The door was closed, and I rang the bell, holding the elevator door open with my hand, rubber and metal against my fingers.

Then the door opened, and there he was. Dark circles under his eyes, regarding me with a steady stare. A brief smile played on his full lips, and I looked away, suddenly embarrassed at everything it implied.

"Come in." His voice was brisk. He turned suddenly, and I followed him in. He shut the door, and flipped two of the locks, loudly. The metallic clang echoed in the room. My escape route had been blocked.

He walked to the middle of the living room and gestured to me to follow him.

"Let me take your jacket." He was suddenly polite, old fashioned. But his manner was still cold and distant. He expertly helped me remove my leather jacket, and he hung it up in the closet, neatly. He turned back and looked me up and down, taking in the soft white t-shirt, slightly see through, revealing a cream balconnet bra underneath. The short black leather skirt. Stockings. High heels. I figured rock and roll with a French edge was what you wore to these sorts of things. Judging by the look on his face, I'd done all right. I ventured a little smile.

"You like?"

"Very nice. You look good in leather."

He was wearing a pair of ripped jeans, faded, torn across the knees and where his leg met his hips. The gap drew your eyes in, made you try to see what was hidden underneath, a mere tantalizing shadow away. His long torso was covered in a vintage Hawaiian print shirt, unbuttoned halfway, showing an expanse of smooth chest. A white belt. He looked the picture of dissolute fashion, put together, but looking effortless. Sexy, yet edgy.

"I like the shirt." The next part came out in a whisper, I hadn't realized I was holding my breath. "And the rips."

He laughed. And just kept staring at me. He reached me in one long motion and ran his hand down my back, and lower, down my legs, slowly. I closed my eyes.

"Nice."

Suddenly his hand dipped below my skirt, and reached in between my legs, brushing the skin at the top of my stockings. I could feel top of his wrist brush against my panties, already wet, then move away. I flushed and looked up at him, his face right above me, controlling. He smiled, like he had discovered a secret, then spun me around so I was pressed up against him from behind. He was already getting hard; I could feel him as he pulled me tight into his hips.

His deep voice murmured in my ear. "When you're here, like this, you're mine to play with. Do you understand? Just nod, don't speak."

I moved my head against him. I could feel his hair against my cheek, the smell of him so close to me. I leaned my head back on his shoulder and he licked the side of my mouth, wetly, and pulled away again. I let out a soft moan, wanting more.

His lips moved around my ear, his tongue darting in and out. "Shh, don't talk." His mouth moved down my neck, and suddenly his hands were covering my breasts, pinching my nipples, hard. I couldn't help the gasp that came out.

"Quiet." His voice was a low command.

I nodded. He pushed me away from him, and the cool air hit my back, which had been so warm pressed against him just seconds before. The contrast was painful. Was he angry?

Then his arms were around me again and his hands ran down my stomach, and made slow, steady circles there. He grabbed my hips and swayed with me, in a slow dance, a delicious friction between his erection and my backside, so close. He moved me against him, and I let myself go with his rhythm. The heat was pooling in my belly. The ache that had been slowly building was now a painful kind of contraction, as though all my muscles were at breaking point. He slowed down and ran his hands up my body, peeling off my t-shirt over my head. He threw it somewhere, and glided his hands down my back, tracing my spine downwards. The sensation was nearly ticklish, I had goosebumps all over my body. I wanted his hands everywhere. As if he'd read my mind, he placed his palms over my breasts.

"I like this." His fingers ran along the top of the lace, with an unbelievable delicacy, gently pressing against the flesh bursting out over the top, avoiding my nipples, which were painfully hard. His hand brushed against one, almost by accident, then twice, then dipped below the fabric and flicked it with one neat fingernail, sending a wave of heat down my body. I bit my tongue, but a groan came out.

"You're shy about speaking out, so you're going to be quiet until I tell you that you can speak. Or make any noises. At all." He turned me around again, and sank down, taking a nipple into his mouth, licking at me through the fabric. I clenched my fists and dug my nails into the skin with the effort it was taking not to moan. I shut my eyes, tight. Then his teeth were tugging at me, pulling, running over the other nipple, biting at the soft underside. I was dizzy from the mix of sensation, his commands, his body so close to mine. Knowing that he was hard. Not knowing what he was going to do.

He straightened up and stood there for a moment, thoughtful. Then his hands were on my shoulders, pushing me down.

"I think you need to be on your knees." His voice a dark threat.

I sank down to my knees, my leather skirt riding up, showing plainly the tops of my stockings. I was trembling. I looked up.

His eyes looked nearly black, and his smile seemed more ominous now. I was losing it.

"Oh, you look good like that. Look straight ahead. That's right, look at my body. What you want. What you're here for."

I was nearly eye level with his crotch and the long rip in the denim. I could see clearly the dark blue boxer briefs peeking through the hole, his thigh, covered in a fine pattern of hair, the bulge that was his erection.

He unbuckled his belt, slowly. Then his long fingers looped around the buckle and freed the whole length of it out of the jeans, in one fluid gesture. The belt made a slapping noise as it whipped through the fabric. The movement was arrested in mid-air, then he snapped the belt back down against his leg at speed, the sound loud and echoing in the silence. His eyes shut for a moment and he gripped the leather in his hand, but did nothing else.

"Unbutton my jeans." His voice was a dark cipher now. A tone I'd never heard.

My hands moved to touch him, and I stroked the silken, burning hot skin, before I reached the buttons. I couldn't help it. He slapped my hand, which made me hit his cock. Hard. He hissed.

"No little girl. Do as you're told."

I moved up to the first button, then the second and third and fourth. His jeans were now hanging open.

"Pull them down."

I held on to the belt loops, careful not to touch him. His soft jeans slid down over his hips, down his legs and fell to the floor. His thighs were strong as he kicked them off and away. He looked enormous in front of me. Tall. Commanding. I watched, fascinated, as he shoved his hand down his briefs and straightened himself out.

"I don't think I'll let you touch me now. In fact, I think you can just watch. Put your arms behind you. Don't move otherwise."

He walked behind me and pushed me forward, my ass up in the air. I heard the swish of the belt through the air before the stinging pain of the leather against the tops of my thighs cut through my thoughts. A cry escaped me, and brought me another hard blow, followed by three more, exactly placed. I waited for the next, but instead Tristan stood behind me, his long leg thrust between mine, pushing against my sex, and swiftly wrapped the belt around my wrists several times, tight. It was warm from his hand. He latched the buckle and pulled it tighter, the leather digging into my skin. My heart was racing. Then he moved away, and pushed me back until I was sitting on my heels.

Standing directly in front of me again, he smiled, that enigmatic smile that didn't reach his eyes, which were darker than before. Then he walked away. His thighs flexed with each step, his firm ass demanding to be touched, moving under the fine fabric of the briefs. As I watched him, he lowered his shirt over his broad shoulders, revealing the pale, creamy skin of his back, smooth and full. He then dropped his shirt on the floor, all without turning around. He knew he had my full attention, and his little striptease, his super consciousness of his body and the power it contained was making me impossibly wet. He was taunting me with his sexuality. I wanted to move, uncramp my legs, ease the burning, but I didn't dare. I felt like he'd memorized my position.

He turned and walked back towards me. "Like what you see? See if you like this." And he came up to my face, and dipped one of his large hands inside his briefs, squeezing his balls, the shape of his knuckles and his cock pushing through the thin fabric. I looked up to his face. He was staring at me. "Don't look away now. I want you to watch me. I know you like it."

And he slowly dragged his hand up his length, then his hands were visible again, He hooked his thumbs around the elastic top of his briefs and began pulling them down, slowly. Finally, his cock sprung free, huge, hard, glistening at the top. He continued pulling them down his long, finely muscled legs, and nimbly stepped out of them, tossing them across the room. And he stood in front of me, his thighs strong, solid, his knees sculptured like his calves, elegant yet insistently male. Then he began stroking himself, slowly, repeating the motion over and over, an arm's length away from me. I wriggled. I couldn't help it. I wanted to touch him so badly, I could taste it. I needed pressure between my legs, and I squeezed my thighs together. My foot twisted, and one of my shoes fell off. He noticed, and he glared at me. And I sat there, chastened.

He stopped and walked behind me, and removed the other shoe from my foot. I couldn't see what he was doing, but he had walked away. "That's why I needed to restrain you. You have no control." I hung my head, and stared at my thighs. Was this it? I heard his footsteps approaching over the heartbeat in my ears. There he was, in front of me again. He tapped me under the chin, and raised my face to look at him. His eyes were searching.

After a long moment, he shook his head, as though he had decided on something.

"You're doing very well though. Considering. Maybe I'll give you a treat." He resumed touching himself, his cock, still full, seemed to swell more under his touch. I watched as his fingers circled his thick erection and pulled. I looked up at his face, and he gestured with a look that I should keep my eyes on what he was doing. His other hand gripped his balls then traced a pattern around his hipbone. I was mesmerized. Just watching him lose control was going to be more than enough to push me over the edge.

I watched as he ran his long forefinger around the head and over the reddened top. He groaned, quietly, and placed his finger on his lips, sticking out his tongue, swirling it around his mouth and his finger, shamelessly tasting himself. It was lewd, an animal gesture, and I couldn't stop watching. All I could think of was that long tongue on me, in me, his big mouth fitting over my pussy, making me wetter. I wanted dirty.

"Little girl." His voice was a filthy growl, and it tore through me. "Want a taste?"

I looked up at him, all need. He laughed. And he slid his thumb over the head of his still wet cock and thrust it in my mouth, letting me run my tongue over his flesh. God, the taste of him, salt, sweat, power. Then he began fucking my mouth with his finger, slowly in and out, opening up my mouth. I moaned, somewhere deep in my throat, it felt so good, so close, almost like having him inside me.

"Mmm, that's good. Here, let's try this." And without any warning, he quickly removed his thumb and pushed his impossible huge wet cock to my mouth. "Suck me off. You know you're good at it."

I opened my mouth, licking him, taking him in little by little, until I nearly had my lips up against his balls, and the head of his cock hitting the back of my throat. The heaviness felt so good in my mouth, and I let him slip out a little so I could take a breath, and swirled my tongue around him. Oh god. It was like the best possible feeling, and the smell and taste of him were so sweet, so strong. More wetness was forming at the head of his cock, and he was starting to push into my mouth, fucking my mouth slowly at first, then speeding up, rocking against me. His breath was getting ragged and his eyes were clenched shut. I gently let my teeth brush against him, and he moaned.

Abruptly, he stopped and put his hands on my shoulders. He pulled out of my mouth, and I took a deep breath of air. His cock was pointing straight out, red and wet and glistening.

"Little girl, look at me." I obeyed, and looked up at him. "I'm going to come. I want to come in your mouth, on your mouth. Will you let me? Please." His eyes were softer now, pleading. I realized I was shaking from need, only his hands on my shoulders keeping me upright. I nodded up at him, the intensity coming off him in waves. "I can't hold back any longer," he grimaced, and thrust his cock back into my willing mouth.

I wanted him to come so badly, I wanted to feel him unstuck, taste him all over me, and my mouth couldn't get enough of him. His rhythm, like before, so steady at first, became more erratic. He gasped for air, and I felt him spasm against me, hot whiteness against my tongue. He grabbed his cock, and pulled it out of my mouth as he kept coming, rocking his hips into air, and the tip of it was on my lips, and the wetness was now covering my mouth, thick, hot. It was so dirty, so erotic, everything I ever wanted, and the noises he was making and the feel of him and him using me like that, coming on me...all these thoughts went straight to my center and I felt my own spasms take me, clutching around emptiness. I cried out, I couldn't help it, as my tongue ran over my mouth, in an imitation of what he had done earlier, I imagined his mouth on me, his tongue buried in me, and I was shaking, falling on to him, his cock against my face, wet, and still half hard. His arms went around me then, and he held me close, through my orgasm.

"Ah, little girl." He kissed the top of my head, and knelt down to be closer to me and kissed my wet lips, licking off the rest, his tongue exploring my mouth. He obviously liked it, liked his own taste. I liked that he liked it.

We held each other tightly, as he murmured sweet words in my ear about how lovely I was, how good it was, as he dropped little kisses around my neck and face. We stayed like that for awhile, until I shivered slightly.

"It's chilly. Wait here, I'll clean us up."

Tristan disappeared towards the kitchen. I heard a door open and shut. I waited.

A minute passed, which seemed forever. Then the door opened and closed again, and he came back in, smiling, holding a washcloth, walking towards me. He undid the belt, and freed my arms. I shook them out, stiffly.

"Good girl. Stand up now." And he stretched out his hand to me and helped me to my feet. I had pins and needles. He seemed to know this, and just held on to my hand while I shook out my legs. I looked up at him, and he raised my hand to his lips and kissed it, softly. "Beautiful. You're doing fine."

I smiled at him, and he gently cleaned off my face with the warm cloth, before easing it gently across the back of my thighs. It smelled faintly of jasmine and mint.

"Shh. Don't speak. You don't need to. You don't need to do anything. How brilliant is that? No decisions. No guilt. It's all on me." His eyes searched mine. "Are you too cold?"

I shook my head. He crooked his head, and took in all of me, appraising what he saw.

"I think I want you close to me right now." He intertwined his fingers with mine. "Come, let's get under the covers, so I can hold you."

I looked up at him, blinking. How could this beautiful man, so hot, so hard, be so sweet and kind the next moment? It was unthinkable, yet here he was. I nodded, and he smiled, a big silly smile, and grabbed my hand, leading me towards the bedroom.

Chapter 18

He led me by the hand, through the kitchen, back to his bedroom, which looked more or less the same as I remembered it. He pulled back the covers on the neatly made bed, and gestured that I should get in. I looked at him for a moment, wondering again if he really was going to hold me, as promised, but his face gave nothing away. I slid in the cool, smooth white sheets, moving over to give him room. I wanted to touch him, feel the reality of him next to me. This was all too dreamlike, and I was still dizzy from what had just happened between us in the living room. It felt good to lie down, and I watched him fold his long body, still naked, under the covers. I was disappointed for a moment not to see his skin as he pulled the sheets up, but it vanished as he snaked an arm under and around me and pulled me to him, effortlessly.

"I want to hold you little girl. Why so surprised? No, don't say anything. Just feel."

I bit my tongue, literally, to hold back the flood of questions I had. But he was right. Would the answers really change what this was? I willed my brain to stop trying to make sense of everything, and focused on the delicious sensation of his stomach against mine, his beautifully soft skin, the muscle underneath, his powerful thighs wrapped around mine, making me feel small, protected. I turned my head to look at his face, so close to mine. His eyes were closed, and there was a small smile teasing gently around the corner of his lips. His eyes flew open, as though he could feel me watching him, and he gave me that searching gaze again. His eyes were so beautiful, not so dark now. Grey and brown, and tiny flecks of blue, almost invisible. But the expression in them gave them their depth. There was a kind of understanding there, a gentleness that surprised me. They gave the impression that he was measuring, weighing things up, just as he had done when I kicked off my shoe. I wondered what he saw and if he could see past me and all the barriers I'd learned to put up. I wasn't sure if I knew how to be open any more.

He kissed the frown between my eyebrows. "Interesting, little girl, interesting. There's something in you that always wants more. But maybe that's because you're only just finding out what you really want. Are you happy now?"

My voice came out in a croak. "I can talk?"

He laughed. "Of course."

I focused my attention on my legs, crushed and tangled up with his, his arm around me, the heavy duvet, and the smooth sheets, his lips, the distant ache of desire that was still there against all my questions, confusions. I couldn't help smiling. What an idiot I was. "Yes, confused. But happy. Very happy. This feels so nice."

He smiled back. "It does, doesn't it? Your body likes me, I think. We'll work more later on your mind." And he pulled me tight to him, and sighed.

I closed my eyes. It wasn't my mind that was in danger. His large hands caressed my back, down to my hip, soothing me. I began drifting off, more tired than I realized from all the tension of the day.

. . .

I woke up, disorientated, cold. I opened my eyes. The room was softly lit, and I was alone under the covers. But I didn't have to look far to find him. He was sitting cross-legged at the end of the bed, naked except for a pair of running shorts, a large black sketch book in front of him. He was drawing. He saw me waking up and smiled. "Hang on, don't move." His hand moved delicately over the page, shading, making marks. "Ok, got it."

"I didn't know you could draw."

"Ah, so many things you don't know. Yet. Are you hungry? I ordered some food for us."

"I am, a little. Thank you. That's really nice of you."

"Why so formal? Of course I'll feed us. C'est normal, like the French say. You'll see." He closed the sketch book before I got a chance to look. "There's a robe in the bathroom. Come to the kitchen when you're ready." And he got up, still holding the book, and walked off towards the kitchen. I watched him. I couldn't get enough of seeing him move, nearly naked, the body filling the room with animal grace, like a tiger pacing slowly in his cage. And I wondered what about him made me think of someone trapped, too large for his surroundings.

I got up, went to the bathroom, and untangled my hair. Was I going to be here all night, or was dinner a prelude to my departure? I ran toothpaste over my teeth, and splashed water on my face. I looked softer, I thought. Maybe life didn't have to be so hard all the time. Maybe.

I tied the robe, and walked out to the kitchen. Tristan was

ladling out some thick buckwheat soba noodles into two bowls. "I got us soba noodles. Do you want some tempura shrimp on top, or pork?"

"I'll have some of the shrimp please."

"I thought you would." He looked over his shoulder at me, and flung a quick grin in my direction before returning to his task of balancing the meat on top of the noodles. He brought the bowls over to the table, then returned to the counter top. He pulled open a drawer, and got out two glazed ceramic spoons and some chopsticks, which he brought over, along with a tea pot.

"Green tea all right?"

I nodded. His careful organization was so appealing, I didn't trust myself to say anything at all, worried that I'd blurt out everything I was thinking. And I wasn't even sure myself what I was thinking yet. My inner polite self shook me though. I needed to say something.

"This looks fantastic. Really. I love Japanese food."

He grinned again. "I know it. Japanese food is just amazing, all of it. I really got into it when I was doing the detox thing. You just feel so much better after you eat it than anything else. Also went with the acupuncture. I thought, do the thing entirely, or not at all." He took a few bites of his noodles, and carried on.

I was finding it hard to eat in front of him, but the food was really good, and he had gone to so much trouble. And he seemed so relaxed. I liked it. I liked this, sitting and eating and talking. Even if it made no sense, considering everything. Or maybe I'd just misunderstood him. I didn't know.

He drank some tea, and as usual, my eyes followed his long throat as he swallowed. I turned to my food. I really couldn't look at him too much and eat.

He carried on talking after neatly managing a bite of his noodles. His eyes met mine briefly, then looked into the distance. "It was a really hard time for me. At first I did a whole week. I thought, I've cracked it. I can do this. It was almost as if my body was agreeing with me, saying you don't need the chemicals anymore, making it easy for me. But then I had a meeting with a friend, in a bar, and I had a drink and a smoke, and it all seemed ok, and another one. And after about five drinks, I thought I should stop, but I felt fine. And eventually I went home. But I couldn't remember how I'd gotten there. And I called a friend, but I didn't remember any of the conversation, just a few hazy ideas. That's when I realized I really needed to stop, and that it wasn't going to be easy. Not at all."

His face was sad, soft and sad. I wanted tell him it was ok, I'd help. I didn't know what to say. But I wanted him to keep talking. "What did you do after that?" I ate some more. I wanted to hear him, hear what he wanted to say. I was going to make him happy, make him proud of me. Whatever that meant.

Tristan carried on. "I was shaken, but I thought I could still do it on my own. Then a couple of days later, there was a party, and some more drinks, and god, I just wanted to be able to have a glass of wine, and not care. But I couldn't. I drank a bottle of wine, ok, I wasn't doing shots of tequila, or snorting coke, but it wasn't what I wanted. I was better, but not enough." He returned to eating, quietly.

I ate more, silently with him, in solidarity. I knew what he meant, maybe not to the same degree, but I'd been there. I was still there.

"I know what it's like." He looked at me, almost surprised.

"I mean, I understand, I think. The day I realized that so many people in my family had ruined their lives through..." I stopped. I couldn't believe I was telling him this. Shouldn't I be perfect for him? No issues? No baggage? "But then I saw myself doing it too. Taking the psychological damage and amplifying it with depressive comedowns and escaping into drinking, coke." He was fixing me with that look again, and I felt like I was confessing something. "I never was as bad as a lot of people, but I was bad for me, you know? And I didn't want to look back and say I'd missed out because it was easier to hide away and get wasted, than get out there and feel fear." He was nodding, so I felt better and carried on. "It's still hard. It doesn't fix everything. But working on it is something. A path. You know?"

His face was thoughtful, stern. "And is this part of that? Facing your fears?"

I nearly choked on my soup. I swallowed hard, and looked at him. Why did everything feel like a test, and the wrong answer would send me out the door? I didn't want to lie, but oh god I wanted him. But I wanted him to want me, whatever that meant, and not faked up me.

"Do you do that a lot? Catch people off guard?"

He shrugged. "It works. But why shouldn't I say what I see? Is it my fault if people let down their guard and I notice?"

"You say that like it's a bad thing. Letting down your guard."

He narrowed his eyes. "Now who's going on the offense? Are you suggesting I like having the upper hand?"

I laughed, nervously. "You have the advantage, in most things, as you said before. People react to the image of you. But you also said you used to like it. I'm assuming that means you're a bit tired of playing up to the image."

He smirked. "Are you interviewing me? Because as you know, I can become monosyllabic in an instant."

"Yeah, I'm interviewing you for my own private fanzine, called 'What The Fuck?'"

His eyes grew wider, and darkened.

I felt a wave of terror wash over me, but I wasn't going to play along with this. "I don't have a stupid fanzine. I just want to know you."

"Maybe you aren't used to having conversations, just interviews." His tone was cutting.

"Maybe you aren't either."

We glared at each other.

He picked up his tea, and drained it, placing the small cup down with unnecessary care. I matched his actions. A waiting game.

He looked at me. And sighed. "You're a very angry girl, Miss Lily. I wonder sometimes who you're fighting." His voice was a long drawl.

"I'm used to fighting. Fighting back. Maybe you aren't used to people caring." I was angry. Why did he think he had it all his way?

"Don't blame people for your own flaws, Lily. I care. I care about many things. And you need to learn to understand that." He stood up, towering over me and the table.

I stared back at him, some of the fear turning back into rage, and back into fear. What had I done?

He walked around behind me and took my arm, pulling me out of my chair, and turned me so I was facing him. I stood my ground and kept staring back at him. If only the closeness of his naked chest was not affecting me. I couldn't look at him.

"Oh little girl. I've never known anyone push away so hard what they want so bad. Except me. Fascinating."

My heart was beating, hard. Stupid motherfucker. Arrogant fuck. The words leapt out before I could stop them.

"You're an arrogant fuck, you know it?"

He smiled. And spoke, very slowly, his voice back to the drawn out vowels and hard consonants. "I think, what works for me, will work for you. Or maybe you don't want to try." He pulled me by the hand away from the table, until we were standing an equal distance from the door to the bedroom and from the door to the living room. "Tell me to stop then. This is your choice." And his dark eyes bore into me as my heart beat faster. "Tell me you don't want me."

I shut my eyes. My body was overruling my brain, again, his voice reminding me of before. My skin felt hot. Oh god, why was I so angry? I felt like slapping him. And I raised my arm with the thought, spontaneously.

And before I could think, or take it back, his fingers were curled around my forearm, gripping me with uncanny force, and his eyes were burning into me.

"Oh no little girl. I'm now taking away your choice. Because what you want is for me to take over. And that's fine. Come." And he started walking towards the bedroom, his grip tightening on my arm.

I hesitated, and he stopped. "Say no, right now, I won't hold it against you. But you have five seconds."

I breathed, my mind whirling. I stared at his hand, circling my arm like it was nothing. Knowing that he'd drop it with one word.

Was that what I wanted? I stepped away, hardly knowing what I was doing. Tristan dropped his hand like it had been burned.

"No." I couldn't look at him. "No," I breathed out again, as I backed out into the living room, tears starting to sting my eyes. I grabbed my clothes and pulled on my skirt. I threw my shirt on, and collected my shoes. I turned around, but he hadn't followed me. I choked down some air, and pulled open the closet door, and put on my jacket, still barefoot, holding my shoes. I rang the bell for the elevator, and figured out the locks just in time for it to arrive. Then I flung myself into it, pulling the door shut behind me. For once, I didn't look back.

Chapter 19

I went rushing out into the street, and was nearly hit by a cab. The driver screeched to a halt, and I looked up, shocked that anyone else was in my world. The self-preservation part of me noticed his light was on, and I flung open the door even while he was shouting. I slammed it shut, the force rocking the cab slightly, and I looked at the driver. He was still shouting, but he was blurry and out of focus. On the second attempt, I managed to croak out my address loudly enough for him to hear. I squinted hard, and saw him press the on button for the meter, before everything went black.

The next thing I heard was a man's voice, repeating something over and over again. I looked up and I saw a dark shadow of a tall man reaching over me. I smiled, and closed my eyes again. It was him. He'd come to save me. The feeling of a rough hand moving up my leg made me jump, and I opened my eyes again to see the cabbie about to climb in the back seat, his hand already between my legs. I kicked out with a desperate force. Surprised, he slammed his head on the door frame and began cursing. I kicked again, and connected with something soft. I didn't wait to see what it was. I clung to the sides of the door and threw myself out of the cab with as much strength as I could manage, and got past him and started running. I didn't look behind to see if he was after me. I just kept running, the sound of my labored breathing canceling out every other noise. I couldn't see anything but the sidewalk in front of me. After I crossed the first avenue, I stopped for a second to take off my shoes. I wasn't sure where I was exactly, but I kept running barefoot, the little pebbles of the street digging into my feet. I didn't stop until I recognized Broadway, and I slowed down. I knew there would still be some people around. I ran across the street against the light, and when I was in the middle section I sat down on one of the filthy benches, trying to get my breath back. But I was still faint, and I turned around, and was promptly sick in the bushes behind the bench. It seemed to go on forever, my stomach clutching with dry heaves, until I managed to slow my breathing enough to turn back around and put my head between my knees. Even so, I kept looking up, not wanting a repeat of being caught by surprise. I didn't think my luck would hold out twice. I finally got to my feet, shakily, and crossed the street, and began walking downtown. I didn't know what I was doing, but I knew I couldn't stay in one place, and I wasn't sure I could go home yet. The last thing I wanted was to see Alice, or have the silence of my room close in on me.

I walked, and walked, until the streets became more familiar, past the 100s, into the 90s. There was the bagel place. They weren't open—wouldn't be open for another two hours, according to the sign, but I saw someone inside, one of the bakers, and I waved frantically. He looked confused, then worried, then he came over to the door, and unlocked it.

"Miss, sorry, we are closed. Come back."

I didn't know what I was going to say, but it all suddenly

came out in a big sob, and when he heard the word "attacked," he opened the door, and pointed to the nearest booth.

"Sit. I bring you tea. Do you want police?"

I shook my head, sobbing again. I tried to mumble "thank you" when he brought a paper cup of tea. He nodded, and backed away, looking worried. "Sit. Rest." That was all he said before disappearing into the kitchen.

I shakily tore open a little white packet of sugar, staring at the pattern of blue words, and watched the white granules slip into the red liquid. I made myself sip it, slowly, burning my tongue, trying not to shake too much and spill it. Finally, when I'd had about half of it, I pushed the cup away to the other side of the little Formica table, and buried my head in my hands. Every thought I started made me feel physically ill, so I kept pushing them away, one after the other, just like the cup. I stayed like that, semi-conscious, hard at work keeping away the blackness, though I was still, deathly still. Finally, they started putting bagels out in the baskets in the shop, and I realized I'd have to go, they were getting ready to open.

I looked down. My t-shirt was filthy and torn, probably from catching on something as I fought my way out of the cab. I started to feel sick to my stomach again, and then I wanted to leave as fast as possible, like a wounded animal, just crawl away, and hide in the darkness. I called out "thank you" loudly as I could, and the man appeared, nodding again, and opened the door for me. "Thank you," I whispered, and he closed the door behind me, and relocked it. Then I was out in the street, and the cold quick wind before dawn rushed up the avenue. The hollowness of my stomach made me feel like I was all icy air, dead, and ready to be broken up into pieces. I saw the benches in the middle, and thought for a moment of curling up there, letting the cold and wind take me, giving up on fighting back. Not yet, not yet, someone said, and even though I wasn't sure if it was my voice or someone else's, I turned back up the slight incline of the street leading back towards the park, and headed towards home.

Chapter 20

I dragged myself up the stairs and got the key in the lock. I blinked at the light coming from the kitchen. This couldn't be good, I thought, and a second later, I heard Alice's anxious voice call my name. We crashed into each other as she ran headlong out of the kitchen, and she threw her skinny arms around me and squeezed, despite my filthy state.

"Jesus, babe, Lil, I've been so worried. Where have you been?" Her words came out in a rush, and before I had a chance to say anything, she carried on. "Are you ok? Where did you go? Let me make you some tea. Come sit down." Then she looked at me, frowning. "Lily, Lily babe, what happened? Don't wash—we'll call the police."

I shook my head. I tried to speak, and held on to the back of the chair tightly. "No, Alice, it's ok. I'm ok. Nothing happened. I fought him off. Not him. The cabbie..." Then I started crying again. "Not him. Not him." I took a deep breath, and Alice hugged me.

"I'm so glad you're ok. I know it wasn't him." She sat down, then abruptly stood up again. "Lily, he was here."

"What?" I shrieked.

"Here. Tristan. He was worried that something had happened to you, and that it was his fault. I've got to call him. He's driving around looking for you."

I stood there, stunned, shivering. My teeth were actually chattering. It was finally all sinking in. "I should call him."

Alice gave me a funny look. "No. He was very insistent. He said you would call when and if you wanted to speak to him. He just wanted to make sure you were ok."

I stared at Alice. Nothing really made sense.

"Go have a bath, you've got chills." She went to the cupboard and took out a shot glass. "Don't argue." And she watched as I drank it down, the burn hurting my raw throat and chest. "I'll talk to him." She pulled out her phone as I headed off to the bathroom. "And Lily?"

I turned around. "Thanks Alice. I'll tell you the whole story. You deserve that much."

"No, that's not it. Lils...I think he does really care about you. Look—he turned up here, looking for you."

I met her eyes. "Maybe, Alice. Maybe. Maybe it's guilt. That makes people do strange things too."

Chapter 21

I slept the rest of the day, and woke up finally in the early evening for some tea. Alice ordered food, and I nibbled at the tofu and rice without a lot of interest. I felt numb. I told her the outline of what had happened, me leaving his apartment, the cab, the driver, walking around, the tea in the closed bagel shop. She applauded my heroics in fighting off the would-be attacker—but when she came to ask me why I'd left Tristan, I couldn't answer her. Truthfully, I didn't know. I'd been angry. So had he. It didn't seem to explain what had happened.

Alice just looked at me, and said nothing for a while. Then she poured each of us a shot, which I tried to refuse again, finally giving in to her.

"Don't you want to know what he said when I called?"

I sipped at the whiskey. It did make some of the hollow feeling better. I tried to answer. "Yes? No? I guess so. I'm sure he said he was glad I was ok. Maybe he wants to know if I'm still doing the secret gig? Figures I'm not professional enough to stick with it after everything that's happened?" I shrugged. My head was pounding.

"Do you really think he's that cold? Really?" Alice looked surprised.

"I don't know what to think. I don't even know what I think about it."

Alice reached out and grabbed my hand. "He wants you to call him. He told me to tell you that. Not now. When you're ready. But soon."

I squeezed her hand and smiled. "I will, Alice. I've got to work with him. I'll smooth it over."

Alice took my other hand. "Babe, you know I love you, right? But honestly—I'm not talking about work. You want him. And I think he wants you."

I finished the drink. "Maybe. I'll call him, Alice. Don't worry."

She waved her hands in front of my face. "Lily, perfection does not exist in this world. Stop. Stop looking for it."

"I'm just looking for what I want, Alice. That's all." I got up. "I'm going back to bed."

Alice rose to her feet, and hugged me. "Babe, you don't know what you want." She smiled at me. "Are you that certain?"

I closed my eyes for a moment to try and make the pounding in my head go away. "I don't know."

I walked down the corridor to my room, and shut the door. I poked at the numbness that seemed to be my brain, and tried to find an answer to her question. There was nothing there.

I tried to sleep. But what Alice had said kept bouncing around my head. And when I finally gave up pretending I was sleeping, I sat up with a rush and grabbed the phone. I knew there were only a few messages I really wanted to hear. He wanted to care? Fine. I'd listen to what he said. See if he'd been rattled, really, or if Alice had been taken in.

I went to the latest message, pressed play and I listened as his voice, deep and liquid, poured into my head. "Hello, it's Tristan."

Did he sound somewhat hesitant? Then he started. "I know you probably hate me, or think you do. I should have warned you. It's intense. Breaking open all those...barriers...makes some people very...angry. They've been holding back for so long—they can't stand it. I think that's what happened to you. Honestly..." and here he paused for a moment, "...maybe me too. Please call me. I think I can help. And Lily," I inhaled sharply at him using my name, "it matters to me. You matter to me. Please don't run before you talk to me, before you finally decide. And..." here he laughed, somewhat bitterly, I thought, "...we are working together. Let's stay friends at least, ok? Can we do that? Please call."

I put down the phone, and lay back against the pillows, and thought about the hollow feeling, and the wind, and how I didn't want to feel better but I did. I looked out the window, at the stars that were hidden somewhere out there, beyond the smog and the lights, and imagined for a moment a world that was different, one that made sense.

I picked the phone up again and sent a one word text. Then I turned it off, and pulled the covers up to my neck, wondering about the power of what I'd just said.

Yes.

Chapter 22

I woke up, and put the music on shuffle, and heard Roland Orzabal's echoing voice singing "Always in the Past" and tried to draw some conclusion from his mix of reassurance and despair. Still no answers, but the numbness seemed less pervasive. I made a cup of coffee, and climbed back in to bed, determined despite the hollow clutching of my stomach to go through all my messages and texts. I listened to Alice's increasingly frantic messages from that night, and his four, calmer, yet equally insistent demands that I call him, ending with his declaration that he was coming over, yes he did know where I lived. So that part was true. Then there was a message from Dave, the editor, checking that I was still on for London next week. I called back right away and left a message in the affirmative that I hoped sounded stronger than I was, wishing I could ask what had made him call. I erased the yoga reminders, and left another message with my agent saying that I was going to be tied up (I laughed when I said it, I couldn't help it) for the next few weeks, and to let me know if anything came up.

The next two days I spent doing nothing. Walking through the park. Trying not to think. Watching the bruises change color. I knew he was giving me time, maybe giving himself some time as well. I organized my schedule for London, cleaned and prepared my packing for next week, made lists, paid bills. I wondered if I'd come back. Maybe this time I'd stay over there for good. Might as well wrap things up here. Make it easier to dissolve if, when, I decided to leave.

When the text came on the third day, asking if I would come over, it seemed almost pre-planned, as though we had mutually decided on a cooling-down period. I didn't think about it too much. It felt like goodbye. I at least wanted to explain though. End on good terms. And when the time came, and I started to get ready, and my first thought was to wonder what to wear, I had to laugh. "Vanity," I said out loud to the mirror, as I tried on one of the sensible but pretty dresses I kept for client meetings. I called a car service—to keep my state of mind on an even keel. And suddenly I was heading downtown, in a very different frame of mind than the previous time.

* * *

"I'm glad you came over." Tristan took my jacket as though we were just repeating the events of a few nights ago, but calmly. I thanked him. Politeness. He asked if I would like to sit in the living room or the kitchen.

"The kitchen, I think. Otherwise I'll feel like I'm working. And it's definitely not an interview." We both laughed, flatly, and stopped at almost the same moment.

"Well, come in. It's cleaner, at least. Would you like a drink?"

God, this was dreadful. It was more formal than the interview. I looked up at him. His usual flirtatious manner was gone, replaced with a neat stranger. I sighed, and he glanced at me.

"Something wrong?" he asked, not unkindly.

"More than what's wrong already? No. No, I'm fine. Could I

have a drink though? But a real drink? A glass of wine or something?" His lips were pinched together. I sat down. "Look it's ok.
I've just been on edge. I'd rather relax." I watched as he stood
there, pressing the bridge of his nose between his thumb and
forefinger.

"No, I'm sorry. Yes, why not? Might as well celebrate the end,
as much as the beginning," he said sharply.

I felt like I'd been sucker punched, and I let out a low whistle.

Tristan turned and the intensity of his stare made me quail
inside. "That's why you're here, isn't it? To tell me that this isn't
for you, that it's against all your principles? Right? Aren't you?"
He spun away from me, and walked to the end of the kitchen and
squatted down in front of a smaller refrigerator. He opened it,
and extracted a bottle. "Here. Let's end how we started. I need
to use these up anyway." And I watched as he tore off the foil,
watched his wrist turn as he untwisted the wire basket, and listened to the small pop of the cork, as he opened the bottle expertly, the French way. No fanfare. No floods of champagne
spilling everywhere. His hand wrapped around the neck of the
bottle, he reached up in the cupboard with the other and thrust
the stems of two champagne glasses between his fingers. He
poured while he was standing, and gestured to me to come and
retrieve my glass. I stood next to him, the top of my head nearly
level with his shoulder, and took my glass, careful not to touch
him. We clinked glasses.

"What shall we toast to?" I asked.

"Why don't you tell me?" he said simply, and I looked up at
him. His eyes had a faraway look that reminded me of that first
time I'd ever spoken to him. It seemed crazy, but I felt like he

needed to know—especially if I wasn't really going to talk to him anymore.

"Why don't we sit down? I've got a story to tell you." I clinked my glass against his again. I was going to need courage for this, and I took a long sip, and let all the bubbles burst against the roof of my mouth. I didn't know how to begin, and I pulled out the chair across from him, and went to sit down, before he put his hand on my arm.

"Look, don't sit over there. Sit next to me at least. And let me start, ok?"

"I don't have to tell you a long story."

"You can tell me whatever you want. But let me say what I need to say first." He pulled out the chair next to him, and waited to sit down until I was seated. It was an oddly old fashioned gesture, and I felt something twist inside me. I put my glass down, and wrapped my arms around my torso and pinched. I'd found that it helped.

He cleared his throat, and his voice seemed to go down a notch. "I'm going to apologize, because I tried to warn you, and stop myself, and I couldn't and I didn't." He stopped for a moment. "Maybe I'm used to..." He looked away. "I didn't mean to hurt you. You're sensitive. I liked that about you. But I think I forgot what that meant."

I started to speak, and he raised his hand to stop me. "Please. Let me finish. Remember what I said to you, about people's expectations? Right? It becomes easier to play to what they want, knowing it's not what you want, banking time against inevitable expectations, and unavoidable failure. I had a friend who used to say 'the triumph of hope over experience.' But he didn't mean it.

Anyway..." He grasped my hand. "I didn't want to hurt you. But I wanted you enough to risk it, knowing it would happen. And whatever I say now will just make me look even more selfish, so I won't." He drank some of his champagne, delicately, then drained the glass, and refilled it, and mine. "But I'm not a bad person." He laughed. "See how stupid that sounds? Justifying myself. When you're the one I've hurt." He held my hand to his lips. I pinched myself harder with the other hand. "I was hurt too though," he whispered into my hand.

My throat tightened, and we sat there, unmoving, his hand still holding mine, both of us silent.

I drank some of the champagne to try and dissolve the lump in my throat that was making it hard to breathe, and he smiled at me, but didn't let go of my hand. "But you had a story. Tell me. I'm sorry, I just wanted to say all that before anything else was said. Go on."

I looked at him, at his multi-colored eyes, and turned away again. I'd never be able to figure out what I meant looking at him. I pinched myself, then stopped. It wasn't working. I ran my hand through my hair, nervously, and thought of what I had been intending to say. My past. Why I'd started writing. Music. Listening to my radio as a child to drown out the noise of everything else that was going on. I turned back to him and tried to face him. My hand was shaking—I returned it to its duties pinching. He looked down and saw what I was doing.

His voice, when it came, was low, and steady. "You know, if you let me punish you, you wouldn't have to do it yourself. You might find it freeing. Forgiveness." He gestured for me to give him the offending hand, and he kissed it softly. I stared at him. "But you'd have to trust me." He suddenly dropped both my hands. "And you'd have to stop pretending. I believed you were heartless, very easily. That's not entirely my fault, you know."

"I don't know if I can." My hands were cold, and I was tempted to sit on them to stop myself from grabbing his warm hands back.

"I know."

Neither of us spoke. Then I said, "Do you want to hear part of my story?"

"Not the whole thing?"

"No, but an important part."

He inclined his head slightly.

I took a sip of champagne, let the bubbles pop, and swallowed, hard. "Do you remember the Brit Awards? In London. Several years ago now. You played with your old band and Mick Jones—a tribute." I said it all quickly, before I could take it back.

"Yes, I remember that—vaguely. It was a rough time actually. I won't bore you with why right now. He was great though. What about it?"

Christ, I'd have to drag his memory back through the whole thing. I'd been hoping he would remember me. I started again. "Remember at the end? The two of you were having your pictures taken backstage. Then you were interrupted—you were about to leave, and suddenly this woman ran up to you and fell over on her face right in front of you. Mick laughed. You picked her up, and asked if she was ok. She told you she was there to write a story, and how it had all been going wrong, until she'd seen the two of you play, and it all made sense. And you talked about how you had to search..." I tried to remember exactly what he said, and the scene came back to me, how he'd picked me up, and that look we'd exchanged. "You said, 'Knowing it means something. Now there's a quest.' Then the two of you left." I stopped. "But I wrote about it. That was the real start for me." Boldly, I refilled both our glasses, and then raised my glass to him, holding his gaze. "That woman—that was me. What you did, what you said—made all the difference. It made me try." I drank some more, and looked at him. He was still silent. I shrugged. "That's my story, some of it anyway. A big piece." I made myself breathe. "Now you know."

We sat there. He still wasn't speaking, but he didn't look unhappy either. I felt like he was studying me, his eyes searching me for clues that I was telling the truth.

Then he spoke. "So that was you. I do remember. I'd often wondered what had happened...to you." A grimace crossed his face. "You seemed so fragile, on the verge of disaster. I asked Mick to turn the limo around...he laughed." He picked up his glass and examined it closely. "Crystal. Delicate—yet strong." He let the glass slip from his hand and I gasped, and reached out to grab it, just as he caught it with his other hand. "See—you have the natural instinct to stop something from being broken, or hurt." He replaced the glass on the table, refilled it, and emptied it in one long swallow. "In this business, they teach you to let people go. They train you to believe that nothing is more important than your 'art', or 'calling', or 'talent', or whatever pretty name they have for pure selfishness and ego at the moment. I didn't have the best reputation, going from one excuse to another. I probably still don't." He looked at me for confirmation. "Honestly, it's incredible that you've made it. It proves maybe you are as tough as you claim." He got up, and walked to the refrigerator, and pulled out another bottle. "Maybe we need to do this—pretend we're starting there—and go back in time, when you were more trusting, and I was more—or less—crazy." He opened the bottle with the same finesse, gestured to me to finish what was in my glass, and poured another one.

I closed my eyes. I didn't know what effect I'd hoped my story would have on him. Maybe it was this, after all. Starting over. Going back into his past, and mine. Tying a little knot, a little anchor, that would give us a reference point. He reached out and took my hand again, and kissed it.

"Please. For everything that might have been, that could be. Can we go back in time?" His eyes had that intense light again. I looked back, and I felt the full weight of what he meant.

"I'm scared," I confessed, but I didn't look away.

He got up, grasping the bottle and his glass in one hand, keeping mine in the other. He walked us to where we had stood the other night, and stopped there, keeping his gaze steady on me while he laced his fingers with mine. "Should I count out loud?"

The same question came to mind– was this what I wanted? His eyes burned into mine, and he mouthed a one at me, then a two. Three. Four. I didn't waver.

"Five. Last chance. Good."

Still holding my hand, he guided me to the bedroom. We stood by the bed and he put down the bottle and the glasses. Then he untied the belt to my dress and it opened. He pushed it over my shoulders, letting it pool to the floor. Then he unclasped my bra, and let it follow the dress to the ground. I stood there, vulnerable, nearly naked. His eyes followed my body down and came back up. He gazed at me levelly. And without warning, he turned my body with his huge hands and pushed me face down on the bed. The shock of it frightened me and I started to say something.

"No. You don't know what you want or what you need. We are going to fix that. Shut your eyes." And his voice was angry and rough, but I obeyed him. "Hold your arms out over your head."

I did it. My mind was completely involved in this game. Nothing else was breaking through, and the peace of that was overwhelming. I closed my eyes, and felt him tie my wrists together with a silk scarf, and pull the knot tight. He made sure I couldn't move my hands. Next, he took another scarf and tied it so that it covered my eyes. I could only see shadows and light through it, nothing else, and I closed my eyes again, feeling slightly panicked. His knee pushed in between my feet and roughly shoved one of them over to the side, opening me up. My heart beat faster.

"Nice." I felt his hands run over my back, over my ass, and down my legs. He must be kneeling down, I thought. I felt completely powerless, and I trembled thinking of his mouth on me. Traitorous body. I wanted to fight him, and I wriggled, moving higher up on the bed.

"No," his voice said, and I could feel his breath against me, god, so warm. The pain in my lower belly grew stronger; the pulse was deeper and I hated him, hated him for this. He blew against me, and I groaned.

"Yes, this time make noise. I want to hear you give in, every fucking painful step." And his mouth was on me, and I felt his long tongue lapping at my clit through the silk pants. Oh god, he was good at this, and I wanted more, the pants gone, his wet, my wet. God. He bit at one of my lips and I shrieked, half in pleasure, half in pain.

He hummed against me, mumbling something. All I could feel was vibration, all I could hear was my pulse beating in my ears. Then his mouth moved away, and I felt his fingers, pulling the fabric to one side. And he buried his tongue in me. I pushed my hips up against him, trying to get more of him in, gasping as his tongue pulsed inside me. My face was pressed into the bed, my upper body unable to move properly with my arms tied. His tongue pulled out and his mouth pressed against my sex, kissing it, wet, his lips rubbing against my clit. I could feel the pressure building, his tongue back inside me, then on me, biting, kissing me like a lover. He was talking again, but I couldn't hear him, my moans escaping me even when I tried to stop them. More, god, more.

His mouth moved away and I felt his hands lifting my hips and grabbing hold of my underwear, ripping half of it away, so I was totally exposed. He ran one finger over my clit, making me buck up, and thrust in, deep, making me cry out. He pulled it out, slowly, and I could hear his mouth, his tongue wetly licking at it, the image from before of his fingers in his mouth in my mind. Fuck. Never, I'd never wanted anything like this before.

I heard him stand up, and I lay there, trembling. I wanted to pull off the scarf and face him, but I didn't, not wanting to disobey, not wanting him to stop. His footsteps took him further away, and it was silent. I lay there, wet, wanton, legs spread, underwear torn, waiting.

It wasn't very obvious anymore who was in charge. If I got up, that would be the end of it.

I jumped when the music started. Droning, strangely tuned instruments, slowly building, layers, repeating, hypnotic lyrics, dreamy and weird. The Velvet Underground. What else? And I waited. I wanted to come so badly I wondered how little it would take. And how he would do it. The music filled the silence, and I let myself be taken away by it. Waiting. Ten minutes must have passed, I thought. I wondered how long I would wait. All fucking night. Whatever it took.

And I lay there, listening. Every inch of my skin felt like it was alight, sensitive, cold and hot, heavy, and painfully alive. I breathed in and out, working through the growing discomfort in my legs.

And then I heard his footsteps coming back. My senses were on full alert, as I struggled to sense where he was in the room and what he was doing.

I heard a deep sigh. And I felt him nearer somehow. Then he spoke. He was right next to me, bending down by my ear. "Little girl, you need this. And I need you. So much. Just remember that." And he moved away again. I heard creaking.

And then he was lying on top of me, his arms holding mine down. But he was dressed. But what was he wearing? I could feel his leather jacket against my back, the snaps cold on my skin. He moved his hips against me and I could feel his huge cock through the leather pants, smooth and strange on my naked skin. It reminded me of the very first night, in the limo, his face thrown back, eyes closed as he let go. The memory made me thrust up against him, trying to feel the leather against my sex. He moaned in my ear. I rubbed against him and he pulled me up towards him, controlling my movements.

But he abruptly pressed me into the bed, holding my hips down. He moved off me and it sounded like he was standing up. There was one hand, spread out on my lower back, warm and holding me in place. I could hear him breathing heavily.

"Tristan, please." My voice was an unrecognizable moan. I was so wet and swollen it hurt.

"Little girl, you're going to learn. Learn what need is. Then you can beg me for it."

I moaned, nearly crying. Twice now, he'd moved away just as I was going to come. Teasing me. Beyond teasing. And now the leather. God it felt good, me naked, him in his rock star leather.

His voice again, dark and slow. "Do you trust me?"

Mine, trembling. "Yes."

Then I heard it, moving through the air, before I felt it, and I heard it, the leather of the belt stinging me, hitting me just at the top of my legs. I heard my voice, gasping pain and surprise.

"Ask me to do it again."

"Please."

"No."

"Do it again."

And he did, hitting the same place with precision, so close to where I needed him. And like he had heard my thoughts, he brought the leather down right there, just hard enough that it felt like a touch, biting through me. I cried out.

"Yes, that's it." He was breathing harder now, and he swung and the belt struck my ass this time, just above where I was aching. He repeated this motion over and over, the whistling of the belt through the air the only warning of what was coming. My skin was stinging, but the pain was sucking up all the pulsing want, all the anger, all the frustration, all the thinking. I was just one idea, and that was to have him do this again, and again. I cried out with each blow; it hurt, but just enough that it created a need. An addiction. I wanted him to touch me; I wanted to feel him, hard, in me. And he then would hit me again. Slowly. The music went on and on and I felt like I was a part of it, losing my boundaries. Crying out with it.

His voice again. "Now I think you're getting the idea. Let's see."

And the belt came down again, right on my clit, once, twice, again, I was losing count, I was crying, "make me come, Tristan, please, make me." Sobbing.

The dark tones of his voice. "Now. Now you can let go." And he whipped me again, the leather stroking over my pussy like his tongue, hard, burning and I started coming, my legs shaking, my hips thrusting into the bed, delirious, crying out his name, tremors running through my entire body.

"Now you're ready to be fucked properly," his voice a threatening whisper just over the sound of a zip and a packet being opened. His leather clad arm around my stomach, pulling me up, pulling my hips towards him and then his cock, the fantastic hard length of it, finally in me, opening me up, touching me where I needed the pressure and I started coming again, rocking into him. His voice, his mouth buried in my neck, whispering, "fuck me, fuck me harder, show me how much you need me, how much you liked me whipping the fuck out of you, let it go."

I thrust back into him, the feel of the leather on my skin heating it up, the burning on my legs and ass insane. He bit me, marking me. I cried out. "You like that don't you? Oh fuck you make me so fucking hard." His voice was incredible, liquid dark in my ear. I felt his fingers at my clit. "I can make you come again." And he pinched my clit, twisting it, making me jump against him. "Oh that's good." And he did it again, and I jumped, making him enter me even deeper and we both cried out. "Oh god, little girl, you're too much." And his fingers worked faster, then stopped.

I whimpered and he laughed. "Not yet, not yet, when I tell you. Let's play another little game. Turn off your brain. You're mine, and I control you and you do what I tell you. And if I tell you to come, you come. And you show me you like what I'm doing." And his fingers came around and pinched my nipples hard and I cried out. "I like it when you scream." And he pinched them again, holding on to them for leverage as his cock moved in and out of me, slowing down, as I started to shake. "No. Not until I tell you."

His hips were rotating against me when he suddenly pulled out. "No, I want it different." And he pushed me up on to the bed. "Get on your hands and knees." He laughed. "Ah, no not your hands. Lean on your elbows. That's it."

I felt his hands running smoothly over my sore backside. "Oh, that's nice. Yeah." And he slapped me, hard, with his hand. It hurt. It felt good. And it made me want him back inside me. I moved back, searching for his body, and his hand connected with me again. "Looking for something?" And I felt his cock again, rubbing up and down my pussy. And it was gone, replaced by his tongue, warm, and wet and soft, licking me in long strokes. I shuddered, and he stopped, instantly. And smacked my ass again. "No. I told you." And he forced his cock back inside me, and pulled out again almost all the way, slowly. I tightened around him, trying to make him stay inside, and we both sighed, together, as he thrust his way back in. "Yeah, girl, do that again. Like I told you."

I tried to keep his cock deep inside me, but his words had made me wetter and I couldn't grip around him now that he was moving faster now inside me. Then he stopped, and I could feel his leather clad legs. He pulled me up, and then down, on to his lap, moving me up and down on him, slowly, as I felt his body behind me. We were silent for a moment, just moving, getting used to the new position. Then he pushed me back down, lying flat on me. "I like you under me. You need to be restrained." He spread my legs further apart, and began exploring me with his fingers. "You need to beg more," he replied to my moans.

"Fuck me, please, now." I needed to come again, I needed to feel him come, I felt a kind of craziness taking me over. Frustration. "I want you so badly, I can't control it."

"Good." He laughed. And pulled out of me. I groaned.

"Tristan, please, you're torturing me."

He laughed again. "I think that was the idea." And I could hear the sound of him stripping off the condom.

"What are you doing?" My voice an anguished howl.

"You'll see." And he walked away again.

Now I did feel like crying. I banged my tied wrists against the bed in frustration. I heard his footsteps coming back in. I didn't care if he saw me.

"Wound up, are we?" His voice was low and soothing. "This should help."

I yelped as he pushed an ice cube inside me. All my muscles tensed up as the coldness spread inside, and the melted ice water ran out of me.

"That's it. Remember you're here for me to play with. Did you forget?" His voice dropped lower still. "Do you still trust me?"

I moaned as he pushed his fingers inside me and flexed them, moving what was left of the melting ice cube around. "Yes," I managed to get out.

"Good." His voice was hard. He pulled out his fingers and pushed in another ice cube. I jumped as the shock of the coldness inside me almost made me cramp up. My voice came from somewhere else, crying out.

Then he ran yet another piece of ice over where he had whipped me earlier. It felt good, cold soothing the soreness, melting fast on my superheated skin. But he slid it down, down to my clit and rubbed it over and over with the ice cube. The pain of it, the coldness, my muscles tensing up. His rhythm, perfect pressure. The feel of his leather jacket against my skin. Knowing he was watching me. My breathing sped up, even as I tried to be silent and stop moving, trying to hide from him that I was about to come.

But he stopped, again. "You don't know that I can tell when you're going to come? It doesn't say much for the lovers you've had before. I think you need to be fucked a lot to make up for that. Do you want me to fuck you?"

"Yes." My voice was a low hiss. "Please."

His voice was tense. "That's not begging. Too polite." He laughed. "Try again."

I felt desperate. Hollow with need. "I want to beg you, but I don't know how." I would do anything now. And I realized I knew nothing, nothing at all. What a joke everything had been that had gone before. I thought I could hear him smiling.

He pulled me to my feet and held me against him, until I got my balance. "Hold on to me." He walked me in the direction of the bathroom, up the stairs, but went left, not right. My thighs were suddenly against the arm of the sofa. "Bend over." I did, and my ass was sticking out, my body lying tense against the pillows of the couch. I felt completely exposed.

"That's it. Yes. Now tell me you want me." And he put a finger inside me. The ice cubes were completely gone, but it was still cooler and wet inside me.

My voice was shaky. "I want you."

"No. Let's start slowly. Repeat after me: I want your cock inside me." I imagined what he must look like, in his leather, standing over my naked body. Smiling. Victorious.

I took a deep breath. "I want your cock inside me."

I heard the telling rip of another packet. "Say it again."

"I want your cock in me. Now. Please. Please."

"I think I can do that. Look at you, open, wet." He slid inside me. "Oh, that's good. Yes. Maybe I'll let you come on me."

"I want to come. I want you to come in me. Please." I felt like I had no control of my voice. Words were coming out, unforced.

"Do you now?" He thrust up, and further in to me and I moaned. "You like that." His fingers found my clit, and began teasing it, and I felt the beginnings of my orgasm. "Oh no, not yet." And he stopped. Again.

I started actually crying with frustration. My words were broken up and rasping out of me. "Please Tristan, please god, I need to come so badly. I want you so much, it hurts, it hurts, please fuck me, hard, I'll be, I'll be whatever you want, please, you're driving me insane, I've never felt like this ever, please, god." I was taking in big gulps of air, frustration and need and pain and desire making me hysterical.

"That's it, baby, let it go." And he sped up, just slightly, angling my hips so he plunged into me even deeper. "You know I want to give you just what you need. But you," and he paused, flicking my clit with his fingers as I sobbed, "need to give me what I need."

I could do it. I had to. I started murmuring, "fuck me please, you're so fucking huge, use me, you make me crazy, I'll do any-thing you want."

He gasped, and pulled back on my hair, making me cry out. "That's it, fuck you're so lovely, you're fucking tight, you're so small around me, squeeze me like that again, clever tricks, oh god." And he sped up again, his breathing heavier. His fingers rubbed against my clit again. "Soon baby." I cried out, making him moan again. "Yeah, that's it." He moved against me, his cock sliding in and out of me, his leather pants burning friction on my skin. He moaned again, "oh baby, soon, oh fuck." And he held my hips down, like before. His voice was altered. "You make me fucking crazy, tell me you want me, little girl, make me come, make me come, so fucking hard."

And he was plunging into me, faster now, his fingers moving circles around my clit. I felt my orgasm start to shake me, tearing me up. And he said, "yes now, now come for me, fuck," and his cock was pulsing inside me, over and over, as his loud cries cut into my body. His sounds, his orgasm going on and on as I tightened around him, coming so hard, rattled, out of control, both of us together as my body followed his convulsions as though we had known all this forever.

Chapter 23

Finally, the aftershocks slowed down, and some kind of sense returned. I could feel him lying on me, heavy and warm, pushing me into the sofa. The weight felt good, solid and comforting. His arms were on either side of me, helping support his body, enclosing us. We lay there like for a while, dazed, and then I felt him pulling out. We both groaned from the change in contact, and I tried to move but couldn't with my wrists tied. He stood up, and pulled me up after him, holding me against him, my back to his leather jacket. I wanted to feel his skin, my mind was whirling, all the things I'd ever wanted had suddenly come out to play and were insisting to be heard. Then he whispered in my ear.

"It's not usually like this, you know." And he kissed my neck, very gently. The contrast was overwhelming.

And I started to cry again.

"Oh, little girl, little girl, it's ok." And he whispered soothing sounds in my ear, as he untied my hands. "No, it's not always like this for you, either. No. No. It's ok. I'm here." He untied the scarf from around my eyes, but I kept them tightly shut, even as the tears were squeezing their way out.

It was too much. I felt like I'd been pried open and everything was at the surface now. No shell, no protective covering.

And there he was, soft and hard, being gentle, sweet with me. Too much.

He turned me to face him. "Open your eyes."

"I can't." I couldn't face him, it would just be too real then, his beautiful face and these feelings and all my needs would collide. I would die.

"Darling, don't be ashamed of who you are and what you've done. Look me in the eye and show me who you are." It was a reminder rather than a challenge, a philosophical idea, spoken in his soft, slow drawl, encouragement instead of a victory call.

And I opened my eyes. And there he was, beautiful, mysterious, his heavy lidded gaze filled with a million thoughts that I didn't know. I looked up at him, taking in all of his face, his messy hair, dark brows, long eyelashes, his strong bones and masculine nose, but I returned to his eyes. There was his real beauty. The intelligence, the questioning, the complications. And we stared at each other.

He placed a gentle kiss on my nose. "Come little girl. So much to talk about, but we'll leave it until tomorrow." He began taking off his jacket, then stopped, and looked at me again. "Unless you want to go home?"

I drew in a breath, sharp and cold. I tried to find an answer to his question in his eyes, but there was nothing. His expression was careful, neutral. "Do you want me to go?"

"I want to hear what you want to do. Tell me."

I played with a snap on his leather jacket as I considered everything that meant. Yes, I was still scared. Yes, it would be easier to go home. Did he want me to? What did I want to do? And all this closeness now...what would happen? Ah, fuck it.

I raised my head to look at him and tried to smile. "I'd like to stay. I'd like to feel you close to me tonight, try and sleep again with you." I couldn't believe I felt shy saying it after all the things we'd just shouted to each other, fucking like rabbits.

His eyes lightened, and he kissed me again. "As you wish, little girl. But let's have a bath first. It's hot under here." He held one side of his jacket and moved it around, as though he were fanning himself. He gave me a lopsided smile and began walking towards the bathroom. Without him there, I felt very uncertain, and I began to teeter slightly. I stuck out an arm, still feeling pins and needles, to hold myself up. But he noticed, and was there, back next to me, in an instant. "Slowly now. I've thrown a lot at you. You've done so well. We don't want you falling down, not now." He curled his arm around me, and placed me in front of him. "To the bath." And he pushed me gently forwards.

The bathroom was warm, the heated towel rack on, everything clean and spotless. Again, in the back of my head, I marveled at his planning. Did he think of everything? Or was he just meticulous in whatever he did? He bent over and began running the bath. He put in some foaming bath oil, that same Jo Malone jasmine and mint scent, and turned towards me. He gave me one of those looks again. "Are you shy? You probably need a moment. I don't mind, but maybe you do." And he walked out, closing the door behind him. I was confused for a minute, and then I realized what he meant. Oh. Oh right. He didn't mind. But I might. Did I?

Not really, I thought. But. That did mean intimacy. Closeness on another level. Almost like a couple. What did we have? And how could you be that close, that uninhibited in one way, and yet reticent in another? Human flesh, so complicated. Or was it the thinking?

I wondered if I should wait for him, but the bath looked so good, warm scented soft bubbles against the black and white tile. I climbed in, feeling slightly guilty. The water was soothing and I was just sinking in, when the bath water hit my bruised and beaten skin. I gasped. It stung like hell, and I lowered myself in, slowly, clenching my teeth. I wasn't sure whether I was sorry he'd missed this spectacle, presenting him with more evidence of his power, or glad I'd shown my wounds to no one but myself. Either way, it was too late now, and the scent was calming. I felt like I'd been running for miles. All my muscles had been used, hard, and were now untwisting in the warmth.

Then the door opened, and he stood there on the threshold, completely naked. There were red marks from where the leather had rubbed against his torso and legs, and his chest was faintly glistening with sweat. His cock was still impressive, even in its normal state, slightly reddened against his heavy balls. He was animal and beautiful, and I felt like I was looking at a work of art. His beauty was so modern, but there was a whisper of something ancient in his proportions, strangely statuesque for someone so pulsing and alive. I returned my eyes to his face, to see him grinning at me. "You like?"

I smiled back. There was no need to speak about it. I was sure it was obvious how I felt.

"Did it hurt getting in?" He looked a little concerned, as he began climbing in the bath carefully opposite me.

"Yeah, it did a bit. Did you hear me?"

He laughed. "Ok, that was you. I thought I heard something." He lay back and groaned, ducking his head under the water. He popped back up, dripping.

Wet was such a good look on him. He glistened, like a seal,

his eyes at once darker and more sparkling in contrast to his almost black wet hair. He seemed to have an entire range of matching bottles and he chose one, and began washing himself, with a sort of sensual efficiency. I watched, forgetting about my own aches and soreness.

He rinsed his hair under the water again, and rubbed the water from his eyes. "Do you want me to wash your hair?"

"I'd love it."

"Here, turn around." I turned gently on my sore backside, and scooted up the tub until I was nestled between his legs. His hands were gentle, and his fingertips began firmly pushing at the tense spots in my skull. I closed my eyes and moaned softly, it felt so fantastic.

"You like?"

"It's wonderful. It feels amazing."

"Funny how much easier it is to talk about someone giving a massage than an orgasm, isn't it?" And he continued adjusting the pressure points in my head, as I tensed up again. "It's only an observation, no need to be alarmed." He snorted.

He rinsed my hair with the shower attachment, and squeezed it out. "Come on little girl, I'm exhausted. It must be three in the morning. Let's try and sleep." He pulled the bath sheet off the rack, and wrapped me in it, rubbing his hands up and down my body. There it was again; that strange feeling of being looked after.

When he thought I was dry, he unwrapped the thick towel and dried himself off, carefully, like he was handling something precious. It was fascinating to see how he cared for his body. It didn't take long, but there was an attention in his movements, the same attention he had paid to me.

"Interesting." It came out of my mouth before I could stop it.

He looked up at me. He had been drying his feet. "What is?"

"Just you. Your attention to detail. The way you look after yourself."

He looked thoughtful. "You get no extra points being careless. If you can't take time over simple things, you miss the larger ones as well." He finished, and folded the towel back over the rack, and flipped the lever to drain the bath.

◆ ◆ ◆

"Come on darling. Come to bed." And he held my hand as we walked back down the little stairs, over to the bed. He flung open the covers, and tucked me in, then went around the other side of the bed and climbed in. Oh, so that was his side, and this was mine. Ok. Then I realized what I'd thought. My side.

I was pushing away my domestic thoughts, when he leaned over and kissed me, sweetly and softly on the mouth. "It's not what I expected," he whispered against my lips. And he leaned back on the pillows and held his arm out. I nestled in, against his chest, and sighed. He kissed my head.

I needed to ask.

"Are you happy?"

I felt him smiling in the dark.

"Yes."

Chapter 24

We slept with a part of us touching each other, close if not cuddled up all night. I woke up a few times, and looked around, confused, until I saw his back and dark hair, rising up and down with his breath. He was sound asleep, and it was soothing to watch him. I curled up, careful not to wake him, and listened to his steady breathing until I fell asleep again.

The next thing I knew, it was full morning, and the bed was empty. I rubbed my eyes, and looked around. The room seemed so normal; it was hard to believe what had happened the night before. Waking up in here. For the second time. But last night was different. What to call it, I wondered. Super charged emotional sexual whirlwind? Something like that. I had a moment of panic. Where was he? Now what? And I sank back down on the pillows, and shut my eyes again. No. I wasn't going to be a coward. I would be who I was. In the daylight too. Whatever, whoever that turned out to be.

I went and washed my face and brushed my teeth with my finger. I'd have to carry a toothbrush if this was going to be a regular thing. If. I sighed. I debated whether to put on my underwear, and decided against it, seeing as the panties were little more than shreds anyway. I'd feel stupid just going out in a bra. Then I saw the robe, and slipped it on. I wasn't ready to march around his house naked and careless.

I took a deep breath and went in the kitchen. There was a pot of green tea, but no Tristan. The door to the living room was shut. I walked up to it and was about to turn the handle, when I stopped and listened. He was talking to someone. On the phone? In person? I held my breath and tried to make out the voices. Yes. Yes, there was someone there. My heart stopped for a moment. Discretion. My presence would raise some questions. I didn't want to eavesdrop, not really, but I was curious to know who it was. I could only hear the low murmurs of their voices. It sounded a bit like his manager. What would he be doing here, this early? He wasn't due to leave until the day after tomorrow, right? Then I would leave the day after that. Reality kicked in. Calls to make. Life to organize. And I didn't listen at doors. Jesus.

I sat down and poured myself some tea. The voices were getting louder suddenly. I was taking a sip of the warm green tea when I heard Tristan's voice quite distinctly. He sounded coldly furious.

"No, I won't drop it. It's really none of your business, is it?"

There was a protesting mumble.

"Yes, you've been great at protecting me. Thank you. Now—leave it alone." I knew that tone of voice, the drawl that meant he was calming himself down. Yes, like the other night, when he did that. That slow down must mean he was holding back. I wondered what the argument was about, but I had my suspicions. There was another growling mumble. Then there was silence. Then Tristan's voice again.

"We'll see who is right after London. And you might want to rethink what you're doing. I'll see you at JFK tonight."

I drew in my breath sharply. So this was about London. And he was leaving tonight. Sooner than expected. What would he see afterwards? I felt slightly sick. The real world intruding back, threatening my beautiful little bubble. I heard the front door open and close, and the sound of the elevator, distantly muffled through the walls. A moment later, Tristan was opening the kitchen door. He looked at me, startled. His mouth was a thin line of displeasure, and I quailed inside, even though I didn't think he was angry with me.

"You're up." There was still a hint of fury in his voice. He stood there, tense.

"Yes, been sitting here for about ten minutes."

"So you heard everything." He stared at me.

Direct, I thought. I needed to deal with this right away before it became more than it should.

"I didn't actually. I heard you getting angry, and something about London. About what, I don't know." I was annoyed that I needed to justify myself, but I didn't want any misunderstandings. And I wanted to know what this was about. " 'You'll see after London.' That's it. That's what came through the wall. I don't listen at doors, you know. I just wanted to drink some tea, and get out of bed, see where you were."

He turned his head, and stared out the window for a moment. Then he looked back at me. There it was again, that look, as though he were about to decide against something in favor of another.

I rushed to speak again, instead of just watching. "Tristan, look, I'm sorry. I don't know what this is about, but it's your business. Ok?"

He nodded, and sat down opposite from me, and poured himself a cup of tea, which he drank from, before he began speaking again.

"Lily, this does have to do with you. Partially. And we need to talk. About London. About what's going to happen."

My stomach turned over. Oh god, this was it. Being discreet. At best. I crossed my arms over my chest and waited for his pronouncement. I tried to feel business like. The only difficulty, aside from his pained expression, was the feeling of the silken fabric of the robe over my bruised backside and swollen breasts. I shook my head. Show nothing. "Ok, let's talk. What is going to happen? And who was that?"

He poured some more tea. A pro. He wouldn't be rushed on this. He took a sip, and jumped up again. "Do you want something to eat? A bagel? Cereal?"

My stomach was one big knot. I couldn't even pretend. "No, thanks, I'm good." I hesitated. I didn't want to push it, but something was wrong. Like ripping open the envelope with the bad news, I wanted it right away. "Tristan, just tell me. I'm a big girl."

He began to smile, just slightly. "Are you?" He laughed. "Yeah, I guess so." He coughed, and shrugged his shoulders. The waves of anger that had been pouring off him before seemed lessened now.

I braced myself. This couldn't be good.

"Look, Lily, that was my manager."

I nodded.

"I'm not going to insult your intelligence. You know how he is. He's particularly prickly about the girls, seeing as we've had some near misses...expensive near misses."

The girls. I closed my eyes for a moment. And now me. What kind of idiot was I?

"He's attached to me. And the money. Of course." He gave a hollow laugh. "Always the money."

I managed to breathe again. "So? What does this mean for London?"

He looked back at me. "London. Yeah. Well, he didn't want you there in the first place, although he gave in. Your piece has been the best, will be the best. He can't ignore that."

"So, London?" I tried to think of the slippery ladder of success.

His voice was all business now. "You'll still do the piece, of course. That's set up. The show is next week. You're going out in a couple of days, now, I'm going out tonight." He stopped. "We won't see each other, except for a brief interview after the show. Of course, you're invited and very welcome to the party afterwards. But..."

I finished his line for him. "But we don't know each other."

"But we don't know each other." He nodded, his lips pulled together in a thin grimace. He looked angry. But at what?

I tried to ignore the aching pain that was beginning to take hold of my entire body. This game was hard. I cursed my sensitive self, and not for the first time, wished I could just be a super bitch about everything. Fuck. It.

"Yeah, well, of course." Was that me? Yes. I seemed to be angry. Where was this coming from? It was almost like there was a complete psychic break, and I was marveling at myself, whoever that was, speaking. "Of course," I repeated. "You said we needed to be discreet. That you didn't do the boyfriend/girlfriend thing. I remember."

He looked at me.

"It's your launch. There's going to be people you need to see, be seen with." I took a breath. There was a sort of burning in my chest. "It's not my first time at the rodeo, however much you're amusing yourself with the idea." I looked away from him.

"Listen, Lily, it's the timing, it's just…"

I interrupted him. "Tristan, don't apologize. I knew what this was. I'm enjoying it, so are you? Great." I took a deep breath. "Look, you're a nice guy. I'm sure. You've got my number, I have yours, the magazine will set up everything. Of course I'll come to the after party. Can I bring a plus 1? There's a lot of people I haven't seen for a while in London, it's a great chance to, um, hook up with them."

Tristan sucked in his cheeks. And looked away. When he turned back to face me, his eyes were studying me. There were two lines on his forehead formed by him furrowing his brow. "Of course. Bring a couple. Bring who you like." His voice was flat and low, without energy.

I stood up. "I've got to go, ok? I need to sort out some things before I leave."

He nodded. "I'll let you get your clothes." And he stood, and walked off, slowly, towards the living room.

I ran back in the bedroom, and threw out what was left of my panties and while fastening my bra at whirlwind speed. I threw the dress around myself, and tied the belt. I ran my fingers through my hair, not really looking at myself. There was nothing there I wanted to see. And I walked back out of the bedroom, not looking back.

Tristan was in the living room, waiting.

I walked past him, avoiding looking at him. Just another trick, I kept thinking. Just another trick. I'm a whore, and he is just another…episode. My shoes were by the chair. The manager must have seen them. Of course he knew I was there. I slipped my feet into the cool leather, welcoming the extra height. I needed the power.

I could feel him watching me.

I turned towards him. He was silent. "My jacket?"

"Oh, right." He loped up the three stairs to the closet, and pulled my leather jacket out, and held it up for me. I followed him and let him help me with it. He ran his hand down over my shoulder, down my arm, to my hand, and grasped my fingers. "Lily, listen…"

I looked at him. The burning feeling was getting worse. Just another trick. I pulled my hand away and put my finger on his lips. God, they were so soft. No.

"Tristan, don't. It's ok. Really." And I kissed him, on the cheek, feeling his stubble under my lips. I breathed in, and closed my eyes. Just for a minute.

We stood there, not moving, not speaking.

I stepped away from him, and pressed the button for the lift. He was looking at me. I tried to look at my shoes, but I could feel his gaze. And I turned my face up to his. His eyes were dark, but not like before, and the shadows under them were pronounced. He looked tired, and beautiful. A little like the very first time I had seen him up close.

The lift door opened on the other side, and I went to get the door.

"I'll get it." And he flipped the locks and opened the door, leaned forward to move aside the cage door of the elevator. I quickly stepped away from him and inside. I pressed the button, and the door began closing. I looked at him, through the little glass porthole, and thought I heard him saying "see you in London." I nodded at him, as he shut his front door and the lift began to move.

I held on to the brass railing with a death grip. Play the game.

And as the door opened to the lobby, I thought—there's an audience. Let's give them what they want. And I strutted through
the lobby, past the handyman, caretaker, whatever the fuck he
was, with the best imitation of high class whore I could manage.
Available to anyone, anywhere, anytime—for the right price.

At least money was a hard limit.

Chapter 25

The cab ride home was a blur. I got into the flat, checked my messages, made a few calls. Drank some coffee. Wanted a nap, decided I would go to the gym and move around. My ass still hurt. Good. I needed the pain, obviously. A pain junkie. Great.

I ran a bit on the treadmill, lifted some weights. And suddenly felt utterly bored and pissed off, and left. I walked along Broadway for a while, then back down Columbus. I didn't want to look at anyone; I just wanted to slip between them. And I realized that for once, I didn't want to be invisible, I wanted the others to be the shadows. A backdrop. And to stay out of my way. A few people managed to move out of the fucking way before I elbowed them out of my path. Not like London.

London. My old home. Now about to be a scene of some painful humiliation that would earn my money for me to continue this shadow existence I seemed to be eking out of the sap of the world. Fine. I'd already put together a list of people I wanted to see. A couple of them would go to any party. I wasn't even sure if they liked Tristan as a musician. Better still. There'd be a certain beauty in standing there, watching him, fucked up, listening to an old friend slag him off in the twang of the middle class London accent. Trying to be street, failing horribly the minute they opened their mouth. Ha fucking ha.

I saw a coffee shop, and decided to sit at a booth for a while, make some notes. At least I had been conscious enough to bring along my bag and the notebook. I ordered coffee, and thought about getting a grilled cheese. My stomach still felt hollow, but my mouth was dry. I had the impression any food would feel and taste like cardboard.

I could still feel the piercing sharpness of his slight stubble against my lips. I replaced it with the thick warm ceramic of the big coffee cup. Thank god for diner dishware. Some things at least didn't fucking change. My lips felt hyper-sensitive; the cool smoothness of the white china contrasting with the hot black coffee. I suddenly put the cup down. I probably looked like I was making out with my cup. I took another quick sip, and opened my book and started making lists. In an hour, I could call London, and set up some appointments. I needed to interview that band too, the one with the annoying girl singer. I was tempted to invite them too, but I knew Tristan would be pissed off. I didn't really want to piss him off. I wrote some more, doodled, ordered another coffee. Nothing seemed to matter.

I looked up at the big white clock over the stainless counter and red topped stools. Nearly 2:00 p.m. Close enough, I could call now. London. Who could I get to come with me? I needed someone really good looking. No. Yes. Better to see if Mark wanted to go. He and I were still fairly good friends. There was some history. He was cool. Not bad looking. Of course, nothing compared to Tristan, I thought. Shut up, I argued with myself, not helping. I wrote down his name. And Sarah and Nick. She was great. We all got on. It was a chance to see them. Come on. I got up and I paid for the coffee, and left, walking towards the park. Thinking.

Mark's phone went to voice mail. His roughened upper class English smoker's voice on the recording made me laugh. We hadn't had sex in a long while, but his voice always made me remember why I'd wanted him.

Sarah's voice mail kicked in too. Fuck. I left messages for each of them, telling them when I was coming in, the name of my hotel, and to call me. I didn't mention the party, not yet. I really did want to see them, not just use them as my backup. They'd have fun, wouldn't they? How long had it been, two, nearly three years since I'd been back?

It was starting to drizzle and I pulled my jacket closer to me, and zipped up my sweatshirt. I just wanted to walk, and walk, and not stop. I called the magazine and told Linda, the editor's executive secretary that I'd be in tomorrow to collect the tickets and the final information. While she was talking, I heard voices in the background. They sounded oddly familiar. No, couldn't be. What would he be doing there? I was obviously overwrought. Paranoia the next stop on that train.

Then she asked me to wait. Dave wanted to speak with me himself. And the phone went silent, then began playing some 80's pop song. I hated being put on hold. Especially to Simply Red. I walked faster, trying to dodge raindrops. Why was I doing business in the park? What next?

She came back on. "Hold for Mr. Fanning." I nodded. Nodding at a phone. Why were we such creatures of inane habit?

I heard his voice a moment later. "Lily, are you there?"

"Yeah, hi Dave. What's up? I was going to come in tomorrow to get the tickets and the write ups, but I can swing back today if that's a better fit."

"Why, Lily, yes. Could you jump in a cab and come over right away?"

My stomach fell again. Things happen in threes, right? Here we go, I thought.

"Yeah, I've just...been running, but sure. What's up though? Can you tell me?"

"Nothing bad—not at all." I dropped my shoulders, and tried to breathe again. "Just developments."

"Ok, be there in about twenty minutes. Don't say I didn't warn you about the sweaty clothes."

I hung up and walked back towards Central Park West. What the fuck was going on? And those voices. No way. It couldn't be. Not possible.

I waited a few minutes, someone got the cab I thought was mine when they rushed out of a building a block up. I swore, and looked at my phone again. Twenty minutes gone already. Another cab finally turned up, and I jumped in, and gave the driver the address. Maybe it was better not to be dressed up. No pressure. A little reality check. The whore off duty, but on duty. Whatever.

We pulled up outside, and I gave the driver some money. "Keep the change," I muttered, and opened the door and clambered out. God, I wished I was wearing something more—serious. Still, people were looking at me. Maybe the casual look was rocking for me. The power in not giving a fuck. Luckily I had my bag with me, notebooks and ID, so I dug out my pass and showed it to the guard, and went through the turnstile, the little black numbers on the side counting me in. One more soul headed to their execution. I didn't totally buy the nothing bad story. Something was up.

The secretary looked me up and down. I fixed her with a stare. Yes, bitch, no heels, and I'm not six feet tall. But I help pay your salary, I thought. And I smiled at her, suddenly feeling very generous. She smiled back at me, warily. No, not looking for girl on girl action. Or am I? I widened my smile. "Hi darling. Could you let Linda know Lily Taylor is here?"

She looked annoyed. "Of course." Ah, she doesn't like being told what to do—at least by me. Too bad. She looked back at me, after speaking quickly into the phone. "You can go in."

I thanked her, and went through the next set of doors. There, at an angle, behind a grey metal desk with two banks of phones, was Linda. You didn't fuck with her, but then again, you never needed to. She was utterly efficient, and never altered her slightly cold manner for anyone, no matter how famous. It worked like a charm at putting people at ease. The one thing that the rich and famous liked was being treated like anyone else. Unless they didn't. Ha. But standing up to them always worked. Never argue with success.

"Hey Linda, how are you?" You also were always nice to her. Of course you were. Dave relied on her impressions of people. You didn't get to make that mistake twice. "Is he ready for me?"

"Hello Lily, good thank you. Congratulations, by the way. Great article." She smiled warmly at me. Well. That was unexpected. Maybe she didn't act the same way with everyone, and I'd just been bumped up a level. That was an idea. Everything I thought I knew, thrown overboard yet again. Why not?

"Thanks Linda. I'm glad you liked it." I smiled, suddenly uncertain how to treat her. She'd changed, now I needed to. But how? Try not giving a fuck came to mind. "You'll like the next one as well, promise." I was going to offer to bring her something from London, but I no longer trusted that was happening, or that giving was appropriate. So I nodded and walked towards the big door and knocked. I heard a muffled, "Avanti," and I stepped into the room. There was Dave, big and imposing as ever, sitting in his large white leather chair behind the glass topped desk, impeccable in what looked like a crisp Gucci suit, on a call. He smiled and waved me in. I took another step and went to sit down at one of the chairs at the desk. But something prickled at the back of my neck and I turned to look at the large Scandinavian bleached wood table in the alcove of his office.

There, sitting at the head, with his manager to his left, was Tristan. He looked cool as always, gazing vaguely towards me through dark sunglasses, as though he were looking off into the distance. The manager was smiling criminally at me. He managed to look condescending and aggressive at once. I tried to smile back.

Dave was off the phone. I stood and he came up to me and kissed me on both cheeks. "Lily, thanks so much for coming by at such short notice." He glanced at my leggings and sweatshirt and sneakers, and then over at the manager, who was watching us. Dave put his arm around me, careless of his perfect suit against my sweaty and damp sweatshirt, and turned me towards Tristan, who took off his sunglasses, as though announcing the meeting had begun. "Tristan, of course you know, and James, had an idea they wanted to run by me, something Tristan came up with, and I knew you would want to hear about it as soon as possible." James looked even more gleeful at this. I looked away from him and over at Tristan. His face was perfectly impassive. The distant rock idol was in place. There would be no help there.

I thought back to when I'd last seen him. No, I wouldn't think about it. He obviously wasn't.

"Come, sit down." Dave moved over to the table, gesturing for me to follow, and pulled a chair out for me. What was going on? I'd just been slipped into business class, and suddenly the servers weren't surly anymore. Shit. I couldn't decide if I was happy about it, or pissed that I'd been happy enough before.

I smiled at him, and sat down as he pushed the chair under me, the perfect gentleman. I glanced over at Tristan and I thought I saw a fragment of a twitch around the corner of his mouth, but it was gone again, instantly, replaced with the business-like mask that covered up his thinking.

Dave sat down, and buzzed for Linda. "Would you all like something to drink? Coffee? Perrier?"

I spoke first. I might as well enjoy the power ride while the quarter was still working. "I'd like some Perrier, thank you." And I sat back, and caught a glimpse of James. His face was hard, and his expression gave off nothing but a kind of vicious malignity. I wondered how and why Tristan had gotten him as a manager. I supposed it was like having a pit bull. Not pretty, but effective. I smiled at him, sweetly, and he looked annoyed. Lovely.

I turned back to Dave. He would need to speak first. Protocol. The complexities of man. I tried to enjoy it. I also tried to ignore the fact that Tristan was sitting right there. I could feel him. His leather clad arms were resting on the table, his long fingers stretched out. I looked away. I could still feel the heat on my skin where he'd whipped me burning against the acrylic chair. I blushed, remembering. Damn.

The drinks came, and when we all had a glass, and some ice, Dave began. I glanced over at Tristan. He was still staring off into the distance, but one of his long fingers was twirling the ice in his glass. He looked over at me, raising his eyebrows slightly, questioning. I looked at his fingers against the ice, and quickly returned my attention to Dave.

"Tristan, we are all very excited about the new release and the tour. Lily, as you know, Tristan is about to release the new record. One week. And then he is going on a short four week tour."

I didn't know that, but I was beginning to think I could see where this was going.

Dave continued. "What they have come up with is the idea of having a tour blog—like a diary. Twitter updates, a regular blog, input from the band and select fans, a daily update on the website, a backstage account of what is going on."

I nodded. My mind was racing.

"There's a possibility of turning the tour into a documentary. They are going to film some of the shows, but we have discussed the idea of making it somewhat biographical as well. AC has agreed to play with Tristan on some of the tour dates, that's a secret by the way, and talk about the old days when they started Devised, rise to stardom, tensions, split. So there would be a lot of interviewing as well. Friends, family. Old girlfriends, possibly even Alixe, Tristan's ex-wife. In the interest of making it a continuing narrative. Real life."

I looked over at James. I could almost see him rubbing his hands together. So this was his plan.

"You're a good writer, have a feel for the music, and would have an interesting perspective on the personalities involved."

Would I? I wondered what made him say that. I had a sudden vision of comparing bruises with a line of women in lingerie.

"Most importantly, Tristan thinks you would be perfect, and actually came here today to request you specifically."

I looked over at Tristan. I couldn't read him at all. His eyes only revealed that he was thinking, their bright intelligence impossible to disguise. I must have looked quizzically at him, because he inclined his head, a careful movement, then returned to his impassive gaze.

I looked back at Dave, who looked at me hopefully. When I said nothing, he continued.

"Of course, it would be a great opportunity for the magazine, which would have first rights on all serialization of the tour. The potential for DVD sales, screenwriting credits is enormous." He turned to me, and I saw him going in for the kill, and realized instantly that this had never been my decision. Which was why Tristan had gone directly to him. If they both wanted it, it would happen. Because they knew I could never watch this job go to anyone else, regardless of how I felt about certain parts of it.

I was cornered, bound up in a golden, leather clad cage. I looked at his manager. He looked so oily and pleased with himself. I felt sick. Of course he'd love it. I'd have to meet up with Tristan's entire life, judge and be judged. And watch him play rock star for weeks. Which wouldn't have been so bad, even amusing, seeing him play the crowd, work the business, getting the girls. But that was before I'd fallen in love with him.

Oh fuck. It was true, wasn't it? Fuck. Fuck.

I looked back at Tristan. I must have looked desperate, because he finally spoke. "Lily, we want this to be special. No hack job, something above the usual. You're the best fit." One corner of his mouth turned up in an almost invisible smile.

Nice choice of words, I thought, as I blushed, from both the praise and the memory of what else I fit. Fuck. Dave looked happy. James was scowling.

Dave tapped the table with his perfectly manicured fingertip. Tristan's eyes darkened. Oh, the pissing contests between powerful men. It was funny—almost. This was a contest between titans. Dave was no lightweight—if he backed the tour, dragging along all the extra publicity the magazine could get, Tristan and his solo career would take off. And then there would be more money. And fame. And of course, more for the magazine. It was a win-win situation. But neither of them would admit to being equals; one of them would have to feel they had the upper hand. And there I was, in the middle. My job, to please them both. While acting as though I didn't really care. I wasn't sure I was really up to it. But I sure had to try. The power behind the throne. The power on the throne. I turned to Dave, first, in response to the finger tapping.

"Dave." I swung my head around to Tristan, and gazed at him. "Tristan." I ignored the idiot between them completely. I turned back to Dave. I focused my admiration on the way his shirt rose an even amount above the dark slice of the single-breasted cut of the suit. "This magazine has given me so many opportunities. I hope you know how much I value your guidance and support. As an editor, your instincts and skills are unparalleled. I've learned so much from you." Dave smiled. He knew what I was about, but he didn't mind his ego being stroked. And he knew I wasn't lying. Now to see how Tristan liked it. A sudden image of me on my knees before him popped into my head. "Tristan." And I kept my eyes steady with his. His arms were folded, each forearm solidly encased in black leather. My knee was shaking. I pinched myself to make it stop. This was not the time. "Tristan.

I've enjoyed meeting and talking with you so much. You know how I feel about getting the word out there about your music, your genius. I think your solo work is your best yet. And it's been thrilling to see you in action." He smiled. The irony wasn't lost on him. "So what can I say to both of you?" I paused and drank some Perrier. Timing. Making them wait, even if the outcome was obvious. "I'd be a fool to turn down an opportunity like this, to work with two such important figures in music. And can I say," I turned to look from Dave to Tristan and back again, "I think you've made the right choice. I'm very excited to be involved, and I think this will bring out my best work so far." I pinched my leg again. Inside, I was quaking. Hopefully none of that was visible.

Dave was smiling, but he tapped the smooth surface of the table impatiently. "Excellent," he said. "We'll consider London a first go. Lily, I've lined up an interview with the head of their first record company. In addition to the still photographer, we'll be sending along a cameraman. For now, it's going to be mostly handheld for the show. Simple things. Direct. Like the music."

I nodded. And looked over at Tristan. He looked more relaxed, but still held a wary tension about his body.

James spoke up. We all looked at him, surprised. "I've unearthed some of the people who followed the band on the very first tour. I'm sure Lily would like to speak with them as well." He had that look again. A line from the song "Red Light" by The Strokes suddenly jumped into my head. "Get yourself a lawyer and a gun." I'd need both, judging from his face.

Dave waved a hand at him. "Great, James. Give me the details, and I'll set up a meet and pass the details over to Lily." I smiled gratefully at Dave. Yes, he did know more than he was letting on, but as long as he was on my side, I had some protection. I wondered how much more he knew.

James was smiling, hypocritically. "Of course, of course. You're her boss, understood."

I felt Tristan bristle, and looked over to see him scowling. More power plays. I turned away and looked at Dave again. This was a relationship I could count on, at any rate. "Dave, that's brilliant. Your organization is always impeccable. I'm sure it will be," here I paused, "interesting to meet some of the crowd that's been there since the start. I'll let you know just how 'interesting' it is." I laughed, and Dave joined in.

Tristan interrupted. As usual, his voice came as a shock, his dark, liquid voice. "Lovely. Lily, glad you're on board. Looking forward to collaborating with you on this."

"Absolutely," I answered, completely straight faced. "Your input will be invaluable."

Tristan's voice was steady. "Obviously." He put his sunglasses back on. "Dave, always a pleasure. Thanks for meeting us at such short notice. But I've got to get going if all of the band is going to get on the plane." He came around the table, and Dave stood to shake hands with him. Tristan turned to me, and placed his hands on my shoulders, and kissed me, lightly, on each cheek, in a strange imitation of what Dave had done when I came in. "Lily, look forward to seeing you in London. Have a good trip." And he and James were gone.

I was standing up, ready to go. Dave was heading back to his usual chair, when he turned towards me. "Lily, can I have a word before you go?"

"Sure. What's up?" His face appeared oddly stern and serious. What the hell? Where did the happy power hungry money counter go?

"Lily, this is a huge thing. For you. To be honest, for the magazine as well."

I instantly felt defensive. "Dave, I know, believe me. I'm sorry if I haven't showed it. I'm a little shocked, that's all. You know what you want, and I hope you wouldn't pick me if you didn't think I was up to it. I'm really very thrilled to do this."

He looked slightly sheepish. "No, Lily, that's not it. Can I be honest with you?"

"Please." I sat down in one of the chairs, but stayed poised on the edge. I needed to be ready.

"Firstly, James."

"Oh, him." I sneered dismissively.

"Lily, watch him. I'm not sure his motives in this are entirely honest, and between you and me, I'm little worried about his management of the band and Tristan as well." Dave picked up a Mont Blanc pen from his desk and examined it closely, before placing it back symmetrically next to his glass. "Although Tristan seems like he can handle himself."

I shook my head to rid it of the images that flashed into my mind. Professional, Lily, professional. And not that kind of handling.

"Yeah, Dave, I don't like him either. And I don't trust him. So I'll keep my eyes open. I think he'd like to see me trip and fall."

"I don't think you're wrong there." His hand went towards the phone, that was always the cue to leave, so I started to get up, but his hand missed the phone and went up to stop me. "Lily, one more thing. It's none of my business, but there...are..." He faltered and I stared at him, astonished. I didn't think I'd ever seen him lost for words. He obviously felt my surprise, and he cleared this throat. "I'm embarrassed to have to say this, I don't know why. But you should know. I feel protective of you. You're a beautiful woman, smart, interesting. They're lucky to have you involved in this project. But of course, Tristan, well, you know the stories about him, don't you? There are just rumors that have floated around for a long time. Anyway. I don't need to give you details, I'm sure you get the idea." He ran his hand through his hand. He was actually flustered.

I wondered what he had heard.

"What if I take you out to dinner tonight? We can go over the schedule." He smiled at me. "Do you like Japanese? There's a new place, sake bar, supposed to be fantastic."

He looked a little more than business like. I thought of my ripped underwear, in the trash in Tristan's house. This was a day of surprises. And here was a perfect way to detach. And someone else would be on a plane. I didn't need to even think about it.

"I'd love to." I gave him a big smile, which he returned. He was a good looking man. The sharp look of those in charge. Besides it was business, right? "I love Japanese food." Hadn't I just said those words to someone else? "We can finalize the interviews. And you can give me your vision of how all this should go." I tilted my head, biting my lower lip. "I'd like to talk about all these big ideas."

He grinned at me. "I'll send a car to pick you up at 8:00. See you later." And he waited until I had left the office before he picked up the phone. Another first.

I walked out of the building into the chilly afternoon sunshine, slightly in shock. What the hell was going on? Was it the fantastic sex, sticking to me like some kind of magic potion? Or just the way I felt about things? I shook my head, and started walking up 7th Avenue. I felt so much energy rushing through me, I thought I'd be sick if I got into a cab. Crowds of people thronged along the streets, waiting at the lights, cars stopping and going, a group of noisy girls shouting to each other. Suddenly I was walking past Macy's, and looking vaguely at the big glass windows. History. So much history. Mixed up with a lot of new unknowns. Sometimes moments felt like they contained past, present and future at once. Catching sight of my reflection, with the mannequins in the background, I thought of all the times I'd walked past shop windows and looked back at myself. I stood there for a minute, watching, thinking about the people I'd known, friends, lovers, family, some no longer around, but the energy remaining, the images overlapping, intertwining.

I kept going, right up to Times Square, an outdoor mall compared to the seedy iconic ruin it'd once been. Manufactured excitement driving the big neon billboards and the tourists, every kind of person milling around. They were all waiting for something to happen. I thought I'd take a picture, remember this strange little moment, and I fished around for my phone in my bag.

The blinking light said there was a message.

> Forget everything I said before. There will be a
> car to meet you at Heathrow. This is going to be
> hard. Please don't make it harder.

I started laughing in the middle of the street, next to the bizarre red metal arena stairs that held the TKTS booth. People went around me, as I stood there, staring at the text. "Please don't make it harder? Whatever the fuck did happen?" I said out loud, watching a couple carrying two large shopping bags emblazoned with the M&M logo quickly change direction to avoid me. I dropped the phone back in my bag, and started walking up to 8th Avenue to hail a cab going uptown, singing "set me free why don't you babe" as loudly as I could in my best Diana Ross impression. The guy collecting money for his charity called over to me, "Hey looking and sounding good beautiful lady. How about some money for the homeless today?"

I fished out a twenty, and dropped it in his bucket. "Wish me luck," I said.

"Keep singing, beautiful," he said. "That works."

. . .

It looked like I had an appointment with destiny. London. Again.

ABOUT THE AUTHOR

Alice Severin thought she was on to something when her professor, a noted poet and translator, told her that her writing was "considerably above the average." Sadly, there was no time to pursue it as she became possibly the only person ever asked to leave that school. So she headed to London, where she quickly found like-minded people backstage and behind the scenes in the music business. Ms. Severin has been a delivery driver, a baker, a teacher, a copywriter, and a performance artist, among other things. She even went back to college.